CRIME HG

RUTHLESS

A gripping and gritty crime thriller

CHARLIE GALLAGHER

JOFFE BOOKS

Published 2018 by Joffe Books, London.

www.joffebooks.com

This book is a work of fiction. Names, characters, businesses, organizations, places and events are either the product of the author's imagination or are used fictitiously. Any resemblance to actual persons, living or dead, events or locales is entirely coincidental. The spelling is British English.

ISBN-13: 978-1-912106-27-1

Dedicated to and inspired by Michael Dodd, who had this dream first.

Author's Note

I am inspired by what I do and see in my day job as a front-line police detective, though my books are entirely fictional. I am aware that the police officers in my novels are not always shown positively. They are human and they make mistakes. This is sometimes the case in real life too, but the vast majority of officers are honest and do a good job in trying circumstances. From what I see on a daily basis, the men and women who wear the uniform are among the very finest, and I am proud to be part of one of the best police forces in the world.

Charlie Gallagher

Chapter 1

The sun beat against the curtains so they were framed in a vivid outline of fiery white. The air hung hot and heavy. William Dryden moved to sit up. He was lying on his side, his left arm numb where it had been crushed, unmoving under his weight. The blood rushed back instantly, a pleasant feeling at first, then like hot little pinpricks. William shook his arm to get the blood flowing. He yawned, his eyes still felt heavy. He wasn't sleeping well at all these days, not since he had abandoned his bedroom for the sofa. He had had no choice: the bed frame had finally given up the ghost — it was still in a heap where it had fallen. He and Janey had ended up in a heap on the floor too, shaken awake. Now the nights meant a sofa each where they would lie fully clothed, no routine, no move to go to bed, just watching their dusty television set until overcome by tiredness. William had fallen asleep first last night, he reckoned. He remembered Janey talking at him. He didn't think he had answered.

Janey lay on the sofa opposite. She was turned away, her legs pulled up so that her knees dug into the back cushion of the sofa, her matted brown hair falling down her back. She had blonde ends, it had all been blonde once. She had dyed it a straw-like tone but her natural colour had gradually reasserted itself and it had grown long, too. She talked about getting it cut, about doing it herself maybe. William had offered but she had just laughed at him.

The feeling in his arm had returned. He planted his feet firmly on the floor and pushed his right hand down into the arm of the sofa. Getting up was never without pain, but the first one of the day was always the worst. He had suffered with abscesses on his thigh on and off for years, longer than he could remember. He'd been putting off visiting the doctor too. He'd heard the official advice often enough and he was well aware of the risks of being an intravenous drug user: unclean needles, raw injection sites and a less than sterile environment overall. Both legs were causing him grief but the right was the worst. It usually got a little better through the day as he loosened up, but he was never without discomfort. He knew he should treat it with antibiotics, a strong course right to the end. He had been told before that it would make all the difference. One day he would do it, complete a course of prescribed drugs. But he reckoned the damage was done. Fifteen years of injecting had taken its toll.

He got to his feet and stood in an arrow of sunlight that penetrated the room where the curtains had fallen apart in the middle. He winced at the light and turned into the kitchen.

Two coffees. Three sugars for Janey. She had one usually, but the first one was always three. He filled two cups. Both were stained brown in a ringed pattern that got lighter in shade the closer it got to the top. He carried the cups back to Janey. She hadn't moved.

'Janey.' His throat was dry and his voice didn't sound like his own. Still no movement. He knew that she could be a heavy sleeper, but . . .

'Janey, coffee. JANEY!' William grunted his frustration. His legs hurt as he bent to set the mugs down on the threadbare carpet. He pulled at her hip and she rolled towards him, her right arm falling as she did so. Her eyes were open, her lips a dark blue, her skin washed out.

'Janey!' William's hand shot out to her cheek. It was cold to the touch. He tapped her cheek with his palm, progressively harder. 'Janey! Janey, don't you ignore me now, Janey. We've got a day planned!'

Janey didn't move. William stepped away. He scanned the room, trying to quell the panic that was rising from the pit of his stomach. Janey's phone lay on the table behind him. He stumbled towards it, his legs still stiff and sore. The coffee cups were kicked over, the fluids trampled into the carpet.

The ambulance took twenty-five minutes to arrive. William spent every one of them sat back on his sofa, his hands covering his face, his body rocking slowly back and forth. He knew a bit of what to do; he knew CPR. But he also knew that she was gone. He just *knew*. And there was nothing anyone could do to bring her back.

Five minutes behind the ambulance came the police. Two coppers: the first a short, bald man who kept his hands tucked into his black stab vest and a woman who tried to talk to him, told him how sorry she was. She was taller than the other copper, she had a slim but awkward build and big brown eyes. She asked some questions about who he was, about who Janey was. Wrote some notes in her pad.

William made it back to his sofa. One of the paramedics stood up. They had pulled Janey onto the floor in front of him. There were white wrappers strewn around her and she had plastic tubes in her nostrils. A machine with lights beeped beside her head. The paramedic shook his head at the policeman. He sat down next to William and took off his hat.

'William, I'm sorry, mate. They've done all they can for Jane, but there's nothing more they can do.'

'Jan*ey*.'

'Sorry, Janey. Is there someone you can call, William? Family or friends who could come round and keep you company for a while?'

'No.' William exhaled in a sort of laugh. It was unbelievable, the realisation of it all starting to sink in. He had no family, no friends and now no Janey. He had nothing left.

'Are you going to be okay? We'll probably be here for a little while longer, William, but we will have to leave. Are you going to be okay when we do?'

'Yeah.'

'Okay. Listen, William . . . In circumstances like this the duty detective sergeant will always come out to the scene. He'll just want to make sure there's nothing been missed here and I've no doubt he'll want to speak to you, okay?'

'Yeah.' William stared forward focusing on nothing. He couldn't think. He couldn't see past Janey lying on the floor in front of him. But he couldn't leave her. She was still face up, her eyes to the ceiling, her mouth lolling open from where the paramedics had put a tube in. Her hands by her side, her legs out straight. They'd cut off her jumper and T-shirt so she was left in a bra that had faded to a tired beige. Her jeans had been unbuttoned and pulled below her bum showing her black knickers. He wanted to cover her, to dress her, to make her look more presentable. She had been a proud woman once and this wasn't how she would have wanted to go. But he couldn't move.

'Can you cover her?' He turned to the police officer who was fiddling with his phone. He stopped what he was doing.

'Cover her?'

'Cover her up. Make her decent. She wouldn't want to just be laying there like that.'

'Yes, of course.' The officer spoke with the paramedics, they were packing their bags. They produced a white blanket. It covered her top half and down to her knees. It had *property of the NHS* stitched into the material. William found himself fixing on the words, reading them over and over. The suited detective sergeant arrived. He must have been just round the corner, waiting for Janey to be confirmed dead.

'You must be William Dryden,' the sergeant said. He was short and squat, and his hair was jet black and untidy. He was well spoken and he instantly looked uncomfortable. Maybe it was the surroundings. The cramped and dirty bungalow, the thick smell of squalor worsened by the intense heat. The sergeant's face flared red and he scratched almost constantly at dry-looking skin on his neck.

'Yeah.' William was still sat on the sofa.

'I'm Detective Sergeant Anthony Keats. It's our policy that a detective sergeant will always attend this type of incident. I'm sure you just want us all to leave you alone, but I promise you I won't take up much of your time.'

'This type of incident?' William repeated back.

The sergeant looked even more uncomfortable. 'Yes. It's what we would refer to as an unexpected death. We need to make sure we have all the details for the coroner before we leave. I have a colleague who will take a statement from you. We will be asking about how you found Jane this morning.'

'It's Janey.'

'Janey, my apologies. We will be asking about how you found Janey and any build up to that moment. We will also ask for a little bit of background, your relationship to Janey, her lifestyle, etc.'

'What do you mean *lifestyle*?'

'Well, at this time, Mr Dryden, we suspect Janey passed after injecting heroin. Is she addicted to heroin?'

'How can you tell that? There are tests that are done afterwards, right? Where you can tell exactly what happened.'

'Yes, and those will be done. There will be a full post-mortem. Janey still has a needle in her thigh, William. She's known to us for bits and bobs — shoplifting mainly — and the last time Janey was in custody she said she was trying to fund a heroin habit. Said she was on four bags a day. Does that sound about right?'

Actually it was more like six these days, William thought, but they didn't need to know that . . . no one did. 'She uses, yeah.'

'Do you take it with her?'

'No. I used to. I've been clean for nearly six months. We were working on getting Janey off, but with her — you know . . .' William took a second; he suddenly felt emotional. He should have done more. He'd told her something like this was going to happen. He'd told her over and over . . . *you never see an old gear head.* They were both too old for this. Janey was slightly older, facing up to turning forty. Neither of them wanted her to meet the milestone with heroin in her veins.

'I know it's hard to get off it—'

'You don't!' William was suddenly angry. 'You don't know how it gets you. With Janey it was bad. She was so deep in, there was no reaching down to her. I tried. You have to know that I tried.'

'I'm sure you did. I'm sure she knew that, too.'

'Doesn't matter what she knew now.'

'Is there anymore in the house?'

'Anymore heroin? No. She lived hand to mouth, Sergeant. Always has. If she has it, she has to stick it inside her. She's got that sort of personality, I guess. Me, I used to have times I'd stick to — a schedule, like. I could stock up for days at a time. Not Janey.'

'Where did she get it from?'

'I don't know.' Of course he did. But you don't go telling the police stuff like that.

'You're sure you don't know, William? I'd hate for there to be a bad batch out there and for more people to go the same way as Janey.'

'I don't know. She had her sources but I've been out of all that too long. I didn't get involved. When you're a recovering addict the last thing you want to be doing is getting involved with the dealers.'

The undertakers arrived. They shuffled into the tight living room. You could tell them a mile off with their cheap, easy-clean black suits and shiny black ties. They stood silently in the background, shoulder-to-shoulder with their arms held to the front, like doormen to the afterlife. The sergeant had seen them too.

'These gents are from the undertakers. My CSI colleague has finished her work so Janey can be taken away. She will be taken to the William Harvey hospital, okay?'

'Okay.'

'The post-mortem may mean a small delay in releasing Janey's body. We will be in touch when that happens so you can start making arrangements. The two gentlemen here will give you some details as regards funerals and things. I'll leave my contact details too, William, and then we'll be out of your way. Any questions for me at this point?'

'No.'

'Okay, great. My colleague will take that statement from you now. Did you want to stay sitting here or is there somewhere else to sit? Just while these men do their work.'

'I'd like to stay here. I can do the statement after. I just want to make sure she's treated right. I know what people will think of her — some skag-head overdose. Janey wasn't like that — no matter what it looks like.'

The sergeant smiled. It didn't look convincing but he made the effort at least. 'I'm sorry, William. I know this is a terrible time for you and all these people are here to make it as painless as possible. We'll leave you for a few minutes until Janey is taken away and then my colleague will write some words, okay?'

Janey was wrapped in a white bag first. It reminded William of the material you got around electrical goods. It was slightly padded and with a zip up the centre that ran from head to toe. Next came a black bag; they put her in feet first. The men grunted with the exertion, despite trying desperately not to. All the while William never moved more than a few feet away. Both undertakers sweated in their jackets. The taller of the two men had a droplet of sweat on his forehead as he straightened his back. He couldn't wipe it away while he held onto the stretcher. They sidled past and out through the front door. Almost immediately the female officer started speaking at William again. He did his best to engage with what she was saying, but he wasn't interested and he soon got the impression that she wasn't either. He signed in three places without checking the words, the image of Janey in that body bag still prominent in his mind.

And then they were gone. The paramedics, the coppers, the fidgeting sergeant. William stood at his window. Through the gap in his hedge, he watched the undertakers close the back doors of a polished black van. They took their seats in the front and the van moved off too.

Everything was gone.

Chapter 2

The car lay on its side, its black under-body turned towards Sergeant Jamie Lee's police car on his arrival just after 11 p.m. It had been hard to pick out in the darkness as he'd pulled his car to a sudden stop. He stepped out to survey the scene. The vivid blue of the car's strobe lights sliced up the gloom. A light breeze concealed the soaking drizzle. He made his way over quickly; he'd angled his own car so as to light up the scene as best he could. He had a hand-held torch strapped to his stab vest and pointed it into the overturned vehicle. There was a clear hole in the windscreen, in front of where a driver would have sat. The passenger window was lying against the road. A female form was half in, half out of it. Her head pressed against the pillar in front of the passenger door, her left arm crushed under the frame so that the hand reached forwards at an unnatural angle. The fingers were dark blue, almost black, the steel of the car providing an effective tourniquet. There was no movement. Her long brown hair had fallen over her face so he couldn't see her eyes. He didn't need to. He already knew they would be lifeless.

'Control from Yankee Zero.'

'Go ahead.'

'Control, I am on scene at the RTC on Alkham Valley Road. There is one female casualty and likely to be another.' The sergeant turned his torch away from the car and in the general direction of where the driver might have been propelled. Sure enough, he saw the heel of a shoe sticking up from the long grass of the verge more than twenty metres away. He broke into a jog.

'Received, Yankee Zero. Is the casualty conscious and breathing?'

Jamie made it to the figure. It was a man, he was lying face down. Jamie rolled him onto his back. He could immediately see a severe head wound, a split that ran from the middle of the forehead up into hair that was slick with blood; it was wide enough for him to see the brilliant white of the skull. The eyes were shut; there was no breathing. James fumbled for a pulse at the neck. Nothing.

James snatched back at his radio. 'Confirm the ambulance is en route, Control. Two casualties. Not conscious. Not breathing. I am commencing CPR on the male.'

Another police car came jolting to a stop beside his own. James was already pushing down rhythmically on the man's chest. He faced the car as it arrived with blue lights spinning. PCs Alan Smith and Angie Boakes ran over to him.

'Sarge, what do you need?' Constable Smith said.

'There's a female in the car. Just do what you can. I'm not even sure we can get her out.'

They had their own torches and immediately turned them on the crashed car and the woman's twisted torso. PC Smith spoke into his radio. James concentrated on the chest compressions. Constable Boakes ran back over with a face mask. She seemed unsure of what to do with it.

'Just stick it on his face. I'll blow into him, don't worry.'

She did as she was told and backed away.

'The woman?' Jamie was already tired; his own voice sounded breathy.

'We can't get to her, Sarge. We've asked for the fire brigade with their hydraulics. It doesn't look good though.'

'No, it doesn't.'

The ambulance was the next to arrive. Two paramedics in green overalls worked around Jamie as he kept up the compressions. He was starting to really feel it in his shoulders and back. The ambulance crew cut the motionless man's shirt off. Two sticky pads were applied to his chest and side, and then Jamie had to stop what he was doing and back away while they shocked him. He took the opportunity for a rest. The man's body flinched as the electricity ripped through him, but it was nothing more than the reactions of stimulated muscular tissue. Still no signs of life. He was instructed to get back on the compressions. The paramedics changed tack, they built a robotic device that bridged his chest, then took over giving the compressions with a padded fist. It was stronger and with perfect timing. Jamie was relieved. He stood up and stepped back, he was breathing heavily. The two paramedics knelt in front of him and assured him that he could do nothing more to help. He looked over to the woman still bunched in the front corner of the car.

'Is there anything I can do for her?'

Neither paramedic even looked up. 'No,' one said. 'There's nothing anyone can do for her.'

Jamie stepped away. Angie Boakes was standing by the upturned car, she was fixed on the passenger. Alan Smith was talking on the radio, updating Control with exact locations for more patrols. Angie had her hand to her mouth. She was new to Jamie's team, new to the force as a whole. She probably hadn't seen anything like it before.

'You okay?' Jamie asked.

'Yeah, Sarge. It doesn't look real does it?'

'No.'

'I reckon it was quick.'

'I reckon it was. I've seen this often enough, Angie. The forces in play are something you just can't comprehend. We all take it for granted that we're safe when we drive home, but when it goes wrong . . .'

'Pissed up, you reckon?'

Jamie hadn't had a look around for causes. He really should do that now. There were stories of a fatal accident a few years back where a car was found one night in similar circumstances, but with four occupants. Three of them were killed instantly and the fourth was worked on by two ambulance crews while three police patrols looked on. In the light of day, it was established that the car had probably swerved to avoid a biker who was coming the other way. The biker had swerved, too, and crashed into a tree on the other side of the road. His injuries were bad but he might not have succumbed to them. As it was, he had bled out silently while everyone's attention was two hundred metres away and on the other side of the road. No one had survived.

'Possibly. That's something that can be worked out in due time.' The sergeant's attention was drawn to more closing car doors. Two more of his team arrived.

'What do you need, Sarge?' One of them called out.

'There's nothing more here. Can you just check there's no other cars involved? Both sides of the road. I want to establish any impact points. Just to be sure it wasn't another vehicle.'

PC Alan Smith came back over, his notebook in his hand.

'The car's registered to an old couple down in Hythe, Sarge. Like, really old. I'm getting Wendy down there to do a door knock. If she can get off her arse that is. Maybe they've sold their car recently or lent it out, but for my money they still believe it to be parked on their drive.'

Jamie looked at the car. It was a Volvo — an old model, he reckoned. They definitely didn't even make these anymore. Consistent with a doddery old couple who needed a run to the shops a couple of times a week. Certainly he didn't think it should be lying on its side on a soaking country lane in the middle of the night.

'Understood.'

'Gives us a problem with informing next of kin. Hopefully they've got ID on them.'

'It would appear I can go have a look.' Alan gestured at the two paramedics. Jamie hadn't noticed that they'd stopped their activity; their bags were packed, the robotic arm back in pieces and packaged in a tough plastic Peli-case.

The paramedic was matter of fact. 'I called it at 11:42 p.m. We were always going through the motions, really. He's basically split his head in half and that's just the injury I can see. We're getting no readings. Not a spark. He's long gone, I'm afraid.'

'He didn't look well. Thanks for your efforts.'

'No problem. I can't do the same for her — confirm life extinct, I mean. Not the way it is. If we can push the car back onto its wheels I can call it.'

'What if it's spinal? The jolt—'

'She's dead. And if she isn't then we need to be doing something right now and I can't do anything until that car is righted.' The paramedic held a reassuring smile.

Jamie considered it for a second. He suddenly felt a small pinch of panic, like they were stood chatting when there might be a chance of doing something for her.

'I thought you said there was nothing you could do?'

The paramedic gestured at the car. 'Her neck looks odd — even from here I can tell you it's broken. I can tell you from her colour that she's got no circulation, so her heart has stopped. But I do like to be sure. Sometimes the box here can get a spark where you'd think that all was lost.'

Jamie raised his voice to instruct everyone to line up on the topside of the car. The bank was in their favour, the car leaning naturally back towards its wheels.

'No one in the middle. Push the boot and bonnet. If it starts coming back towards us we all jump well out of the way. Understood?' Jamie received confirmations. 'On three. One, two, THREE!'

The car dropped to its wheels on the first heave. The woman inside was thrown away from the door. She ended up over the centre console, her head in the driver's seat. The paramedic went in through the driver's door. It took less than a minute for him to reappear, shaking his head.

'I just like to be sure.'

'I'd much rather you were, too. Thanks.' Jamie turned to Angie. 'Can you cancel the fire service? We can get her out now. Are we happy there's no one else involved?'

'No one else involved, Sarge,' Alan answered. 'There's one set of skid marks and a tree with a chunk taken out of it. Looks like they overcooked a bend.'

'Cut and dried then. Did you search the driver yet?'

'Yes. Nothing that's going to help immediately, I'm afraid. He's got a wallet with some cash in it, some train tickets and a card for a casino in Ramsgate. It looks old, but they should be able to tell us who it was issued to.'

'They should. But that won't be quick and it won't be enough.' Jamie turned his attention back to the car. The paramedic had left the driver's door open. The passenger door was damaged and wouldn't budge. A little more of the woman's face had been revealed; she had come to rest peering across at them all. Her eyes were wide open, her mouth too, like she'd screamed at death with all her might. The leg and arm on her left side were both twisted and a straw-coloured fluid stained her ear. She was wearing a black dress, a short, white cardigan unbuttoned on her top half and strappy black shoes. She had a black handbag in the footwell on the passenger side. If she had ID, that's where it would be. Jamie knelt on the driver's seat to lean over. As he put more weight on it, he could feel her head roll into his knee. He tried to ignore it and leaned forward a little more, rainwater running off his nose. He snatched at the strap, scooping up the bag. He retreated quickly back out of the car.

He searched the contents of the bag. Angie held the torch. He found a black smartphone with a damaged screen that still woke up when he pushed the button on the front. It was security locked. He also found a packet of tissues, two lipsticks, two crumpled twenty pound notes and a small, circular mirror.

'No ID,' Angie said.

Alan Smith was back. 'Sarge, Wendy woke up the elderly couple who own the car. It's nicked.'

'Of course it is. You don't carry ID if you're stealing cars, I suppose.' Jamie rubbed at his face as he considered his options.

'So what do we do? Wait for someone to call up and say that their loved one is missing? Last seen planning on stealing a car with their other half?'

'We could. But there might be a quicker way.' Jamie pulled the driver's door back open. He still held the woman's smartphone. Her right hand was under her head, pointing towards him as he leant in. Her eyes stared directly at him. He took a firm hold of her index finger. Even through his blue glove it felt cold.

'Sorry, love,' he offered.

He held her finger against the button on the phone. He felt the phone vibrate a rejection. He was holding his breath as he tried again, this time with her thumb. The phone unlocked, the screen changed. Now it showed a smiling woman cuddling up to a curly haired dog that was nuzzled up under her chin. It was the same woman. She was almost unrecognisable with life behind those eyes. Jamie opened up the call screen. He moved to the screen marked *Favourites*. The first name read *Rhi xx*. He tapped the name and the phone immediately made a calling tone.

Chapter 3

Rhiannon Davis woke in some confusion. She was on her bed, still clothed, and the only source of light was the television. The canned laughter in some American comedy series came through very loud, but there was something else, something she couldn't quite work out. Her phone was ringing.

She sat up with a start and started the hunt for her phone. It was on at the bottom of her bed. She checked the screen and smirked at the caller ID.

'Hey, Aunty Mel.'

'Hello.'

A male voice? And not one that she recognised. Her aunt had a new boyfriend but she'd met him a couple of times and he had a northern accent. This voice didn't.

'Who is this?'

'I'm sorry to call you so late. I'm Sergeant Lee. I'm a police officer based at Langthorne Police Station and I'm trying to work out who the owner of this phone is. I hope you don't mind me calling, only you were the first person listed.'

Rhiannon's heart had been racing but now she relaxed and let out a breath. It was the police. Her aunty liked a drink any weekend she wasn't working. No doubt she had left her phone in some bar and someone had handed it in. It wouldn't be the first time she had lost it and it probably wouldn't be the last.

'I don't mind. Where did she leave it this time? Did someone hand it in? People *can* be nice.'

'Can I take your name, please, love? Just so I know who I'm talking to.'

'Rhiannon.'

'Thanks, Rhiannon. And whose phone am I holding, love?'

'My aunt's — Melissa. Melissa Cooper.'

'That's great, thank you, Rhiannon. Do you know Melissa's date of birth at all?'

'Why do you need that?'

'I don't necessarily, Rhiannon. Don't worry. It just means I can create a record of finding the phone.' The man paused like he was still expecting it.

'It's the first of May, I know that much. She's thirty-five, so . . . what's that? 1982?'

'Sounds about right. And you said she's your aunt, Rhiannon, is that right?'

'That's right.'

'Do you know where your aunt lives, Rhiannon?'

'Well . . . yes. She lives with me.'

There was another pause.

Rhiannon was starting to feel tense again. 'Is she okay? How did you get hold of her phone?'

'I tell you what, Rhiannon, I'd rather return this phone tonight — it looks like an expensive one. Let me know your address and I'll drop round with it, okay?'

'Now? Okay. It's 101 Linwood — in Langthorne.'

'Linwood, I know it. I'll be with you soon, okay?'

'Okay, thanks.'

The call ended. Rhiannon opened the Facebook app on her phone. She scrolled down her timeline and stopped at her aunt's last update. She rarely did anything without putting it on social media. Sure enough, ninety minutes earlier, a selfie with a raised drink and a lopsided smile, her arm draped round her new man's neck. It looked like he might be holding her up. The post had a caption, *Mel is feeling lucky — date night with this gorgeous man.*

Rhiannon stood up to get herself a glass of water. She flicked off the television and headed downstairs where she turned on all the lights so the police would know she was home.

* * *

Jamie Lee angled his book so that Angie Boakes could see it. She copied the details over.

'The age is about right,' she said.

'It is.'

'Do you want me to come down with you?'

'Probably, Angie. We'll see what comes back from the checks first. But I'm pretty sure it's going to be our girl.'

Angie had already unclipped the radio from her chest. She called Control and stepped away.

Jamie's phone went off in his pocket. He pulled off his gloves hurriedly to accept the call. 'Sergeant Lee.'

'Jamie, it's Keith from the crash investigation team.'

Jamie felt a tinge of guilt immediately. 'Hey, Keith. Sorry to wake you up, mate.'

'You would have been criticised if you hadn't by the sounds of it. Don't worry. I got a few details from your message but, tell me, what have you got down there?'

'We have a single vehicle RTC. The subject has left the road and ended up on its side. Two casualties, both confirmed life extinct at the scene and both remain in situ. There's no sign of any other vehicles involved. The presumed driver has been thrown from the vehicle. He is as yet unknown. The female passenger is still in the vehicle and we may be able to identify her within the hour. If we do, I will be letting the next of kin know tonight. It would appear that the vehicle is stolen. We'll conduct some more enquiries around that, but the victims of the theft are elderly, so it might be that they are revisited in the morning.'

'Sounds like everything is in hand. I've been to the Alkham Valley before for the same sort of thing. That's quite a busy route come the morning, is it not?'

'It is. But there are workarounds. We can get diversions in place before the traffic arrives, I will put a call in to Highways.'

'Okay. There's little point me coming out in the middle of the night. I will aim to get to the scene for six a.m. The rest of my team can join me when they get in. Are you okay to hold the scene overnight?'

'We'll find a way. I reckon I can hold it with three officers.'

'Great. I'll get some sleep and I'll be with you at six a.m. Are you the night shift or the late turn, Jamie?'

'The night shift. Assuming I'm not tucked up, I'll meet you here for a proper handover. But right now you know about as much as I do.'

'See you in the morning.'

Angie had been hovering in the background with her work phone in her hand. As Jamie ended his call, Angie angled the phone so the screen was towards him. The digital image of a female looked out. She looked stern, her eyes flushed red as if she had been crying. She was backed into a grey board that revealed that she was five feet six inches tall.

'Melissa Cooper, 101 Linwood,' Angie said. 'This is the mugshot from her arrest for drink driving in 2014. She was never charged — she must have passed the test when she got back to the station.'

'That's her, though, right? Just different hair?'

'It looks like her, doesn't it?'

'Definitely. Okay, Alan will need to stay on scene preservation. Can you jump in with me and we'll go and talk to the next of kin.'

'Yeah, no problem. Who did you speak to?'

'Niece. And she didn't sound very old.'

* * *

The door opened and Sergeant Lee got the instant impression that Rhiannon was a pretty girl. She was wearing a white vest top and small cotton shorts over her slight build. She had long, tousled hair that fell over deep brown eyes, full lips and sleek cheekbones. She bit down lightly on her bottom lip and stepped back, her bare feet squeaking on the wooden flooring.

'You must be Rhiannon.'

The girl's expression was changing. She'd appeared instantly bright, had rolled her eyes in an exaggerated gesture. *What's my aunt been up to now?* Now two police officers had stepped into her hall, their expressions stern, their hats tucked under their arms. Jamie had seen it play out the same way before — people could always just tell.

'Is there something wrong?' Rhiannon said.

'Rhiannon, is there anywhere we can sit?'

She looked even more uncertain. The living room was off to the left. It was in keeping with what Jamie had seen of the house so far — clean, but lived in. Rhiannon moved a clump of magazines from a sofa then sat in the armchair opposite. She bent one leg under the other and rubbed at her foot. She looked nervous all of a sudden. Jamie and Angie both sat.

'Your aunt was involved in a road traffic collision. She was a passenger in a Volvo car. I'm sorry, Rhiannon, but your aunt's injuries were very serious. She passed away earlier tonight.'

Rhiannon stared back. She swallowed hard and looked from one police officer to the other.

'Dead?'

'Yes. I'm so sorry.'

'Oh,' she said. Her voice was weaker, her eyes suddenly looked different — like they were missing something. Jamie had delivered the death message a few times now — too many — and it was always the eyes that carried the first reaction. It was like you could see a spark going out, never to be replaced.

'Is there anyone else here?' Jamie pressed.

'No,' she said. Her head dropped, her chest suddenly rising and falling as she sucked in more air, a sure sign of someone fighting back panic.

'I'm so sorry, Rhiannon. This is the part of the job I really hate.'

Rhiannon picked at her foot. She still stared out like she was waiting for an emotion.

'How old are you, Rhiannon?'

'Sixteen. Seventeen soon, though.' She spoke quietly. She took a couple of deeper, slower breaths.

'And is your aunt your primary carer?'

'Yeah, for about a year now. Oh God! What happens now? It was such a stress last time, when my mum—'

Jamie and Angie exchanged a glance. 'What happened with your mum, Rhiannon?'

'She gave up.' Her breathing was rushed again. She lifted her eyes and they flashed with anger.

'Gave you up?'

'Gave everything up. Except the drink. The social people, they said she had to quit the drink or they would take me away. She tried. Just not hard enough.'

'So your aunty stepped in?'

'She saved my life. They were planning to put me in foster care. It was sorted and I was all ready to go. I begged Aunty Mel, but I didn't need to. She didn't even know anything about it. If she had known, she would have offered from the start. And she works shifts, so it's difficult — my aunty does, I mean. She's a nurse . . . I guess my mum, she didn't talk to her about it. Too embarrassed or whatever.'

'Your mum will have to be told — about her sister, I mean. We'll need someone to formally identify your Aunty Mel too. Do you want me talk to your mum? Maybe something can be arranged with Social Services. Maybe she can sort herself out in the circumstances and you can go back there? Not straight away — I'll have to sort something out in the short term, but thinking longer term?'

'Formally identify? So it might not be Mel, it might—'

'It's her, Rhiannon. I'm so sorry. These are formalities.'

Rhiannon suddenly leant forward, her head in her hands. She took a minute. 'I can't go back to my mum. Not while *he's* there. Why are all men such arseholes? My Aunty Mel . . .' Finally, the tears came. Rhiannon sobbed into her hands. Angie moved to sit next to her and wrapped an arm tight around her shoulders.

'I'll start making some calls,' Jamie said to Angie, who nodded.

'And put the kettle on for some tea!' Angie called out. Jamie made his way into the kitchen.

Chapter 4

The pain in William's leg was too much, and he fell the short distance from his squatting position onto the kitchen floor. There was nothing left. He knew he wouldn't find anything, but desperation had him turning out the contents of his kitchen cupboards for a forgotten bottle of alcohol.

The parade of shops was just a few streets over. A couple of minutes for an able-bodied man, but today the pain in his legs was particularly bad. It was always worse in the mornings. He was out of painkillers and he hadn't put in his repeat prescription at the doctor's for more. The doctor's surgery was just a few doors down from the shop. He would try today.

* * *

The walk to the convenience shop took him ten minutes in total. He'd stopped to rest on a couple of low walls when the pain had gotten too bad. It felt like his whole right thigh was on fire, the pain pulsing in time with his heartbeat. An elderly Asian woman looked up from the counter as he entered the store. Her long dress and scarf looked out of place in the muggy interior. William himself had the cold sweats and his hand had a visible shake as he reached for a litre bottle of cider. It was on the bottom shelf of the chiller and he struggled to straighten with it in his grasp. He limped to the counter.

'Four pound.' The woman thrust out her hand for the payment. He felt in his back pocket for his last five-pound note. His pound coin change was discarded on the counter top, his cider pushed into a thin blue carrier bag and the woman sat back on her chair where she was largely concealed behind the counter display. He left as quickly as he could manage.

William licked his lips as he stepped back out into the sun. His attention was dragged to the left where the door to his doctor's surgery opened. A woman poured out backwards, she spun to face him, pushing a buggy with a wailing child inside. He'd go later for his pills.

He turned into his road and found a low wall under the shade of a large tree. He needed a rest, maybe a little something to take the edge off the pain, too. The cider hissed from the neck and the sickly-sweet scent immediately filled his nostrils. He took a deep swig, the blue bag stuck to the condensation covering the bottle.

'Will, man!' The voice was jovial but William didn't recognise it immediately. He squinted against the sun at the man standing over him.

'Damon,' Will said. Damon Allcott. He was the sort William knew *of*, rather than anything else. He was part of the drug supply scene in the area, himself an addict, too, William reckoned. He always seemed to attract a lot of bad people or police attention, two things William sought actively to avoid. Damon stood straight on, his right hand tucked into the front of his tracksuit bottoms. He was looking worse than William remembered: gaunt and pale, his mousey-coloured hair flat down one side where he'd slept on it. William reckoned he'd lost weight, too.

'Man, I heard. Sorry, man. Shit!' Of course he'd heard. A heroin addict overdoses and word travels fast. It was a sick world. The underground knew that Janey was a twenty-year addict; they knew that it would have taken a strong hit to kill her. They would want to know where she'd managed to score something that good. Perverse.

'Yeah, thanks. I don't know where she got it from. I never got involved in her shit, Damon. That's not my scene anymore. I can't help you.' William struggled to his feet. His thigh burned. He tried to shake it out; sometimes that helped. He was aware of where Damon was standing — all but blocking his way — and he didn't move.

'Your leg giving you shit, Will? You could do with some help, mate.'

'I'm fine thanks, Damon. I'm nearly home.' He could sense Damon alongside him, hanging just off his shoulder.

'I don't mean getting home, I mean like daily shit. Without Janey it's gonna be tough, right? For a while I mean. She ain't gonna be grafting with you no more is she?'

Grafting. William had always hated the word. Criminal-speak for earning money on the wrong side of the law, but call it *grafting* and it almost sounded like an honest day's work. His and Janey's graft was shoplifting for the most part — meat and perfume mainly. They had a good outlet for both. It was quick money.

'I'll manage.'

'Maybe you don't have to. I got a guy who needs a place for a few days. He'll pay rent, like. Keep you in a bottle or two a day of the old moonshine. Not that shit though. The good stuff. Whatever you like.'

'Thanks, Damon, but I want to be on my own for a bit.'

'It would be just until you get on your feet. A hundred quid up front pays until the end of the week. That sorts you out for a bit, right?'

William stopped his walk. A hundred quid. He could use the money. Of course he could. But all he had ever heard about Damon Allcott was to stay away from him. He was bad news.

'Thanks for the offer. I need to sort the house. There isn't the room for two anyway. I'm good for now.'

'I'll bring him round to meet you. He's a good guy. He can help you get the place straight.'

'No thanks, Damon. I'm staying on my own for now.'

Damon grinned widely and patted William on the shoulder. 'I'll bring him round, just for a drink,' he said, and then walked away.

Chapter 5

Rhiannon woke up confused. The room was bright and white everywhere — the walls, the ceiling, the crisp sheets that she lay under. She felt a sudden panic. Nothing was familiar. She didn't know where she was. Her eyes flicked round the room and fell on her bag bundled clumsily under the window, her battered old Converse pumps spewing out of the top. And she remembered. She remembered the phone call, she remembered the late night police visit, she remembered crying with the kind lady police officer. She remembered her aunty.

She could hear scuffling outside her door, the movements of other people. She could hear voices but not words. She turned on her side and stared at the white wall. There was a light tap on her door. She ignored it but the door pushed open anyway, a hesitant push, just enough for a voice to be projected through.

'Hey — you okay in there?'

Rhiannon sat up. She stared at the door, the source of the voice still hadn't revealed herself. She guessed the girl was around her age.

'I'm okay,' she said. The door pushed open further and the girl stepped into the room. Her blonde hair was pulled back tightly, revealing a face with a lot of makeup and intricately shaped eyebrows.

'You the new girl, then? Came in last night?'

'I did, yeah.'

'I'm Sam. Like Samantha, obviously, but I'm Sam.'

'Rhiannon.'

'Okay, cool.'

'You live here?' Rhiannon asked. She rubbed at her eyes.

'For like a couple of months. Not long. They just moved a couple out to their own places. That's what I want, but you know, I gotta be eighteen. Or seventeen with a deposit and a job — but who's got that, right? But that's like a month from now.' She paced across the room to Rhiannon's bag and picked up the trainer that had made it to the floor. She cast her eyes over it; she didn't seem to approve. 'What's your story then?'

'My story?' Rhiannon said.

'Everyone here's got one.'

'I dunno. I got told it was just for now. The police brought me here last night. I had nowhere else to go.'

'We all get told that. *Just a few days*. That's what I got told. But once you're here you don't go nowhere until they find you a place to live on your own and the council won't even put you on a list until you're eighteen. This ain't no short stop.'

'We'll see. It was all a bit sudden last night. I don't really know what's going to happen to me at the moment.'

Sam's attention was back on Rhiannon's bag. She picked it up, her hand pushed into it and she pulled a few items of clothing out. 'This all you brought?'

Rhiannon stood out of bed and grabbed hold of her bag. She pulled it away. 'It's all I've got.'

Sam was smiling. 'I've got loads of clothes and I reckon we're about the same size. You can borrow what you want. It's rough coming here with nothing. I did that. I got myself a good man, though. He buys me everything. You should come out with us. There's a group of boys. Maybe we can get you a man, too. Unless you already got one?'

Rhiannon shook her head and then dropped her bag back onto the floor. 'Sorry, I'm just a bit tired I think. Thanks for the offer. Maybe I'll take you up on it later.'

'Don't worry. There's breakfast downstairs. Rose always does a cooked breakfast when we get someone new. But you need to hurry or all the good stuff will be gone!'

'I'm not hungry, thanks anyway.'

Sam took one last disapproving look at the clothes she had tipped out onto the floor and left.

Rhiannon stepped out of bed and pulled on some shorts. She pulled open the curtains and looked out over the busy Hythe Road in the town of Ashford. It was the next stop up the motorway from her aunty's place in Langthorne. The house was on a busy road, a major link between the motorway and the town centre. It was morning rush hour and the road was choked. She looked down at the square drive that was as wide as the house. The house itself was a big square, too, detached and divided up into more bedrooms than were ever intended. She stepped out of her room. There were three more bedrooms off the corridor and a large room on the opposite side that acted as a communal living room for the girls upstairs. It had two sofas with brightly coloured throws opposite an old tube television and a fridge that hummed loud enough for Rhiannon to hear it from her room. As part of the tour the previous night, she had been told that it was only girls in the house. Rose was an emergency foster carer, the first port of call for the police in the area. The officers were on first name terms with her and they had all stood around for a while, swapping stories involving previous occupants of the house. Rose had shown Rhiannon to her room. It was basic: a bedside cabinet and a tall wardrobe with a creaky hinge.

The stairs were creaky, too. Rhiannon made it to the bottom and then stopped and went back to the large kitchen. A circular table that looked like it'd seen a lot of wear stood in the middle. Sam was already sitting there. Rhiannon smiled weakly. Rose was filling rough-cut bread with fried bacon — it smelled delicious.

'I was just going to bring this up to you, my love!' Rose smiled too; it looked very natural. She was a large woman. She wore light blue jeans that sat high on her waist and looked like a cheap fit below a black top. Her hair was down; it was thick and brown with a clump of grey gathered around the roots.

'Thanks,' Rhiannon said.

Rose gestured at the table. 'Sit down. Do you like sauce? I have red or brown.'

'No, thanks.' Rhiannon sat.

Sam was hurrying her food; she stood still chewing. 'I gotta get to college. We'll talk later, though, yeah? About meeting the boys. You'll like them.'

Rhiannon watched her leave.

'You've met our Sam then, love?' Rose scooped up Sam's dirty plate and cup.

'She came in to see me earlier. She seems nice.'

'She means well, I'm sure. She doesn't hang about with the best people, though, Rhiannon. You seem like a clever kid. Don't get caught up with that lot.'

'I'm not really planning on getting caught up with anything to be honest. Am I seeing Social today? Are they being told about what's gone on?'

'They know. The police referred you last night. It was Social that got hold of me. You got lucky, love. I've been full for most of the year. I just got a girl out into her own place. Would you want that?'

Rhiannon shrugged. She really hadn't thought about it. She hadn't really thought about anything other than living with her aunt. They were good together. Aunty Mel was cool, really laid back. Rhiannon had her own life. She'd finally found a place to settle and now it had all been stripped away from her overnight.

'Listen to me. You don't need to be worrying about all that right now, love. You just take your time. The Social will do what they do, but all the time you need to be here you're welcome, okay?'

'That's great. Thanks, Rose.'

'Not a problem. Now, you want some tea?'

'Sure.'

* * *

There was a knock at the door. William was laid out on the sofa. The television was on but it was just background noise. He'd been lying awake in the fog of strong cider. He'd been staring at Janey's empty sofa.

The knock came again, an urgent pattern. William wasn't expecting anyone. He hadn't had a visitor in months. He felt the pulse in his head as he rose to a sitting position. He was suddenly very hot and he pulled his shirt away from his collar.

Damon Allcott smiled a greeting. A black lad stood next to him, he was wearing an all-grey tracksuit, the top unzipped but the hood pulled over his head. He was tall and strongly built, and he wasn't smiling.

'Will, how you doing, man?' said Damon.

'Doing fine.'

'This is my guy, Aaron. I was telling you about him earlier, yeah?'

'I told you, Damon, I don't have room for anyone. I just want to be left alone.' William's head hurt. He closed his eyes to the bright sunshine for just a second. It was long enough for Damon to get his foot in the door.

'Can we do this inside? I don't wanna be talking about this out on the street, you know what I mean? It's a respect thing.' Damon's smile had gone. William hesitated.

The two men stood firm and he stepped back. He suddenly felt like he had no choice. Damon stepped straight through the lounge and into the kitchen. He peered into the bedroom, checking they were alone. He had a carrier bag in his hand and he pulled a bottle from it.

'Rum. I hear it's your thing, right? Aaron here can turn out and get you some coke mixer if you want — whatever you need.'

Aaron moved into the lounge. His nose wrinkled. He was carrying a holdall that William hadn't been able to see behind his back. He put it on the floor next to the sofa, reached into his pocket and pulled out a clump of folded notes. He counted some out quickly and dropped them on the cluttered table.

'There's one hundred there for a few days.' Damon spoke for him.

William eyed the money and the bottle of rum that was now stood beside it on the table. He still didn't like the idea, but it was clear to him that they weren't here to give him a choice.

'A few days,' he repeated back.

'Just a few days. And he'll help you sort this place out a bit. I know you've not had the chance to get it sorted. Then he'll be gone and you're a hundred quid up! Happy days!' Damon said.

'Just until the weekend.' He felt it best to lay down exactly what he saw as being a few days.

The two men exchanged glances.

'Until the weekend,' Aaron spoke, finally.

Damon slapped William playfully on the arm. He strode into the kitchen and returned a few seconds later with a dirty glass. He broke the seal on the rum and poured a good measure. 'Here you go then, mate. Get this down your neck. I reckon Aaron here is good for another bottle or two before the weekend comes, don't you worry about that.' He held the glass out and William took it. Damon looked encouragingly at him and he necked it. The liquid was smooth on the back of his throat, much less harsh than the cheap cider he'd had in the morning. It was good. William hadn't had something this good for a long time. Damon was already pouring him another and William held the glass for him. He felt a pat on his arm and Damon made to leave. He said something but William focused on the drink, on the hit of the liquid, the warmth in his throat, and that familiar feeling as it mingled with his bloodstream. Aaron was on his sofa. William shrugged. He scooped up the rum and walked a few paces to Janey's sofa. He sat down clumsily and patted the cushion affectionately down one end. He hadn't moved it since two nights before.

He heard his front door shut. Aaron still sat opposite him and was fiddling in his bag. He pulled out a basic-looking Nokia mobile phone and switched it on. He tapped on the keys for a full minute and then put it down on the table. William had downed another shot. He let his head sink back into the softness of the sofa and rolled his head a little to focus on the television. *Bargain Hunt* was on. He and Janey had liked this. They would play along, a team each. William had never won. Aaron's phone beeped. After just a few seconds it beeped again, William recognised the sound of messages coming through. They were steady, every thirty seconds or so. After a few minutes Aaron was back tapping on his phone. He stood up.

'You want another?' He gestured at the bottle.

William smiled. 'At some point,' he said.

'I gotta go out.'

William kept his eyes on the television until he heard the door click shut.

Chapter 6

Rhiannon's first impression was that Danny was tall, almost too tall for his age, as if the rest of his body hadn't been able to keep up. He wasn't good looking, at least not in the traditional way, but he had a swagger when he walked over. He carried himself with real assurance and everyone else seemed to stop and wait for him to speak. She was captivated. Danny had deep brown eyes to match his skin tone, his hair was rolled tight to his head and had a pattern of straight lines cut into the side that also went through his eyebrow. He lit a cigarette, narrowing those eyes as the smoke drifted upwards. His presence belied his seventeen years.

'So this is Rhiannon.' Sam's eyes were lit with delight. 'I told you she was pretty, right?'

Danny smiled. He looked Rhiannon up and down. He was biting down on his bottom lip. 'You did say that. I should have known you would be right too.'

Rhiannon felt her face flush warm. She had never been any good at meeting new people — definitely not boys. Yet here she was, in the middle of a group of new people and being called pretty. She had nothing to say.

'She's gonna be staying with me for a while. Don't know how long,' Sam said.

'Lucky you. I'm sorry to hear about all your shit, Rhiannon. Sam said about your mum an' that. About what happened. Shit time.'

'My aunt . . .' Rhiannon managed.

'What?'

'It was my aunt. I lost my aunt.' She said a little louder.

'Your aunt. Right. Sorry to hear about your aunt.'

'Thanks.'

He pulled a cigarette higher in the packet and offered it to Rhiannon. 'You smoke?'

'No thanks.'

'You sure? It helps, you know, if you get stressed or whatever. Helps me at least.'

'I don't smoke.'

'Drink? We got a few beers an' that.' He gestured behind him. They were in Victoria Park, a large park in the middle of Ashford with benches in among mature trees, concrete paths and a defunct fountain as a centrepiece. Most of the group had found a place to sit in the shade of one of the trees. Rhiannon looked over. She could see they were swigging from bottles.

'No thanks.'

'You don't drink either then?'

'No. I grew up with drinkers. It can put you off.'

'I respect that. So what do you do? For fun like?'

'I don't know. My aunt and I used to have fun. Right now I can't see me having fun ever again.'

Sam cut in with an awkward chuckle. 'Well, I'm sure that ain't true. You just need to hang out with us lot a bit.'

'Thanks, I'm sure you're right. I got to get back to the house for now, though. I have a meeting with my social worker.'

'Sack it off! Them boring bastards never did a damned thing for me. They're all fucking useless.' Sam said.

'I have to go today. I need to know what they have planned for me at least.'

'Fine. We'll probably still be here when you're finished wasting your time. I want you to meet Rosh. He's my man. He'll be here soon.' Sam walked a few steps away and took a seat at the foot of the tree. She accepted a bottle of beer.

'You should try and come back. Just to hang. You don't have to drink or smoke!' Danny chuckled.

Rhiannon felt herself blushing again. 'I shouldn't be long.'

Rhiannon's social worker was called Theresa Hart and she had an obvious affinity for purple. Rhiannon had met her on a number of occasions and she couldn't remember her wearing any other colour. Today she even had purple tassels sprouting from her thick, dark hair that was clumped in a loose band to keep it from covering her face. She wore a purple top tucked into a black dress with some purple stitching. Her black tights finished in purple shoes and the same purple featured on oversized bangles that clacked together on her wrist as she readied her pen over a notepad.

'So, Rhiannon, I haven't seen you for a little while now. You're sixteen — seventeen in October?' Theresa looked up, her expression soft. She expelled a dramatic sigh. 'Such a terrible time.'

Rhiannon wasn't sure if she was supposed to reply. She didn't.

'She's a strong little one, I could tell that straight away.' Rose was sat on the smallest sofa in her lounge and she was beaming, her gaze flicking from Rhiannon to Theresa.

'Oh yes, our Rhiannon here is right little trooper. When I think of the things she's been through, but she gets back up okay. I'm just here to try and make it a little easier, does that make sense?'

Rhiannon shrugged. She didn't feel like getting back up. She didn't feel like getting patronised either but she bit her tongue. Theresa was always a little dramatic. Rhiannon had learned that you had to let her get her little bit of drama out of the way first before anything got done. And you needed to flatter her ego a little.

'I appreciate your help, Theresa. I wasn't sure who would come out and I was glad when you turned up.'

'Yeah, we go back a bit me and you, right?' She reached out and put her hand on top of Rhiannon's.

Rhiannon felt awkward and wanted to snatch it away but she resisted the urge. 'What happens now?'

Theresa took her hand back and sighed again. 'Well, you remember when we spoke the last time and your aunty . . . well, she sort of stepped in at the last minute there didn't she? We were all set up with a foster placement for you. That particular family no longer has the space, but don't you worry about that. I'm certain I can get you a permanent placement in the next month or so. Your circumstances put you right to the top of the pile, Rhiannon, and people out there, they're going to want to help you! How could they not?'

'A foster placement? The police officer, he said you could go back to my mum. Maybe she's sorted herself out.'

'She hasn't, Rhiannon. You can take my word on that. And you remember how it was when you lived with your mother?'

'Better the devil you know though, right? A foster placement, I mean, that's some complete stranger.' Rhiannon could feel her voice breaking a little.

'I organise care for vulnerable young persons, Rhiannon. *Better the devil you know* is not something I keep in mind when I do that. I would rather you were kept away from devils completely, do you understand what I am saying? I have your best interests at heart, Rhiannon, and I will not put you back into that environment again.'

'My mum, she might sort herself out. You know, after all that's happened.'

Theresa sat back. She chewed her pen a little. It was another pause for the sake of drama. 'She just might you know, that might just happen. But she might go the other way, Rhiannon. She might just react to all that's been going on by hitting the bottle harder than ever. We both know she doesn't deal with things well — with normal everyday things. This might just hit her for six. You know me, Rhiannon, I won't rule anything out, and if your mum wants to see me and wants to convince me that she is capable of giving you the home you deserve then I will sit and listen. And if that's the best thing for you then that's where you will go. But she hasn't been beating my door down since you went to stay with your aunty.'

'I know, but she knew I could have a better life with Aunt Mel for now. She knew she could give me a more stable environment while she was sorting herself out. She didn't want to let me go, but she knew she had to. It might be different now. If I could just talk to her, tell her that I'm going to live with a complete stranger, maybe—'

'I'll talk to her, Rhiannon. I'll let the dust settle a little, let her come to terms with losing her sister and then I'll go and see her. Not with the intention of asking her to provide a home for her daughter, that isn't something I will be asking for. But I will talk to her. And if she asks me, if she says she wants to take you back in, then I will start the ball rolling for her to be effectively assessed. With her past though, Rhiannon, with all that we know about her, it would be a long process. It will take months. And in that time I need to be sure you are in the right environment. This is all for you.'

'I could stay here, then.' Rhiannon flicked her attention to Rose, who quickly disguised a reaction.

'Rose, here, is set up as an emergency service. The police bring people like you to her when they are caught out in the middle of the night. She has Anais here, who is Rose's long-termer, and she has Sam who we are looking to house in the near future. Rose needs to have a space for the next emergency, Rhiannon.'

'You might not have met Anais yet. But I won't kick you out, my love,' Rose said. 'You are always welcome here. You can stay until there is something right for you to go to.' Rose was beaming again.

'And this new family,' Rhiannon challenged, 'who says they are right?'

'The assessments are stringent. The people on our books, they're all good people. Professionals usually, upstanding members of the community who want to make a difference, who want to provide positive environments for the young and the vulnerable. This is such an important time for you, Rhiannon. I can't get this wrong.'

Rhiannon could feel the panic rising in her again. She had spent so much of her life anxious and unsure that it had become the norm. It didn't bother her usually, but with her aunt she had tasted how it could be to have a settled life. She knew how good that was and she yearned to have it again.

'So how long until I'm somewhere else?'

'Like I said, you're top of the list. A month — two at a push. Until then, you can stay here with Rose.'

'You're very welcome here, Rhiannon.' Rose said again.

'Thanks. I just want to be settled somewhere. The last time I was up in the air, when you told me you were taking me away from my mum, that was the worst time. It's the waiting. If you're going to move me I would rather you take me now. It's fine here, I'll probably like it, but that's worse. I don't want to be sat somewhere I like waiting to go somewhere I might not.'

'I know how frustrating all of this is. I know you didn't want to be going through this again, Rhiannon. I didn't want you to have to do this again either. But be a little patient. That is why this next move is so important.

Because we need to get it right. We need to make sure it is the last move you have to make.'

Rhiannon checked the time. The meeting had lasted twenty minutes. She knew there was nothing more to come from it. 'I need to get back out.'

'You have an appointment?' Theresa looked a little taken aback.

'No.'

'There are a few more bits I need to go through with you, Rhiannon. Some paperwork.'

'What paperwork?'

'You know the sort of things. I need to fill out a form for your mental health assessment, we need to be sure you're not depressed or suffering in ways we can't see.'

Rhiannon got to her feet. She peered down at the pile of forms Theresa had pulled from a purple folder. She suddenly flashed with anger she couldn't control. 'I lost my aunt. She was my best friend. My mum doesn't want me — that's if she still realises who I am. And you're telling me not to get too comfortable because I need to go and live with a bunch of strangers just as soon as you can sort it out? I *am* depressed. I *am* suffering. You can put that on your form if you want — you don't need me here for that.'

Rhiannon walked away. She heard Rose calling out. Rhiannon's anger dissipated immediately; she felt bad for Rose. But she kept walking. She could make her apologies later. She crossed the hall and got to the front door. She pulled it open then pushed it shut again loudly and moved quietly to the stairs opposite. She knew from experience that adults only ever spoke the truth about children when they weren't around. She flattened herself against the wall. There was a dramatic sigh and then a voice.

'She's really been through it. I genuinely don't know how she's managed to stay so bright and so *normal*, you know?' It was Theresa's voice. It carried well.

'I've seen some really messed up kids who have been through a lot less.' Rose was quieter. Rhiannon found herself holding her breath as she listened.

'And that's just what you get in the handover notes, Rose. You get the case summary — that's not half her story. This girl, her mum's been an alcoholic just about all of her life — then she took in a man. We're pretty sure he was abusing her in all sorts of ways. We're certain he beat her. And what did her mother do? She chose the booze and this man over her own daughter. How could she do that?'

'It happens all too often. I wish I could say I hadn't heard of it before. I'll hear of it again, too. I don't doubt there's a queue of wonderful young children who are being damaged as we speak by their own parents. And then when they start acting out, they'll be kicked out for the rest of us to pick up the pieces.'

There was another sigh. 'She's different though, you know. Rhiannon, I mean. She should be damaged, she should be acting out. But when she's in school she's top of her class and her behaviour . . . when I first started talking to the school about her home life, no one there would believe me. They were about ready to praise her upbringing.'

'She's a special kid, alright.'

'Somehow. Somehow her mum didn't manage to mess her up yet, like she has everything else in her life.'

Rhiannon had heard enough. She tugged the heavy front door open roughly and slammed it shut so hard the glass panels rattled.

Chapter 7

William was very suddenly awake. His shirt was damp with sweat and it clung to him as he sat up on the sofa. A young, black lad sat opposite and was fidgeting on the table. The table had been cleared of the clutter William was used to. He rubbed his eyes and fixed on a small device that whirred as it flickered with twenty-pound notes. When it stopped the male scooped up the wad of notes and wrapped a band around them. He didn't look over.

'Who the fuck are you?'

'Mo.'

'Mo? Who the fuck are you?'

'Aaron said it was cool to use his place.'

'His place? This isn't his place. This is my fucking place!'

The lad shrugged. He couldn't have been any older than sixteen. He wore a white vest and his arms were stick thin. His hair was shorn close to his scalp and he had baggy jeans that were hanging so low on his body that William could see the brand of his underwear.

'Aaron here?'

'No.'

'You know where he is?'

'No.'

'You want to get the fuck out of my place!'

The boy had continued working with his hands. He stopped what he was doing and looked over. 'Aaron said it was cool. Talk to Aaron. If he tells me to go, I'll go.'

'This ain't Aaron's place!'

'He's staying here right?'

'Well, yeah, a few days.'

'Then it's his place.'

'Jesus.' William's head thumped. His throat felt dry and he struggled to his feet for a glass of water. He drank a pint in one go. From his position in the kitchen he looked back out over the table.

'So you're fucking drug dealers. I mean, it's not a great shock. I guessed Aaron was in that sort of game from the start, you know. I've seen a million of him before. He can be what he wants but I won't have it here. I can't have it here.'

He got no response.

'Mo!'

The lad did nothing to hide his impatience. He finished what he was doing, his movements deliberate, and only when he had made it clear he had finished did he look over.

'What do you want from me, man? I ain't the person to talk to if you got beef. Aaron tells me it's cool then it's cool. You got a problem with that then you need to speak to Aaron.'

'Are there drugs here?'

'It's my business what I got. But I ain't no common drug dealer. There's some of that rum left, right? Aaron said you like the drink? Said that you just need to be on that shit and it don't matter what happens. Best you don't know.'

'Not here. I don't give a shit what you've been told or who you've been told it by. I don't have drugs here. Not dealing. The cops round here, they get a whiff there's a setup in a house and they'll be through the door. I can't have that. Not here. This isn't that sort of place. This is my old mum's house. I got lucky. When she died, the council let me have it. Round here it's only supposed to be old people. It's quiet and I like it. You'll mess everything up if you got drugs here.'

'I told you already, I ain't no common drug dealer. Don't be worrying yourself.'

Suddenly there was a knock at the door. The curtains had been pulled and the only light was from a weak bulb hanging over the table. Mo moved to the wall so he could get an angled view through the gap in the curtains towards the front door. He looked a little tense. Almost immediately, his body relaxed. He moved to open the front door. William couldn't see the door from his position and he couldn't move quickly enough on his leg. He stayed still, listening for the conversation.

'Hey!' Mo greeted the visitor.

'Need a reload.' The voice was urgent, it sounded similar to Aaron but it wasn't him — the same accent that London street gangs always seemed to have. He'd heard it a lot recently.

'Already?'

'Business is good!'

William heard the scuffle of feet. He stepped round to see another black guy entering the house. He was around the same age — a little older maybe — definitely stronger built. He gave no reaction. It was as if William wasn't there at all.

'Who are you?' William demanded.

The man did now look over. He looked William up and down. 'I'm with Aaron.'

'I asked who you were, not who you were with. This is my house. What are you doing in my house?'

'This is Aaron's house. Who I am don't mean nothing.' He stepped a few paces towards William and looked him up and down again. He sucked at his teeth, his expression one of disgust. He stepped in closer, so close William could smell the sickly energy drink he held in his hand. He was dressed similarly to Mo, baggy jeans that were tied off tight over his thighs, his underwear visible over the top, a black T-shirt and a Nike rucksack with string handles that hung loose on his back.

'This is my house.' William held his ground.

'Keep your mouth shut and you might be able to stay here. You're just as pathetic as Aaron said, man. Now get back in your fucking corner before I put you there. You don't know who we are — and you don't want me showing you.'

'You're a fucking boy! Two boys who think they can come in here and tell me what to do. I've seen a million of you and not one has impressed me.'

'This impress you?' The boy held eye contact, his right hand came up smoothly, William was sure he was holding a blade. Though William didn't stare at it directly, he thought it was a large kitchen knife, but he kept his eyes on the boy whose face was now a sneer. He felt something sharp push into his cheek, just below his eye.

'That doesn't impress me at all.' William leant into it a little.

'Maybe I should run it through your gut. See if that does the trick.'

'You ever done that before? You ever stabbed anyone? Takes nothing to carry one of them. Takes nothing to pull one either. Takes a bit of something to stick it in someone. Trust me on that.'

The boy stepped back. William was suddenly aware that he couldn't move quickly in any direction. The knife spun in the lad's hand, it was thrust back towards him. The lad struck him hard in the thigh with a closed fist that was bunched around the handle of the knife and increased the power of the blow. The pain was instant and excruciating. William's legs were so tender to touch that the boy might as well have used the blade. The pain took him off his feet and he fell onto the kitchen floor where the cold tiles pressed against his cheek.

'You stand against me again and the next time you don't get up, you get me?'

William tried to get his breathing under control. He didn't want to show how much he was hurting. He didn't reply.

'Pathetic fucking rummy.' He heard the boy spit. A warm clump of it fell onto this neck and chin. He recoiled.

The boy stepped away. From his vantage point on the floor he could see Mo standing a few paces away, still with the same expression and facing the lad who had just punched him to the floor. Mo handed him a package and then held out a small, round tub with the lid off. The lad declined it.

'I'm good.' He stepped out of sight.

William didn't think he had left as Mo looked like he was still watching him. He heard some breathing noises, a sharp intake of breath and then a scuffle of clothes. The front door opened and closed. Mo sniffed and walked out of sight. He appeared a few seconds later with the bottle of rum. There was two-thirds of it left. He placed it next to where William had managed to drag himself and was now sitting, propped against a kitchen cupboard. Mo went back to his table and got busy again. William knew it would be some time before he'd be able to get up. He reached out for the bottle.

Chapter 8

'I'm so glad you called!' Rhiannon looked up to see Sam hanging out of the passenger window of a smart-looking white car. It pulled alongside her. The rear windows were blacked out. Rhiannon could see through the front to the driver. She didn't recognise him. He was black and had a bit of a baby face. Rhiannon didn't think he looked old enough even to be driving the car.

'I know I said I would walk back, but I didn't fancy the crowd, you know.'

'Shit meeting?'

Rhiannon nodded.

'They always are,' Sam said. 'No crowds then. Just my fella and Danny. Get in the back and I'll introduce you!' Sam almost squealed with excitement. Rhiannon pulled the back door open and she saw Danny, who scrambled immediately over to the seat on the other side.

'Hey!' he said.

'Hey.' Rhiannon could feel herself blushing all over again. She wasn't sure why and it angered her a little. She didn't want to be out blushing at boys. That was for other girls: silly little girls who hadn't been through what she had in the last few days. Maybe this was a bad idea. Maybe she should have gone somewhere quiet, where she could think about what she was going to do next. No one had said anything helpful in the meeting with Social Services but one message had been clear: they would never allow her to go back to her mum.

'You okay?' Danny said. Those brown eyes seemed to carry genuine concern.

'I'll be fine.'

'You wanna talk about it?' he persisted.

'Nah.'

He held his palms up. 'Then I won't ask again.'

The heat in Rhiannon's cheeks intensified. 'Sorry, it was shit. There's nothing much else to say.'

'Well, we should go somewhere that isn't. You hungry or anything? I would love a milkshake. My treat, yeah?'

Sam had turned and was beaming into the back. 'You two are so cute together! Don't you think they're cute together, Rosh?'

'If you say so, woman.'

Sam slapped him playfully on the arm. 'Don't call me that!'

'You are my woman!'

Sam turned to the back. 'Rhiannon, this is Rosh. He's my *man*. So you wanna go to McDonald's?'

'Sure. Hey, Rosh, nice car!' Rhiannon called out. She rubbed at the leather. They pulled away. Rosh didn't respond.

'It's a BMW!' Sam squealed.

McDonald's was ten minutes away. Rosh abandoned the car on double yellow lines and strode inside, leaving them all trailing behind. He then barked his order at the young girl stood behind the counter. Already, Rhiannon didn't like him. He seemed to speak down to everyone. He struck her instantly as brash and obnoxious. They all ordered to take away and were quickly back in the car. Rhiannon hadn't spoken to Danny on the journey. She had looked over a couple of times and exchanged a shy smile, but Sam was in control of the stereo system — and the volume. Conversation was impossible. Rosh moved them a little further away to where he found a parking bay and immediately tore at his brown bag of food. He switched the engine off and the music turned off with it. Rhiannon dropped her window. She only had a milkshake; everyone else was eating something.

'So this car, is it yours, Rosh?' *Rosh*, she thought, what sort of a name was that anyway?

'Mine to use,' came the curt reply. Rhiannon could see the back of his neck through the headrest. He made no effort to turn and engage with her.

'So it's not yours.' She pressed, disliking him more every second.

'It's a company car.'

'What do you do for a job?'

'I don't answer questions, that's for sure.'

'Rosh!' Sam hit him harder on the arm. 'She's my friend. She's just making conversation.' Sam turned to the back. 'It's his boss's car. Rosh lets me drive it sometimes too. Maybe he'll let you drive it later if you want to? When it gets dark, like.'

'It's okay. I'll wait. I wouldn't like to drive it without the actual owner's permission.'

The silence that fell was a little awkward. Rhiannon had intended for it to be.

'So, how long are you at the house for?' Sam said.

'I don't know now. I don't know what they're going to do with me,' Rhiannon mumbled. She watched a family of four walk past. She had seen them round a table in McDonald's. The two parents were led by two toddlers, holding hands and giggling. They had a balloon each and were dressed the same. *Not a care in the world*, Rhiannon thought.

Sam faced her in the back. 'They don't know their arse from their elbow that lot. Fucking useless. I ain't ever heard of them sorting someone out, doing a good job.'

Rhiannon turned her face away, looking back out of the window.

Danny nudged her gently. 'You fancy a walk? There are some shops, nothing much. Rosh don't mind picking us up in a bit, right?'

Rhiannon found herself smiling, she did want to get out of that car and away from Rosh. But she wasn't sure that was why she was smiling.

* * *

McDonald's was part of Ashford's pedestrianised High Street. As they turned into it, an old man was singing as loud as he could while sat on top of a wooden box. His singing was terrible, a little slurred even, and he was beating the box out of time. Danny's and Rhiannon's eyes met and they chuckled. Rhiannon peeled off to find a bin for her cup. She dropped a coin with the busker on her way back.

'You're different.' Danny had thrust his hands into his pockets and stopped walking to watch her.

'What do you mean?'

'I dunno really. You're not like the rest of us, are you? I mean, you don't really belong here, having all this shit.'

'I don't know who does. Anyone can have a bit of a rough time.'

'I dunno. It's difficult to explain. I just think you should be with a good family. With a proper mum and dad, in a posh house and in school an' that. You don't drink, don't smoke, you don't talk shit like we do. I mean, you're not Sam are you?'

'Only Sam can be!'

They both chuckled. 'You know what I mean though?' Danny said.

Rhiannon shrugged.

'It's not like you're better, I mean, maybe it is. I think that's it . . . you're better than all this shit. You're better than a loser mum and a kid's home. You shouldn't be here. You ever feel that?'

Rhiannon started walking down the High Street. Danny walked alongside her, his hands still in his pockets.

'Sometimes I think things will never be any different. I get frustrated. I try to be a good person. I think that good people have good things happen for them. I do worry that I won't ever have that. And I don't know why.'

Danny pulled his hand out of his pocket and hooked his arm around hers. He pulled her in closer and she smiled at him. They both smiled as they continued walking.

* * *

Aaron walked through the front door of William's bungalow on his mobile phone, holding two pizza boxes. He dropped one on the table in front of Mo, who was still busy. Aaron continued through to the kitchen and ended his call. William could hear running water. Aaron walked back in and addressed Mo.

'Strong day. Business is good down here.'

'The drug business.' William called out from where he was sat on the sofa.

Aaron turned to face him. His expression didn't change as he spoke to William. 'I'm gonna need you to use your bedroom. You can't be out here.'

'What the fuck?' William pulled himself up straighter, though his mind was foggy with alcohol. 'What the fuck are you talking about? I've been waiting for you to come back so I can tell you to fuck off. You need to leave. I know what you lot are doing from here and I won't have it.'

'You know nothing. You need to go into your bedroom and you need to stay there. It'll be for a few days.'

'Get the fuck out of my house! Get out tonight and maybe I'll stay quiet about your little setup here. I'll give you a few hours' head start. That should give you enough time to get back to London. I know that's where you're all from.'

Aaron walked over so he was stood directly over where William sat. William suddenly felt very vulnerable. Aaron was a big man, even bigger up close. William had been a fighter once, dirty and headstrong. He was never the biggest, but his attitude and determination had always carried him through. He couldn't be that way anymore.

'I'll make you two promises,' Aaron hissed. 'You'd do well to listen to me. If you do as you're asked, if you go into your bedroom and stay the fuck out of my way, you'll be just fine. That's my first promise. My second promise . . . if you don't do what I ask, you have my word: they will never find your body. Do I make myself clear?'

William could only reply with a jerked nod.

'I'll have your bedroom cleared. You can come out to shit and heat your food. Anything else is none of your fucking business. It's a very simple rule. Stick to it and you'll be fine. We clear?'

William gave another nod.

Aaron managed a smile of sorts. 'I gotta go back out. You want some more rum?'

William nodded again.

'Of course you fucking do.'

Chapter 9

Rhiannon felt tired all of a sudden. She was sitting in the communal living room of her temporary home after spending an hour in town with Danny. They'd bought another milkshake and then he'd walked her to the bus station. She hadn't wanted to meet back up with Sam or her obnoxious boyfriend. Sam was still out with Rosh. Rhiannon didn't know where they would end up, but Danny had hinted that he might know and this had reinforced her decision to come home early. Rhiannon was watching some terrible American police show where a body was discovered in suspicious circumstances and a group of attractive forensic scientists took the rest of the forty-minute episode to piece together how it had got there and who was responsible. Her aunty had loved it; she always made Rhiannon watch, trying to second-guess what technique they would use to crack the case this time. Rhiannon had always protested, but tonight she found a strange comfort in having it on in the background. She still hadn't cried for her aunt, not really, and she was starting to feel almost guilty about it. Meeting Danny, walking hand-in-hand with a milkshake and pulling faces in glass shopfronts — it had been a normal day. How could she have had a normal day so soon after her poor aunt was gone forever? She wanted to be sad, she wanted to sob, to mourn her loss. But she just felt empty, accepting that this was how her life worked out, as if she was never going to be settled with people she loved without something going wrong.

Her vision blurred as she gazed listlessly at the television, lost in her thoughts. She was suddenly aware that the channel had been changed when the audience's laughter in a panel show cut through her thoughts. She turned to a girl who now sat on the sofa opposite. She must have removed the remote control from the arm of Rhiannon's chair. The girl still held it out and the channel changed again. She had something in her other hand, which she gnawed at absently.

'Hey,' Rhiannon said in greeting.

The girl did nothing to acknowledge her.

'I'm Rhiannon. I came last night? I guess you're Anais, right?'

The girl still ignored her completely.

'Or should I just call you rude bitch?' Rhiannon felt her neck and cheeks suddenly burn with the one emotion she was getting good at: anger.

'What did you call me?' The girl faced her now at least. She had a larger build and was pale-skinned. Her hair was so black it had to be dyed, her lips two flashes of scowling red.

'I said hello.'

'So what? You think you can talk to me just because you're the latest freak they stick in the emergency squat through there? Another down-and-out street rat.'

'Oh, well it seems I misjudged you. You're not a rude bitch after all.'

'I'm whatever I need to be for you to stay the hell away from me. I'm sick of it. I'm sick of you lot coming in here thinking you own the place.'

'I was just sat watching the TV.' Rhiannon was suddenly overcome. She felt like she might break down and cry. She wasn't upset or scared — just furious. She couldn't speak; she didn't have the words. She got to her feet to leave; she didn't want this thing to see her cry.

'Yeah, fuck off!'

Rhiannon didn't reply, she walked towards her room.

Anais still called out after her. 'Rose told you this is a shared room, right? Well, it ain't! This is my room. You can stay the hell out!'

Rhiannon still said nothing. She got into her room and pushed the door shut. She leant on it for a few seconds, waiting. Sure enough the tears came.

It took a few minutes for Rhiannon to get a hold of herself. She felt angry all over again. Not at Anais — she was just a rude bitch who Rhiannon wouldn't normally think twice about. It was more the thought that she had walked away, that her emotions had got the better of her. She stood up and rested her hand on her door handle, ready to go back out and shout Anais down, to tell her what she thought.

Her phone vibrated in her pocket. It was a message from Danny. He said he was outside and he wanted her to come down and meet him. It was nearly 10 p.m. Rose had a curfew of 10 p.m. She had just a few minutes — just time to go down and tell him about the curfew.

She slipped on her trainers and picked up a hoody. She put it on quickly and checked her makeup as she stepped out of the door. By now, the night was cooler and the street outside was quiet. She checked both ways, her attention caught by a flash of headlights. She strained to see where it had come from; it was a car parked around six cars down and she walked towards it. She could see it was the same white car she had been in earlier. She hesitated, dipping her head to see the front-seat occupants and expecting it to be a squealing Sam and her obnoxious boyfriend. It was just Danny. He was smiling.

She pulled open the front passenger door and the interior suddenly lit up with a soft white. She slid into the leather seat and pulled the door shut. The light faded to off.

'What are you doing here? And in this car?'

'I wanted to come and see you.'

'Does Rosh know you've got the car?'

'No. And, like you pointed out earlier, it's very obviously not down to him who uses it!'

'Who is it down to then? He said it was a work's car, right?'

'It is.'

'So how come you got it?'

'Because I'm in the same line of work. I need to run an errand in it. It's a drive out. I was wondering if you fancied coming along for the ride.'

'What line of work?'

'I guess I'm a courier. Not often. I just help out sometimes. Do you want to come along or not?'

Rhiannon turned to face the front door of the house. 'I can't. Rose has us in for ten. She'll be checking on me any minute.'

'She don't own you, Rhiannon. No one does. Kids skip out of these places all the time. It don't mean shit. This Rose, she'll expect it from you. She probably won't even mention it.'

'I don't want to upset her, you know. She's been good to me.'

'You got your phone?'

Rhiannon could feel it digging into her buttock through her back pocket. 'Yeah.'

'So she can call you, right? You can tell her you're fine.'

'I shouldn't. Maybe tomorrow night? I'll tell her what I'm doing so she knows not to worry—'

'Maybe I can't do tomorrow night. I thought it would be nice. I didn't want to ride on my own. But don't worry, you better get back in before she checks on you.'

Rhiannon took a moment. He was pissed off, it wasn't difficult to tell. She really didn't want to disappoint him. And what would it matter anyway? The first thing Rose would do was call and she would just say she was running late and she was fine. After what she'd been through, no one was going to be too hard on her for getting in late past a curfew. And she was certain Sam wasn't back yet.

'Okay.'

Danny perked up. 'Okay you're going in or okay you're coming for the ride?'

'I'll take the ride out. But it's one hour, that's all.'

'One hour! Cross my heart.'

Rhiannon reached for her seatbelt. It clicked shut. Danny's gaze lingered on her.

'What?' she said.

'Nothing! You're just different.'

'So you keep saying and I still don't know what you mean.'

'I'm not sure I do either,' Danny said. 'Do you want a go? We can head somewhere quieter.'

'A go?'

'A go. A drive.'

'No, I don't drive.'

'It's an automatic, it's real easy.'

'It's real expensive is what it is.'

'Nothing can go wrong, and I'd just say I was driving. Come on, your mate Sam's had a go in it. You don't want her to have that over you, right? She drives it loads.'

'No. Thanks but I'm not bothered. It looks complicated too, I'd look silly.'

'It's easy!' Danny started pointing at different components of the car. 'This button starts it. This is the gear stick. You just need to have your foot on the brake and knock it back so the "D" lights up. Then it's good to go — the right pedal makes it go faster and the left pedal is the brake. Oh and "R" for reverse. Easy as that! You can't mess up, and if you do, the car even tells you.' Danny pointed at the car's internal display; it suddenly changed to a diagram of the gear stick and instructions on how to use it, the car also bonged impatiently. Danny had obviously done something wrong.

'I'm sure it's all very easy, but I'm good, thanks.'

'You can't even mess up the seating position. The boss is programmed in to the "Number One" button, you just push that when you're done and he'll never know you were in his seat! It goes right back to how he sits. Come on, give it a go!'

'No!' Rhiannon instantly felt bad. He was trying to be nice and she had snapped. 'Sorry, I just really don't want to give it a go. I have to be back soon anyway so we should probably get going. I can't be out too long. Maybe I'll give it a go another time.'

Danny didn't seem bothered. 'You're right. Let's get this done.'

It was twenty minutes later when the car came to a stop. They had talked for the first half of the journey, re-living their walk around the town. Danny had been too cool to make a face in the reflections of the shop windows at first. When Rhiannon finally convinced him to play along, he'd chosen the exact moment a window dresser had stepped out. For a few moments at least she'd been consumed with laughter, enough to forget everything else.

The car was warm and comfortable and they quickly left the town behind, so there was nothing to see outside but blackness. Rhiannon was fighting heavy eyelids, but she snapped to attention when the engine fell silent.

'Are we here?'

'Yeah. I won't be a minute.' She had to narrow her eyes; the interior was again a bright white that faded as the door closed behind him. She peered out. He was walking towards what looked like a small industrial unit. It was part of a row of maybe six or seven that pushed away into the distance. There were no other cars or people that she could see and just one orange light above one of the doors. The door that Danny entered.

Rhiannon pushed her door open to stretch her legs. The car lit up again. She pushed the door shut and the night returned. It was a beautiful clear sky. She could see a little more of the industrial estate. It appeared there was one road in, one road out and a low fence wrapped around as far as she could see. Beyond this fence were occasional silhouettes of trees. A couple of the other units had boats outside, which made her think that they might be near the sea, or a river at least. In truth she had no idea where she was.

The door that Danny had entered drew her attention, it opened again — with such force that it smacked off the wall. A figure came out of it, it was moving towards the car and it was moving fast. It was Danny, and he called out as he got to her.

'Get back in the car! Get in the car!' He sounded panicked. It made Rhiannon panic and she fumbled over the door handle. Suddenly two bright headlights came from nowhere, illuminating Danny as he sprinted to the driver's side. He threw himself into the seat and the car started. Danny pulled away, swinging the car 180 degrees and accelerating away. The road was uneven and bumpy. Rhiannon said nothing until they made it back to the road and turned right. The BMW accelerated strongly and shifted Rhiannon around in her seat. Danny's breathing was quick, still a little panicked. She waited until he seemed to relax a little and had stopped checking his rear-view mirrors every few seconds. He made a few more turns and got himself lost in a housing estate. He pulled the car over.

'Sorry, Rhiannon.'

'What just happened?'

'It wasn't supposed to be like that.'

'What wasn't?'

'I pick stuff up, stuff gets left for me, I pick it up and I take it back. That's it.'

'That isn't what just happened.'

'No. There were people there. They said there was no stuff for me to take. I told them my boss wouldn't be happy but they didn't care.'

'What stuff? What people?'

'I don't know what people! I don't know anything! I turn up, pick up and I take it back.'

'Pick up what?'

'Jesus, Rhiannon, I don't ask. You shouldn't ask either — there are some things you just don't ask about.'

Danny was suddenly upset. Rhiannon assumed he was upset at her. She bit back. 'You said this was a drive out — you sold it like it was a drive in the country. I think I've got every right to ask what you were doing if you're going to make me a part of it, don't you?'

'Sorry,' Danny said.

Rhiannon sat back. This was the first time Danny had come across as anything other than supremely confident. He had backed right off — almost meek.

'Are you taking me home?' Rhiannon demanded.

Danny peered out. He had killed all the lights on the car. They were parked in a residential street that was washed in a dull orange light from fixed street lamps. Their position was elevated, enough that they could see some of the surrounding roads too. Nothing was moving.

'Yeah. I'll take you home. I am sorry though, yeah? I shouldn't have involved you in this. I swear this has never happened before. This is some easy shit normally.'

'Forget about it.'

The BMW fired and Danny pulled away.

Chapter 10

William woke on his living room floor, his buttocks still pushed against the back wall. He had slumped onto his side, his right hand still wrapped around the empty bottle of rum. It had been two-thirds full when he had started. He was aware of people walking past him, the rustling of black sacks — they had one in each hand. His eyes focused on two teenage white lads. He thought he recognised them from around the town. He watched them walk out of his front door in single file. They returned seconds later. They no longer had the black sacks.

'What's going on? What are you doing?'

'We got, like, fifty quid,' one of the lads said. 'We're nearly done, mate.'

'Fifty quid for what?'

'Aaron wants us to get rid of a load of shit. Everything in there.' The two continued into the bedroom once occupied by William and Janey. William got unsteadily to his feet. His right leg was stiff but the pain was dulled by the alcohol. As he used the wall for support, the room seemed to move a little around him. He made it to the threshold of his bedroom. He had to step back as the two lads came back out with two more sacks each. He stepped in the room after them. The window was wide open, the curtains that had been pulled shut over it for as long as he could remember were gone. The curtain pole remained and now held wisps of material as if the curtains had just been ripped from the pole.

The bedroom looked out on the rear garden. His mum had kept it nice all the while she had the mobility but, when she got ill, nature had taken it aggressively back. Now it was six-foot tall grass, weeds and brambles and they pressed at the window like an invading army. William could see that an area had been flattened. A chest of drawers and his broken bed frame had been thrown out. His mum's old wardrobe was still against the far wall. It was a large, flimsy unit, three doors wide but the middle one had been hanging off. That was now missing and the clothes that had been spilling from its belly were missing too. Most of those had been Janey's. He remembered the floor had been covered in clothes and shoes and the top of the wardrobe had been layers and layers of books. Janey was a big reader: Stephen King, Dean Koontz, James Herbert — all the classic horrors. All were gone. Now the top of the wardrobe supported a digital aerial with two metal prongs sticking out. The aerial lead ran to a flat-screen television that clung to the wall and that William had never seen before.

William made it back into the lounge just as the front door was closing. He pulled it open almost immediately. The two lads had a shopping trolley with *Sainsbury's* on the handle. It was laden with black bags, the wheels clunked as they kicked up against the uneven stone path.

'Hey! That's my stuff, you can't just take that!'

The lads stopped. 'We got paid to get it all out and to get rid of it. We ain't robbing it, we're dumping it.'

'I don't want it dumped!'

'You need to speak to Aaron, man. We got told, we need to do what he said to get paid.'

'Janey's stuff. You can't just take Janey's stuff!' William took hold of the trolley handle and pulled it back towards the house. He immediately felt a shove in his chest. He stepped back, the handle slipped from his grasp and the lad who had pushed him stepped in between him and the trolley.

'You got a problem, you speak to Aaron. He said to take it away and he said not to take no shit about it. He said he'd told you about it too. We're going.'

William stepped back so he was squared up to the lad; he was suddenly filled with rage. 'You don't just come here and take my stuff. I don't care who told you what. This is my house.' William couldn't see the blow coming, the first he knew of it was when he felt the force to his stomach and the air suddenly left his lungs. He was forced to stumble back, the pain in his leg suddenly so bad that it took him right to the floor. His breath still wouldn't come. He lay gulping on the floor and could do nothing more than watch as the two lads pushed the trolley away. The second lad stepped back towards him.

'You got a new TV at least. It works. I tested it. There's no remote though. We didn't have time to get that too.'

William watched them leave for good.

It took a couple more minutes for a complete recovery. He made it to a tentative sit first, then back to his feet. It was the first time he had been alone for a few days and he slammed the door shut as he limped back into his home. No sooner had it shut than he heard it push back open again. He turned to see Aaron strutting through. The black guy who had hit him in the thigh earlier was with him. Neither of them acknowledged William.

'So what happened?' Aaron sounded upset. He moved to the sofa and sat down. He looked back up at his colleague with his arms crossed.

'I can only tell you what I got told. He went there and he says he got chased off. They said we owe them money and there was nothing coming our way until they had it. They said, like, ten grand.'

'Ten grand. That's about right for what he was picking up. It's always been the same though. We never pay upfront.'

'I know that, Aaron.'

'So why did they want it upfront this time?'

'I don't know, man. He asked the question and got told to fuck off. It got heated and they made some promises if he didn't leave, you know what I'm saying?'

'Yeah, I think I do. My boy should be able to handle that, though, right? Was he carrying?'

'I guess so. We always do on pickups, right? But he had to be away clean — he had his bitch in the car outside. I think he was worried it might spill over.'

Aaron had been shaking his head, sucking his bottom lip, looking thoughtful. Now his attention snapped up as if he had been stung. 'Say what?'

'He was worried, like. He had a bitch out in the car. I don't think he wanted to start pulling in that situation, you know?'

'No, I don't fucking *know*! What bitch? And why the fuck would he be taking some girl out to a meet?'

The lad offered a shrug. William saw real fear in him.

'Where is he? I want him here. I want him to come and tell me what the fuck happened and I want to know why I need to be running back up to the city for a reload. This hits business and I don't accept that, you understand?'

'I understand, Aaron. I'll give him a call.'

'You do that. And you tell him to get over here. And you tell him to bring that bitch with him too. Seems he likes bringing her along to his shit anyway. I don't work with no fucking amateurs.' Aaron stood up. He kicked the table so it shifted across the floor.

‘Oi!’ William stepped forward. ‘Why don’t you fuck off home and kick your own table!’

Aaron turned wide eyes and flaring nostrils towards William. ‘Well, if it ain’t the rummy. Your bedroom should be sorted by now. I told you to stay in it and I meant it. I see you out here again and I’m going to start taking out some of my frustration on your good leg. And you should know that I got a lot of frustration inside me right now.’

‘Why don’t you just fuck off?’ William reacted.

Aaron was on him in an instant and William was on the floor before his senses caught up. The right side of his face stung, his vision flashed black. He was on his hands and knees. He could sense that Aaron was stood over him.

‘Why beat on the leg when I can beat on your worthless fucking face instead? Let’s pretend that room in there is your fucking rock rummy. Now go crawl back under it.’

William felt a kick to the ribs on his left side and a shot of pain in his right thigh as he crawled towards the door. He struggled to speak. ‘You can have that room, too. I’m out of here. I’ll find somewhere else to stay. You can have the whole fucking place.’

‘No can do, rummy. While you’re here I know you ain’t talking to no one about nothing. I reckon I need to get some control over you, make sure I keep it fresh in your mind what happens if you go talking about my setup here.’

‘You making me a prisoner in my own home?’

Aaron smiled. He dropped to a squat so he was closer to William. ‘I don’t need to make you no prisoner, rummy, do I? You understand your situation. You need to get out to the shops an’ that, you fill your boots, but you come back here when you’re done. I’m making a real dent in this town. Soon it will be mine. People are talking to me already out there, rummy. If you think you can go shooting your mouth off I’ll know about it before you get home. My advice is to crawl back under your rock and to stay there for as long as possible.'

The pain in William's leg remained. He made it to the door, he used the handle to get to his feet. He scanned the living room, he settled on a framed picture on top of the wooden shelf over the fireplace. 'I want my picture. Give me the picture and I'll get out of your way.'

Aaron walked over to it. He picked it up. 'This one?'

'Yeah. Give it here and I'm out of your way.'

Aaron dropped it to the floor. He stepped forward and William could hear the crunch of the glass under his foot. He picked it back up. 'You can have your worthless picture, rummy. You cause me any more problems and it won't be the only thing broken up into little pieces. You understand?'

The picture landed at his feet. Most of the glass shook itself out. The beaming couple and the six-year-old girl looked up at him from the floor. He picked it up and brought it hurriedly to his chest.

Chapter 11

A scraping noise made Rhiannon jump. She'd been lost in her thoughts at the big table in Rose's kitchen. She looked up to see Sam perched on the offending stool.

'You scared me!' Rhiannon said. She'd been thinking about Aunty Mel, about the happy times, about karaoke in Benidorm last September when Mel had managed to get a last minute cheap deal. They had shared an apartment. It was so bad they had stayed out late every night to put off going back there. Despite this, it had been the best week of Rhiannon's life. For just a few days she was able to understand what it was like to be truly carefree, to put life and all its troubles on hold.

'Sorry, Rhiannon. I didn't, like, sneak up or anything.'

'Nah, I know. I was just thinking about stuff.'

'About your aunt?'

'A little.'

'It's shit. It's proper shit. It'll take some time, but it will be cool. I know what you said, but you will be happy again. We're young, right, babe? There's loads of good times to come.'

Rhiannon forced a smile. 'I'm sure you're right.'

'There's Danny for one thing. You like him right?'

'He seems nice.'

'And fit too!'

'He's nice. I don't know what I'm doing at the moment. I wasn't really planning on getting involved with a fella.'

'Don't stress. You don't need to be doing boyfriend-girlfriend. Doesn't mean you can't have some fun, get him to spend some money on you, right?'

'I like the sound of that at least! How do the boys make their money, Sam? They're in the same business right?'

Sam suddenly looked more serious. 'Yeah, I think they work together.'

'Doing what?'

'You know what, Rhiannon? I don't ask much. You see how Rosh gets. He doesn't like questions. They do some courier work, I think. Deliveries. Shit like that.'

'Do you know what they deliver?'

'Nope. Nothing illegal though. These boys are good boys. Rosh ain't ever even been nicked.'

'He told you that?'

'He didn't have to. What's this about? You worried about getting involved with a bad boy? You shouldn't worry about that. It's the good boys you want to worry about anyway. Them boys will bore you shitless.'

'Like I said, I'm not sure I want to get involved with any boys — good or bad.'

'Shame. 'Cause I got a message from Rosh. He wants to pick us both up and take us out this afternoon. I was thinking maybe the bowling alley or summin'. He said to make sure I asked you, too — for Danny.'

'He didn't say that, did he?'

'He did! Look!' Sam pulled her smartphone from her pocket. Rhiannon held her hands out.

'Okay, fine. I believe you. Have you not got school this afternoon?'

'*College*. And, no. I only do a half day on Thursdays. So what do you reckon? You fancy it?'

'I dunno, Sam.'

'You can stay here if you want. But Anais has Thursday afternoons off too, so she'll be home soon. Rose is out, so it'll just be you two getting real cosy.'

'I was going to ask you about Anais. What is her problem?'

'She's a bitch, that's her problem. She doesn't like people. That suits me to be honest. I never wanted to hang with the bitch anyway. She's literally got, like, no friends. So now you have to come out, otherwise you'll be here taking her shit.'

'Fine. I'll come out for a bit.'

Sam looked Rhiannon up and down. 'I think the boys will be about half an hour. Do you want to get changed?'

Rhiannon was wearing her usual: tight fitting jeans with rips at the knees, Converse trainers and a black fitted T-shirt with cut back sleeves. She chuckled. 'Well, no. But you clearly think I should.'

'I just never see any harm in showing a little flesh, you know? You dress like you want to cover it all up. You've got a great body. Show it off a bit.'

'This is pretty much all I've got to wear.'

'You could *sooo* get in my dresses! Let's go try some shit on — see if we can't bring out the slut you've been hiding.'

Rhiannon chuckled again. 'Clearly I haven't been hiding it well.' Then a thought occurred to her and the laughter fell away.

'You okay?' Sam said.

'Yeah, of course. For a second there you just really sounded like my Aunty Mel.'

'The slut bit?'

'Yeah.'

'I think I would have liked your aunty.'

* * *

The rain had come on quick and it had caught William out. He had seen the clouds gathering through the bus window and the rain was already heavy by the time he was spat out through the hissing doors into the centre of Langthorne. Eazy Cutz barbers was just a couple of hundred metres' walk, but he was limping heavily and pretty soaked through by the time he bustled through the door.

Nik Jenkins's chair was occupied by a young lad with a tattoo that covered most of his neck at the front and Nik was stood over him. He acknowledged William in the mirror but didn't break from his small talk with the client. William fell clumsily into one of the seats in the waiting area and listened as Nik went through his small-talk repertoire. First up were the football fixtures for the weekend, then came the muggy weather at nights and the rain today. It was just five minutes or so until Nik thanked the tattooed man and closed the door.

'You look like shit, Will.' Nik's full and pointed beard shook as he spoke.

'Well, thanks a lot, man. You look like you haven't shaved in months yourself.'

'I shave every morning, mate. So what can I do for you?' Nik was already sweeping the floor. William stayed seated.

'What can I do for you, Nik? That is the question.'

Nik stopped what he was doing and checked the shop door. It was still empty. 'I'm not really doing much at the moment, Will, you know. I don't like to have too much on the go.'

'Very sensible. So what doesn't stick around for long? Maybe we can help each other here.'

Nik looked thoughtful. He emptied a dustpan over the bin. 'Look, perfume. It's always the best. The Issey Miyake stuff. I can always get rid of that. I got a few people that will take that straight off my hands.'

'*Flowerbomb*?'

'Yeah, that's the stuff. It's one of the most expensive scents out there so it always goes if it's offered at a price.'

'Anything else? What about aftershaves, the last lot of Calvin Klein went well, right?'

'Yeah it did, but that was just before Christmas, weren't it? I never struggle round then. I'll be honest, mate, I got more call for perfume. The women will buy it all year round, the only time the aftershave really goes is when the women are buying that for the blokes.'

'So perfume. Issey Miyake, maybe Calvin Klein. Anything else?'

'Any of the new stuff out. They always go well, but just don't go too mad. I don't want so much shit that it's hanging around.'

'Don't worry, I understand. We're a tenner a bottle right? Like before.'

Nik frowned. 'I dunno, man, that was just before Christmas, like I said, so I could punt that out for a bit more. People still knew they were getting a deal but they wanted it. This time of year people will take it or leave it if the price isn't right. I will need to punt it out for a bit less and it needs to be worth my while.'

'So what are you saying, Nik? 'Cause I'm the one taking all the risk here.'

'I'm saying a fiver a bottle. That's all I can do and you're not the only one risking your arse. Most of it will only go for a tenner, tops. I won't get more than that and I've got a business and a clean record to consider.'

'Some of this shit is seventy quid a bottle. Surely you can punt it out for more than a tenner?'

'Seventy quid to your well-heeled Debenhams' customer with a nice display box and a receipt. The black market tends to value shit differently.'

'You don't need to be telling me, Nik. I can't remember any other type of market.'

'You okay, though, Will? You don't look your normal self. Did you lose weight and gain a limp?'

'Something like that.'

'You been to the doctor? Looks nasty.'

'Nah. I will go, I'm not a big fan of the doctor.'

'Who is. Where's the partner in crime today? You already got Janey out scoping the scene?'

William took a second. 'No, mate. I lost her. Just a couple of days back. Seems the drugs finally got the better of her.'

'Lost her? Oh shit, you mean lost her like she's gone? Gone?'

'Gone, gone. Overdose. All accidental. She knew the risks. We both did. I can't say I didn't see it coming but there was just no telling her.'

'Shit, man. I'm really sorry.'

'Me too.'

'You gonna be able to pull this off now? I mean you were a team effort right and now you've got a shitty leg an' all.'

'I'm not totally useless just yet, Nik. I might struggle for a fiver a go though.'

'Fine. Seven quid a bottle if I can move it straight away, but I get to be choosy.'

'That'll do.'

* * *

William stood back out in the rain. Langthorne was home to one of a chain of chemists that also sold a large selection of perfumes and aftershaves. It was a short walk but his aching thigh meant it took him twice as long to get there. This gave him plenty of time to consider his options. He and Janey had been good at this. She was becoming quite well known in the town, all the shop staff and security guards knew she had previously been done for shoplifting and she was banned from most of the shops. It had been rather ironic that this was the best thing that could have happened; it had provided them with an opportunity. Janey would walk into the chosen shop with real purpose and would fill a bag with the most expensive items she could find. She would then hurry towards the door, dropping the bag just before the exit and continuing through and out onto the street. Any security guard worth their salt would make her their complete focus but would hold off until the moment she left the shop. Prior to this point there was nothing that could be done; it took someone to *leave* a shop with stolen items to commit the act of theft. Only Janey would never be in possession of any stolen items when she left, the bag dropped on the threshold. Security would still fuss over her; she would be searched, reminded of her ban and sent on her way. William, in the meantime, would have filled a similar bag. Only this one would stay with him.

Today he would need to rethink his options.

The shop was busy. The weather is important to the shoplifter. Sunny days were the best as they brought out the more casual shopper. Crowds of people would wander in and out of shops, browsing at their leisure and it was easy to blend in. On rainy days there were very few browsers; people were in the shop to buy something, to steal something or to stand still and watch the rain for their opportunity to leave. It was very difficult to disguise which of them you were. The security guard spotted William the second he walked in. He was Nepalese — a lot of ex-Gurkha soldiers would turn to security when their military careers were spent. He was alert, his uniform immaculately pressed. William expected him to be quite the foe.

The shop was on two floors. The perfume was mostly on shelves behind the counters on the ground floor against the right-hand wall. The top floor was a mezzanine level. There were escalators to the left up to the photography and baby section. William could see two women gassing at the lift door, the call-button illuminated. They were stood over buggies, one with a toddler squirming in her grasp. They stopped their talking momentarily to move into the lift. William made for the escalators. He arrived at the top at the same sort of time and moved towards the back of the floor. He was aware that the security guard had watched him up the escalator. He knew how he looked, he knew his appearance would put the guard on high alert. But the guard was still on the ground floor and he would be out of his line of sight.

At the back of the top floor were rows of prams for sale as well as nappies, creams and toys. He picked out a baby doll and ripped it from its box. He tucked the doll in his rain jacket — the one advantage of grafting on a rainy day. He stood back up as the two mums ambled towards the front of the floor. He made it to the lift and called it. The lift arrived and he dropped the empty box between its doors. They immediately jolted back open and stayed that way. The woman with the toddler holding her hand was walking slowly, slow enough for William to get to her while she crossed along the top of the escalator. He glanced into the pram — empty — he shoved it sideways into the moving stairs. It bucked and twisted against the metal shelves as they rose up, but it soon tipped sideways down the stairs. Both women screamed, and William added to the confusion with a shout of his own. Then he turned and made his way as quickly as his leg would allow back to the lift. The adrenalin helped with the pain. He kicked the box out of the way and pressed for the ground floor. Within seconds he was walking past the commotion. The Nepalese guard was trying to retrieve the pram. It had made it halfway back up, the contents from underneath the pram strewn all down the metal stairs. Other members of staff were helping as best they could. William threw the baby doll under a rail of clothes. He shouted again, pointing as he did so. The rest of the staff came and he heard another scream from behind him. Everyone's attention was elsewhere.

William made it to the counter. He scooped what he needed off the shelves in seconds, the bottles fell into a big 'bag-for-life.' He had sewn layers of foil around the inside. It wasn't a sure-fire way to beat the sensors but it rarely failed him. It didn't today. The alarm stayed silent. He walked away from the commotion and into the street where he could mingle back with the dismal day and the shoppers with their heads down.

William made it to Eazy Cutz and found it empty of customers. Nik must have reacted to the sound of the front door; he appeared from the back room swigging from a coffee cup. 'You want one?' he offered.

'No, I need to get out of town, really.'

'I see. Did you make a noise?'

'Nothing that will come back to you. The classic diversion.'

'Nothing naked, I hope?'

'No, the old push-the-baby-down-the-stairs routine.'

Nik balked on his coffee. 'You pushed a baby down the stairs?'

'Of course I didn't! Smoke and mirrors, Nik. You want these or not?'

'What did you get?'

'Thirteen bottles – Calvin Klein. Most of them boxed, they will need the tags removed. You can still snip the tags right?'

'Yeah, until they change them.'

'Well, okay, you'll be fine with these. So thirteen times seven, I make that ninety-one quid. Call it ninety, yeah?'

Nik had a comb behind his ear. He used it to reach in to the bag to move the bottles around. 'I'm not sure I want all of these, mate. There's definitely a couple that aren't worth anything much. Did you not get any Issey Miyake?'

'I didn't have the time to be choosy, I went for the Calvin Klein display. Most of it is CK.'

'And some of it isn't.'

'Like three bottles aren't. They're still worth money though.'

'Not to me.'

'Fine . . . listen . . . seventy quid, the lot. That's your ten CK bottles and the three others for nothing — you can still get a fiver each for them I reckon. That's fair, right?'

Nik bit on the comb. 'Fine. Put them out the back – usual place.'

William limped through a door marked *private.* It had a small kitchenette and a further door with a toilet and basin. Under the sink, the pipes had been boxed in by sheets of wood. It eased apart and William stacked the perfume in the void behind. By the time he walked back into the shop with his bag empty, his cash was already counted out.

'Cheers, Nik.'

'Are you back on it now then? I haven't seen you for a while is all.'

'We all have to make our money, Nik. I need to eat. I need to come up with something different long term. Today's idea won't work again. I might get picked out when they review the CCTV footage as it is.' William saw Nik react. 'Don't worry! I walked a route that is well off-camera, there's no coverage up here.'

'Well, pop back in for a haircut when you know what you're doing. Just make sure you give it a rinse first.'

William couldn't miss Nik staring at his hair. He didn't miss his expression of disgust either.

'Thanks mate. I'll bear that in mind.'

* * *

Rosh hadn't been obnoxious toward Rhiannon all afternoon, but then he hadn't really been anything to anyone. He had hardly said a word. He bowled in silence and ignored the playful banter and the giggling around him. Rhiannon could see that Sam was becoming more and more frustrated. Rhiannon knew an argument was imminent. It came on the way back to the car.

'What's up with you?' Sam demanded. Rosh didn't reply immediately and Sam was back at him. ''Cause you been a dick today. I know you think you're the big man, and that might be, but you don't get to treat me like this. If you got issues with me then you need to be a man and come out and say it like it is.'

'I ain't got no issue with you,' Rosh growled.

'You got an issue with my friend?'

'No. She's nothing to me.'

'Don't speak about my friend like that. Why you been acting all sulky?'

'I'm not sulky. Get off my case, yeah?' They had made it back to the BMW. It was parked in the centre of Ashford, the bowling alley still in sight behind. Danny stopped short of the car, he was looking around. He addressed Rosh. 'Listen man, there's a bus route, yeah? Passes right by here. I'll get Rhiannon home. You two go sort yourselves out, yeah? Don't worry about us.'

'Get in the car.' Rosh's tone was still a growl. He lowered himself into the driver's seat, the car started and his door was pulled shut. Danny's face contorted a little — anger, Rhiannon thought. Danny pulled the passenger door open and stooped.

'Nah, man, we're going to take the bus. So whatever this is, you can sort it out. It's nothing to do with us. You just need to sort it.' He pushed the door back shut and stood beside Rhiannon. The driver's door swung open and Rosh stepped out. He was plainly furious.

'You need to get back in the car, bruv. We need to be somewhere and we need to be there now. And the reason we need to do that is because you think this is all a game. One that you can play when you want to. This ain't a game, bruv. Get in the fucking car.'

'What are you talking about, Rosh? Where are we going?'

'Get in the fucking car! Last time I ask nice. He's already pissed off. The last thing you want to do is turn up late. He's expecting us. He's expecting us all.'

Everyone looked at Rosh. Rhiannon looked away and over at Danny and Sam. She could see in their faces that they knew who Rosh was talking about. Neither of them looked happy about it. Danny had been angry. Now he looked uncertain.

'Get in the car,' Danny said. It was directed at her.

'I'll get the bus on my own,' Rhiannon said. The driver's door shut. Sam got in the passenger side. Danny stepped away, towards Rhiannon and he lowered his voice.

'Please,' he said. 'There's obviously some issue with Rosh. I just want to make sure Sam gets home okay. Can you help me with that? Rosh has his moods, you know? I just want to make sure she's okay.'

'Who are we going to see?'

'It'll be a stop-off on the way home. It won't involve you. I'll deal with that and then I'll make sure you both get home. Please come with me — I need your help.'

Rhiannon sighed. She didn't think that was a good idea at all, but this was the first time Danny had asked for her help and she felt obliged, as if she couldn't say no.

'Okay,' she said.

They both climbed into the back of the car. Rosh pulled away immediately.

Chapter 12

It was a bungalow. It looked small and the front garden was unkempt compared to all the neighbours'. Access was through a low gate that was jammed open and round a conifer that was growing wild and covering much of the path. Rhiannon didn't like the look of the place.

Rosh and Danny had gone in on their own to start with. Danny had assured her that it would be a quick stop, but after a few minutes Rosh came back out to the car alone. The two girls were told that they were staying for a drink and Rosh shepherded them across the garden. An old mobility scooter was parked against the house and a puddle of brown-tinged water had collected on the seat. The dirty white plastic front door was open. The letterbox was missing and there were scuff marks on the bottom. Rosh pushed it open and let Sam and Rhiannon step past so that they could go in before him.

'Who have you brought me?' the solidly built black man grunted. He looked older than both Rosh and Danny and he had the air of being in charge. Rhiannon felt a shove in her back. Rosh was standing behind her. She had to take a step forward to keep her balance. It took her over the threshold of the bungalow.

Rhiannon faced the seated man. He was sat on a grubby sofa. His head was bent; he was rolling a cigarette. He didn't look up. Rhiannon got an instant bad feeling: about the place, about the man sat in front of her and about how he had implied that she might have been *brought* for him. As Rosh prodded her towards him, she looked at Danny. He was a couple of paces in front of her and facing away — towards the seated male. He didn't turn to greet her either.

'What is this?' Rhiannon said. No one answered and no one looked at her. Everyone looked at the seated man as he finished rolling his cigarette. He stacked it neatly against two others and immediately started on another. Rhiannon cast a nervous look around the bungalow. Rosh, Sam and Danny were packed into the small living room. A boy a few years younger than her sat at a table in the middle the room. Her overriding impression was that it was a filthy place to live. All the soft materials — the curtains, the sofas, the carpet — looked grimy. The carpet in particular was a mass of stains and patches where the floorboards were pushing through. It had fresh-looking drag marks on it and patches of darker tones as if someone had recently pulled heavy items of furniture out of the property. The table was cluttered with a set of scales, some empty clip bags, a few packs of foil, a large pack of condoms and discarded containers from various takeaway food outlets.

'Listen, Aaron,' Danny said, 'you wanted to speak to me. This has got nothing to do with her.' He turned to Rhiannon very briefly. He looked unsure, scared even. The seated man, Aaron, looked up and fixed his eyes on Danny. He made him wait for his reaction.

'Are you questioning my decisions?'

'No. I'm not questioning anything. She just don't need to be here.'

'Sounds like a question to me.' All eyes were now on Danny. He squirmed in the spotlight. 'What happened?' Aaron continued.

'I dunno, man. It was a stitch up, nothing like normal. Them cunts need—'

'What happened?' Aaron spoke over him.

Danny shook his head. 'I got there, I used the code. I go into the place and the gear wasn't there waiting like it usually is. I look around and suddenly there's, like, four of them . . .' Danny stopped talking as if struggling for words.

'What happened then?' Aaron raised his arms so that they ran along the back of the sofa. He looked comfortable.

'They said they wanted money. They said, like, ten grand. I told them I didn't have no money. I said this wasn't how it goes down. I been doing this a while now and this ain't ever how it goes down—'

'What did I tell you? In your training? What did I say?'

'I got trained, yeah. I got a lot. I don't know what you want me to say? When?'

'Your training. When we talked about meets. When we talked about going to see these people, to do business. What did I tell you?'

'I don't know, man. There was nothing I could do, there was four of them and they weren't in the mood to just hand it over. They were never going to hand it over.'

'They would have done. They would have handed it over. This was a big opportunity for us. I told you, I told you all. I said that we would be tested. This isn't a fucking game, Danny. This ain't something we play at until a bigger bully comes along and tells us we can't play anymore! I told you we were going to get tested and I told you it would happen more than once. I told you what we need to do when this happens. What did I say?'

'You said we stand them up.'

Aaron suddenly sprung to his feet. 'So you *were* there! I told you we would have to stand them up. Face them up. Were you carrying?'

'Yeah, of course I was. I always do.'

'Right, so show me how you would stand me up? Come on!'

'Aaron, don't do this, man. I didn't have no choice — no chance. There was, like, four of them.'

'Stand me the fuck up, Danny. Pull the blade.' Aaron stepped towards Danny. He stomped his foot on the ground and Danny reacted: he snatched his hand to his waistband and then back towards Aaron. He clutched a black-handled, hunting-style knife in his hand.

'Jesus, Danny!' Rhiannon recoiled. She stepped back into Rosh, who once again shoved her forward. He was blocking the doorway.

'Shut your bitch up, Danny. Shut her up or I'll talk to her instead of you. Your choice.'

Danny turned to Rhiannon. His eyes were wide with terror, his voice a little more than a stammer. 'Stay quiet, Rhiannon . . . you'll be just fine . . . just stay quiet a minute.'

Rhiannon stepped to the right, she could feel Rosh; he was so close her hair was moving with his breathing. She felt him grab hold of her right bicep. The grip was firm enough to hurt. She stayed quiet, tried to take in the environment again, tried to identify exits. Straight ahead was a kitchen area that was open to the lounge. A door hung open on the left side, she could see it was the bathroom, and a door to the right was closed. She guessed it would be a bedroom. There was a back door in the kitchen. The floor around it was thick with a layer of dirt that didn't look like it had been disturbed for quite some time. An overflowing bin blocked it and in any case she could see thick, green branches from the rear garden pushing up against the glass of the top half of the door. There were just two screw holes where the handle should have been. She didn't think an exit that way would be viable.

'So now what?' Aaron stared at the knife that was levelled at his forehead.

Danny shrugged. 'Fuck, Aaron, there's no need to—'

'Don't drop it! Keep it on me. You need to point it right between my fucking eyes.' Aaron stepped forward again. He pushed his forehead into the blade. Rhiannon could see that Danny was straining to keep it held out. 'This is how you stand a man up. They tell you there ain't no gear, they tell you they want your money and you pull your blade and you rest it right on their fucking face. And you stare into their eyes, Danny. You can tell everything you need to know about a man when you have a blade to his head.' Aaron pushed forward more firmly; he was leaning with his head, his weight supported by the point of the knife.

'What are you learning about me, Danny? What do you think about me now? Now you've got me at the end of your fucking blade? It goes both ways, you see. This is how I get to learn about you. I can see you ain't got what it takes to use it, you couldn't do it if you had to!'

Aaron's hand suddenly reached out and slapped the fist that held the knife. It caught Danny out. Aaron slapped it again. 'You're never going to use that are you, Danny? You never fucking would. No wonder they chose you to test . . . No wonder they fancied their fucking chances. Maybe you should have sent your bitch in, rather than making her sit in the car. You could have waited outside while *she* got the job done.'

Aaron slapped the knife again. This time he followed it up with a lunge at Danny. He caught him with a closed fist on the side of his face. Two more quick punches were enough to knock Danny to his knees. Aaron hit him again, now he was stood over him and they were ground punches. They hit the top of Danny's head and were enough to knock him all the way to the floor. Rhiannon could hear the blows; they were sickening against his skull. Danny didn't make any noise, he didn't protest, he didn't seem to try and protect himself. On the floor he wrapped his head up in his arms. Aaron took to kicking him. He swung his foot hard three times. Finally, Danny yelped in pain. Rhiannon tried to pull away from Rosh's hold. He tightened his grip, her muscle shot with pain and she yelped herself.

Aaron now turned to look at her. 'And who is this then? So this is who you took along? Is she part of the gang now then, Danny? Are you making these decisions without me?' He stepped closer to Rhiannon and looked her up and down. 'Some white trash you picked up off the street. Is she more important than us? We're supposed to be brothers, Danny. You took an oath to serve, to be a part of something you said you would die for. Are you choosing this bitch over all that? Is that what this is all about?'

Danny rose to an unsteady sit. He was bleeding from a gash above his right eye. He shook his head as if regaining his senses. 'She's nothing to do with this. She wasn't even there. I didn't take her in.'

'You took her to the meet though, right? She was waiting for you outside like a good little bitch? I lost ten grand's worth of gear in that meet, Danny. I lost twelve hours of trading. We are here trying to build something. Do you have any idea how damaging it is for me, at this stage, to shut the door for twelve hours? It might just have fucked everything. You owe *me* that ten grand now, Danny. That's how this works. But don't worry, your half of the debt is five grand. I want the other five grand from your bitch here.'

'She's got nothing to do with this. She came out for the drive.'

Aaron swung his boot into Danny's side again. He fell into a foetal position. 'Out for a drive? In my car. To a meeting. That you both fucked up. Listen to me Danny and listen to me proper . . . You owe me five grand each. Your half I can get from your takings. Unless you want to impress me and go get it off the real men who mugged you off. Your bitch though, she's gonna have to stay here and earn her half.' Aaron turned to Rhiannon again, lingering on her body. 'Lot of fellas like them young round here, I bet. She's a pretty thing — got that innocent look about her. She can do tricks for fifty quid a go. Easy, right? But I need a hundred a day from her, minimum. If she gets any more than that then she can keep it or she can pay off her debt quicker. Depends if she's secretly enjoying herself!' He leered right at Rhiannon. 'You ever fuck a man for money, white trash?'

'Aaron, she's got nothing—'

'Shut the fuck up, Danny! Don't think you can stand up to me now when you couldn't stand up to them cunts last night. I don't respect you enough to listen to you right now. This is how it's gonna happen.' Aaron turned his attention back to Rhiannon.

'What are you talking about?' she stammered.

'Oh come on, you're not so naïve now, are you? You owe me a debt. The debt's got to be paid. I'm not like your pussy boyfriend here. I always collect.'

'I don't owe you anything.'

Rhiannon saw the movement towards her but Rosh still had her in a tight grip. She could do nothing to stop Aaron taking a handful of her hair. He pulled her off her feet. She squealed in pain. He let go immediately, his hand now grabbing for her neck. He used his weight and had her in a powerful ground pin, her neck crushed in his one hand.

'You white girls. You think because you're young and pretty that people will give a shit. Let me tell you, I've seen it all before . . . people forget very quickly. You owe me five grand. You will get it by fucking the local scum. Because that's all you're good for. You understand me?'

Rhiannon couldn't breathe. Her hands scrabbled against his grip, but he was so strong it was nothing more than desperation. He was fixed on her, his eyes locked into hers. She managed a gargling sound.

'I'll take that as a yes. You be sure to come see me if you want to change your mind though, yeah?' Aaron pushed off her neck to get back up. He went back to his seat. The same posture, his arms pushed out either side onto the back of the sofa. Danny was still on the floor, his wide eyes locked with Rhiannon's. He looked relieved, as if he was relieved that Aaron had let her go while she could still breathe.

'Who's this?' Aaron suddenly gestured at Sam. She was stood over the other side of the room. She had her hand raised covering her mouth as if she was in the middle of a silent scream.

'No one,' Rosh said. 'She's her mate. I had to bring them both or they wouldn't have come.'

'She with you?' Aaron flicked to Rosh.

He shrugged. 'For a fuck maybe.'

Aaron grinned wildly. The grin turned into laughter. He slapped his knee and nudged Danny with his foot. 'You see, Danny, your brother, here . . . he knows a bitch and he knows their place in this world. You need to start learning and you need to start learning quick. Now get the fuck out of here and I don't want to see you again until you've been back and reloaded. This will happen again — you will be tested. They will have marked you out as the weak link now, Danny, and when they do test you I want them to be impressed. I want you to make a fucking statement. We are not here playing at this — you understand me?'

Danny struggled to his feet. 'Yeah, I understand.'

'And get this one out of my sight.' Aaron pointed at Sam. She still had the same stance. Danny took hold of her lightly and she pushed him away. He came back a lot rougher, he grabbed her hard by the arm and dragged her through the front door. He had time to exchange a furious look with Rosh before it slammed shut. He hadn't even looked over to Rhiannon. She was back on her feet, massaging her neck. Rosh moved back behind her; she could feel he was close again.

'We got a contact at a whorehouse two roads over. Czech girls, Czech madam. They ain't gonna like you!' He chuckled. You can make good money, though. You could pay me back in a week if you wanted to. Hundred a day, though, that's your minimum. It might not even be a lot of fucking — men will pay for your innocence. I'll get the word out. I want you started tonight. I'll walk you over myself.'

Rhiannon stood still. She wanted to run, to fight for the door, but she couldn't move. The panic in the pit of her stomach was like a weight that rooted her to the ground.

'I'll go first.' The male voice came from the rear of the house.

Rhiannon looked up. A man had appeared at the door to the bedroom. He was older, white and dishevelled. His face was dark with stubble and dirt and he had a white shirt that hung open and was ringed with sweat marks. He licked his lips as he peered over. Rhiannon broke into tears.

'Rummy!' Aaron sounded delighted. 'I never knew you had it in you! You like 'em young, do you? Who the fuck would have known, right?'

'I like what I like. That's my business. Is she available or what.'

'Straight to business! Fifty quid a fuck, rummy.'

Rhiannon watched through her silent tears as the man stepped more into the room. He had a limp and grimaced with every step. He dropped money on the table.

'A hundred. You said you wanted a hundred a day, minimum. That's today's. She stays with me tonight. No one else.'

'Rummy! I don't think you understand the rules of this game. She's a tom. That means she gets paid by the fuck, not by the night.'

'It's late. One hundred's what you want from her per day. You've got that. She stays with me. Or I take it back and you get the hassle of getting the word out quick and walking her across the estate.'

Aaron still smiled. 'Okay then, rummy. You get your night. I guess you're a lonely old pisshead since your ex did the honourable thing and upped and died. Be gentle though, yeah? I get the feeling she ain't seen a real man before!' Aaron laughed loud.

The man nodded towards Rhiannon and limped back to his room.

'Bring her in!' he called out. Rosh still had hold of Rhiannon's arm and she felt him pull on it. She wanted to pull back, to fight, to run. But she found herself shuffling to the bedroom door. She was shoved into the room. It was bare, save for a broken wardrobe and a wooden chair against the wall and a filthy mattress on the floor. A large TV hung precariously on the wall. It flickered in silence.

'And, rummy!' Aaron's voice boomed through the open door. 'She don't get out of here tonight, you hear me? Not tonight. Not until I walk her tomorrow. She has a debt to work off. You understand?'

'Close the door.' The man growled. Rosh backed through it, and turned his head as if waiting for permission. Then he pushed it firmly closed. Rhiannon turned back to face the man.

'Please,' she managed. 'I'm so scared!'

The man peered past her at the shut door. He spoke in an urgent whisper. 'Listen to me . . . I'm not going to touch you. I promise, okay?' He held up his hands. 'You're in a lot of danger. They *have* to believe that I did what is expected. Do you understand?'

'That you touched me?'

'I just paid for sex. They have to believe that I got what I paid for or that piece of shit is going to send out word that you're on the game and there won't be much I can do to protect you.'

'Why are you protecting me?'

'You'll have to stay here tonight. I need time to think, time to sort out where we go from there — how we get you out of here for good.'

'Can't you just call the police?'

'No. Hell no, we can't do that. These people will kill you for even thinking it.'

'Are you drunk?' Rhiannon could smell the alcohol on his breath, his eyes looked a little glazed and some of his words might have been slightly slurred.

'Not drunk enough, I can assure you of that.' He stood up. Rhiannon noticed the grimace on his face again. 'You can have the bed tonight. I'll take the floor.' He bent down, this time he grunted in pain. He picked up the corner of the mattress and let it slap back on the floor. He did it again, and again.

'What are you doing?'

He looked over. 'It's been a little while, love, I'll be honest. But this is kinda what I remember sex sounding like.'

Rhiannon backed away; she did nothing to hide her disgust. She found a place to sit in the corner against the wall.

'Jesus,' she said, her face rigid with shock.

'He won't help right now. Do me a favour, love . . . get that chair — *quietly* — and jam it under the door handle, would you? I need to be sure we don't get anyone come check on our progress.'

Rhiannon did as she was told. The man kept up the slapping of the mattress for a couple more minutes. When he stopped she heard a shout and a cheer from the other side of the door. Their eyes met and Rhiannon could do nothing to stop the tears. She buried her head in her hands and sobbed.

Chapter 13

'You saved me last night.' Rhiannon reckoned she had slept less than an hour in total. Her new friend had slept much better. His snoring was testament to that.

'For now, and you're welcome.' He was still fully clothed. They both were. He sat up and leant against the wall. She saw that same grimace on his face. It looked as if every movement hurt him.

'I never got your name.'

'No. I'm William. This is my house, believe it or not. Or at least it was.'

'Rhiannon. Rhiannon Davis. What's the matter with you? Are you in pain?'

'My leg. It gives me stick is all.'

'Are you on painkillers or anything?'

'No, I don't like the doctors. I don't trust them.'

'My mum never trusted them either. She had a bad back. She was in a lot of pain, but the doctor couldn't give her anything that she could take with the booze. He told her that she was drinking too much, too — the only person who ever did. She said she never trusted him after that. The truth is she just didn't like him.'

'Are you making a point?'

'Alcoholics don't like people who tell them they're alcoholics.'

William chuckled a little. 'That's not entirely true. The committed alcoholic you see, now he or she doesn't need to be told.'

'That's you then, is it?'

'You're very sharp.'

'You don't have to be sharp to spot a drinker. The shakes, your nose, your surroundings.'

William struggled to his feet. 'Well done, you. And speaking of my surroundings we need to get you out of here. You got an alcoholic mother to get back to.'

'I don't live with her. The Social won't let me.'

William pulled the door open a crack to peer through. He turned back to look at Rhiannon. When he spoke it was a whisper. 'Well, wherever you live, you need to be there and not here.'

'What about you?'

'What about me?'

'The man, Aaron, he said you were in charge of keeping me here, right? If I'm gone you'll get it in the neck from him.'

William pushed the door back shut. 'There's no movement. They'll be asleep. You need to get going. Don't worry about him, or me. I'm just some sad old drunk to him. I'll tell him you overpowered me — that will please him enough that he might just laugh it off. He'll have some other plaything by the end of the day. As long as it isn't you. You need to go. Now!'

Rhiannon stood up. She still had her shoes on. She scooped her phone up and pressed the button on the front screen. It was completely dead. William pulled the door open and she peered out into the living room. The sun was just up. There was nothing to stop the daylight in William's room but the curtains had been pulled across and the lights were off out in the living room area. It was just light enough to see shapes. She could see the back of the sofa, but she couldn't see who was on the other side.

'Is there no other way out?' she whispered. Her attention turned to the bedroom window. It was a tired, white UPVC unit, stained black with damp. The only part that might open was a thin strip along the top. The handle was black, too, and thick brambles bumped against the glass as the breeze shook them.

'No. Just make a run for it. The door never gets locked. It's a bit stiff so you might *think* it's locked. Just twist it all the way and give it a good tug.'

'It will make a noise though?'

'It might. Once it's open, just go. They won't catch you.'

Rhiannon wasn't sure. She opened the bedroom door and peered back out. Her eyes were better adjusted; it looked lighter. She could see a bundle of something on the sofa that faced her; it was too small to be someone. There was an open bag on the floor at one end and clothes were leaking out. She could hear the sounds of breathing, rhythmic and long, like someone asleep.

'I can't!' she breathed.

'Go!'

'What if he catches me?'

'Just go, and don't let that happen.'

Rhiannon tiptoed into the living room. Her footfalls sounded to her like the loudest thing she had ever heard. She grimaced with every step. She snuck past the sofa. She could see a long shape on it, under a cover of sorts and turned away from her. The head was covered. She made it to the front door. The handle squeaked as it turned. She held it and peered back over at the sleeping figure, holding her breath. Still no movement. Beyond him she could see the bedroom door was still ajar. William still stood at it; he opened it wider to signal for her to go.

She pulled at the door. It didn't budge. It felt like it was locked. She turned back to William, starting to feel the desperation. She shook the door and it rattled loudly. The figure stirred. William waved again for her to go. She rattled the door harder, used all her strength. It didn't budge.

'We found the key.' A man's voice, a figure sat up on the sofa. He shook his head and rubbed at his face. 'You ain't gonna be able to get out without it.' He stood up and stepped towards Rhiannon. He was holding a key out on the end of his finger, mocking her. It was the thin boy who had stayed silent last night.

'Let me go.'

'I got my instructions,' he said.

'Let her go, Mo!' William shouted. 'This don't involve her. What good is she here?'

'Five grand, I heard.'

'He knows she don't owe that. Aaron's playing with the girl. You don't need to be part of that, Mo. Let her go. I'll say it was me — I let her out.'

'Aaron said you would. He told me to make sure you don't. It don't matter what you say, rummy, this is self-preservation. I ain't gonna be the one pissing him off.'

William had moved closer. Rhiannon looked at him. Her panic started to build again — the realisation that she was a prisoner.

'She's going, Mo.' William snatched for the keys. He was quicker than Rhiannon expected; he took them from Mo in a single movement and moved to the door. Mo was back at him. He had a slight build and he was a young man but he was quick. He hooked his arm round William's neck from behind him and pulled him backwards. William stumbled away from Rhiannon but still held the keys tightly in his right fist.

'Get off me, Mo!'

'Give me the fucking keys back, rummy!' Rhiannon saw Mo's hand snatch downwards. He brought out an evil-looking blade. He hooked his arm back around, the blade pushing lightly into William's neck. Rhiannon covered her mouth, William was looking directly at her. He seemed assured. Rhiannon could see the colour of his skin had gone white where the pressure of the point pushed into his throat.

'What is it with you boys and your knives? What happened to a good fist fight? That's what men used to do, I swear it. You boys . . . you're playing.' William was almost smiling.

'You ain't got a fist fight in you either, rummy.'

'Put the knife down and we'll give it a go.'

'Give me the keys!'

'She's leaving.' William was close enough to reach the door. He pushed the key into the lock.'

'Turn that key and I'll slit your throat.'

'No, you won't.' The key turned. William was looking right at Rhiannon again. 'Pull the door, love. Go home.'

'Don't you fucking move!' Mo still held William with his arm hooked round his neck, but the knife now pointed towards her. She pulled the door enough for a slit of daylight.

'Go on love, go!'

Rhiannon pulled the door wider. She stepped out. When she made it to the gate she broke into a run.

* * *

William took a pint of water back to his bedroom. Mo eyed him furiously and he waved him away, calling him a boy for the final time. William lay back on the mattress. It smelled sweet for once; Rhiannon must have left some of her perfume on it. He ran through his options in his mind. He was pretty sure he had finished the last of the rum the night before. He would need to get out for some more supplies and he reckoned he would be back to funding it himself. He had some money left over from what Aaron had given him and from his grafting the day before, even after paying to keep Rhiannon out of harm's way — for now at least. He lay thinking about Rhiannon. She had immediately looked out of place, a true flower in a compost heap. He hoped she never looked back.

He could hear Mo's voice through the wall. Not enough to be able to pick out words, but he guessed it was a phone call. He also reckoned he knew who he was speaking to. This was confirmed around fifteen minutes later. He knew it was Aaron, just from the way the door was opened. The man seemed to be heavy handed in everything he did. The door slammed off the wall, the footsteps were heavy and came right to his bedroom door, which was opened just as heavily. The chair against the handle folded as if it was made of matchsticks.

'Rummy!' Aaron stepped into the room and fell on top of where William was lying. He was already swinging his giant fists. William felt a blow to his head and two hammer blows to his body. His head stung and his vision blurred, he felt a shot of pain in his ribs. He tried to get his arms out for protection but felt his left wrist get swept up in a firm grip. His arm was pushed outwards and he took two more blows to the face. He tried to lift his right arm out in a push, but it was useless. Everything was fading, the pain, his vision, the sounds of Aaron's rage. Until it all slipped away.

* * *

Rhiannon didn't stop running until she made it to the bus stop. She jumped onto the first bus that showed up and found a seat at the back. The bus was near empty, and from her position she could see anyone who might get on. The trip from Langthorne to Ashford was around thirty-five minutes. After fifteen minutes, the bus left the town of Langthorne and she felt herself relaxing. Inevitably she was overcome with sleep. She took off her hoody, rolled it up to form a pillow and rested against the window. It smelled of damp and stale cigarette smoke but she didn't care.

She got to her stop and felt worse for the sleep. She yearned for a shower and a comfy bed with clean sheets. She was as quiet as she could manage opening the door to her temporary home, but it was no good. Rose had been waiting for her. She was at the door before Rhiannon had even pushed it open.

'Oh, Rhiannon! What happened to you?'

'Hey, Rose. I'm really sorry — I got caught out. The buses weren't running.'

'The buses? You should have called. Two nights in a row, late and then this!' Rose gestured at her. 'You look like you slept on a park bench. You could have called me out. I would have come and picked you up, Rhiannon. I just needed to know you were okay.'

'I'm fine, Rose. It won't happen again. My phone died. I'm really sorry.' Rhiannon's voice broke a little and her tears caught her by surprise.

Rose's stance softened immediately. 'Oh, Rhiannon, don't be upset. You're here and you're okay, that's all that matters. Have you eaten even?'

Rhiannon was suddenly aware how hungry she was. 'No, actually. I'll just do some toast.'

'Go shower, my love. Go get yourself all freshened up and I'll put some toast in.'

'Is Sam in?'

'No. She was in late and she left for college this morning.'

Rhiannon plugged her phone into its charger the second she made it back into her room. It took a few minutes for it to have enough life to even turn on. She had left the shower running just down the corridor, it was calling her. She Googled the local doctor's surgery. It came up with a telephone number. She pressed on the number and it started calling.

* * *

Something vibrated. It was close to him, William could feel the vibration as well as hear it. He opened his eyes, his right eye didn't function, he could barely see out. His face stung, his lips and mouth particularly. He reached a hand up and pushed at his mouth and winced immediately. Flexing his jaw got the same reaction. He felt a tooth move in his gum, the pain was enough to make him wail. The vibrating stopped. William struggled sit up. He had been lying on his side and his lips were stuck to his pillow with dried blood. He had to peel the cotton away.

The vibration started again.

Confused, he looked around. There were no places for anything to hide. Sure enough, a mobile phone lay on the floor. It was plugged into a charger on the wall. He recognised it as being the one he'd lost ages ago.

The screen gave no clue as to who was calling. 'Hello?' His lips and mouth stung with speaking.

'William? William Dryden?'

'Yeah.'

'It's Rhiannon. From last night. Are you okay? Did that Mo leave you alone after I left?' The concern was genuine, unmistakable. William hadn't heard that in a while. His face flushed, a tear rolled out that he couldn't feel until it made it to his chin. He wiped it away.

'Yeah.' It was all he could manage, lying beaten and in pain his sudden emotion still caught him out.

'I found your phone. It was under the wardrobe. I took your number, I hope you don't mind.'

'No.'

'Are you sure you're okay? Are they there? Can you not talk?'

'Not really.'

'Okay. I called to tell you I made you an appointment. With the doctor.'

'What?'

'The doctor. You need to get yourself sorted out. You shouldn't be living with that sort of pain. It's 4 p.m. — the appointment, I mean.'

'I can't. Shorry.' The tooth that had been flexing now came loose in his mouth. He spat it out, catching it in his hand. He fixed on it; it was a bloody mass. 'Oh, Jesus!'

'Are you drunk, William?' The concern slipped immediately. She sounded angry now.

'No.'

'You're just as hopeless as Mum was. You need to start looking after yourself. You need to make this appointment at four. They'll help you with the pain but they can also help get you off the drink. You do want that right?'

'Shure.' He felt a fresh drip of blood over his lips.

'So you'll be there?'

'I can't. Not now.' Every word was agony.

'You can. Why can't you? If you don't make it then I will make another appointment and I will walk back to that house to make sure you come. Believe me, William, I will.'

'You can't! You don't understand. You need to shtay away.'

'You are drunk. Just be there William. Please.'

The call disconnected. William dropped the phone. He shook his head. He surveyed his body for more injuries. His ribs were sore, the back of his head had a lump. The inside of the wardrobe had a full-length mirror. He had to wipe it with his sleeve to remove a layer of dust and grime. His reflection made him gasp. His right eye looked like a split tomato and it leaked a clear fluid. His nose was swollen at the bridge and was tender to the touch. His lips were swollen, too, and he had dried blood over most of his face. He pulled his shirt open. He had bruising on his chest and arms and his left shin was severely bruised with an open gash that trickled blood. He couldn't stand. Not for now at least — he'd have to build up to it. He lowered himself as gently as he could back onto his side and closed his eyes to the world.

Chapter 14

Rhiannon woke to bright sunshine. She hadn't closed the curtains or managed to get under her quilt. She was still wrapped in just a towel around her body and a second one wrapped round her hair.

'Fuck! What happened to you?' Sam's voice was urgent. She was sat at the end of the bed. She must have been what had woken Rhiannon.

'What happened to *you*, you mean,' Rhiannon grunted. She shifted to a sit. 'You made it back okay, then.'

'I sent Danny back for you. He sent me a message, like, an hour later and said he was back with you, and Rosh and you were fine. Rosh sent the same.'

'Well, they weren't.'

'Jesus.'

Rhiannon sat up. She hugged herself, suddenly feeling the cold from being wrapped in a damp towel.

Sam was lingering on her, especially her body. 'Did you, you know, did they make you?'

'No! But only because I got very lucky.'

'Lucky how?'

'I don't even know. Right bloke, right time I guess.'

'Danny?'

'No. Definitely not Danny.'

'I thought it was weird, you know. I haven't heard from them today. Not Rosh, that's not normal for him. I thought they had gone back and sorted you out. I figured you had stayed out, maybe over at Danny's.'

'Nope. I slept on some manky mattress thanking my lucky stars no one was raping me. How was your night?'

'Jesus, Rhiannon, I know you're angry, but it wasn't my fault. I couldn't do nothing.'

'You could have not taken me there in the first place. You could have not introduced me to those people. We should both be staying away from them — all of them.'

'Yeah. You're right. I mean what sort of a man does that? Leaves you there. I didn't know, though, right, Rhiannon? I mean, I checked up. I thought you were cool.'

'Yeah, well I wasn't. And I've got to get sorted.' Rhiannon pulled her phone from where it had been charging. It was half past two.

'You got somewhere to be?'

'Yeah. Soon, too.'

'You want to hang later? After, like?'

'No.'

Sam got up off the bed. She flashed angry herself, but it was nothing more than an expression. She walked towards the door.

'I'm just tired, Sam, that's all! I didn't sleep much!' Rhiannon called out.

'Sure, I understand.'

* * *

William pushed the door and bundled through. The room consisted of a reception desk on the left, two rows of chairs back to back through the middle and a third row against the right-hand wall under high windows. An elderly woman sat closest to him, dressed as if in her Sunday best. She had a tartan bag on the seat next to her and she wrapped her arm around it as William let the door close behind him. On the opposite side of the room was a small play area. A little boy played with a wooden puzzle. He crashed two wooden balls together that were suspended on wire and squealed loudly. Engrossed in her smartphone, his mother didn't seem to notice. A few other patients were scattered across the waiting room. In the front row he saw the girl from the house — Rhiannon. She was staring at him, her eyes wide, her hand over her mouth. She got to her feet slowly. A few of the waiting people noticed; they flicked from her to him and back again.

He dipped his head and stepped forwards — shot of pain through his thigh. He tried not to give any outward sign. He made it to the seat next to the girl and fell into it.

'Jesus! They did that because of me!'

'They didn't say why!' William tried to expel laughter, but his laughter turned to a grimace. His jaw was still sore, his mouth and gums hurt with speech. It was still a lot better than first thing though.

'You have to tell the police. What did they do?'

'Nothing like what they'll do if I tell the police. Don't worry, I'll be fine.'

'You don't look fine.'

'It looks worse than it is.'

'What did he hit you with? Look at your eye, your lips! It looks like they hit you everywhere.'

'Listen, kid, I appreciate you making a call — for caring about my leg. But I can't go in there. I only came here to make sure you understand that you can't go back. To the house, I mean. And I can handle this from here. I don't need you calling my doctor.'

'Well, you're here now. If you can handle this then you might as well go in and talk to the doctor. He's the other side of that door. And your appointment . . . it's five minutes. I read up a bit about abscesses. They only get worse. If you let it get too bad, it will kill you.'

'I know. Trust me, I know how bad they can get. But I can't go in there looking like this. I know the system. They might tip off the old bill, and right now I could do without a visit.'

Rhiannon suddenly became animated. 'That would be perfect, surely? If someone else called the police, that's nothing to do with you. They can arrest the arsehole that did this to you then. Or at least get them all out of your house.'

'It don't work like that, love. The police won't be bothered about me, especially when I tell them I fell down the stairs. I can't go telling them what happened. No one can.' William locked eyes with Rhiannon to reinforce his message.

'It might scare them off at least.'

'Or they will go again on me, and this time they won't stop just because I lose consciousness.'

'They beat you unconscious?'

William shrugged. 'Yeah, I think so. Look, I'm fine.'

'But you're not. You're in pain every day with your leg. Go see the doctor. I feel so bad they did that to you because of me. Because you let me go. Please just go and see him, so I at least feel like I've done something for you.'

'William Dryden?' a man called out. William looked up and the man seemed to be staring right at him. He had grey hair and a neat, white beard. He wore a checked shirt tucked into chinos and he lifted his glasses and one eyebrow in expectation. William sighed in resignation.

'How did you even know my surname?' William hissed towards Rhiannon. The doctor nodded and turned towards the corridor. William was supposed to follow.

'Oh,' Rhiannon pulled a crumpled envelope from her pocket. She handed it to William. 'You should have this back. I took it from your place this morning. It was stuffed behind your radiator. I guess that's where you keep the important stuff.'

He unfolded it. It was an NHS branded letter, dated from late the previous year. It had all the information she would have needed to make the appointment. He smiled at her, despite the pain in his mouth.

'You found my phone, charged it and took the number and then found a letter so you could make me a doctor's appointment for my leg?'

'Yeah, pretty much.'

'I'm not used to having someone look out for me you know.'

'Mr Dryden?' The spectacled man called out again. He was further away, stood at an open door. 'Shall we?'

William struggled to his feet. He took a step and the muscle spasmed, he stumbled and Rhiannon steadied him.

The man called out again, 'Is your daughter able to help you in at least. She doesn't have to stay beyond that.'

They exchanged glances. 'No, I can manage.' William walked a few more steps. The man stepped into his examination room. William turned back to Rhiannon. 'Look, thanks, okay? But you need to stay away. From all of this. As far away as you can.' He continued his walk.

* * *

'Why are you still here?' William's meeting with the doctor had been short. Neither man had an appetite to drag it out it seemed. 'I did what you wanted, right?'

'What did he say?' Rhiannon said.

'What I expected.'

'Did he look at your face?'

'He held eye contact if that's what you mean.'

'You know what I mean.'

'My nose is broken. That's about the worst there is. He reckons my jaw is just bruised, it might have dislocated but it isn't now.'

'You should still get an x-ray.'

'He said the same, wanted me to go to a hospital. No point though. There's nothing they can do about it.'

'You should listen to the doctor.'

'Why are you still here?'

Rhiannon stood up. 'I wanted to talk to you. About those men at your house. I want to know more.'

'Why? I told you to stay away. That's all you need to know.'

'My friend, Sam . . .'

'The girl from last night? She should stay away too. Simple as that.'

'Yes, she should. But I don't think she will. What do I tell her to convince her? She doesn't seem to see what they're like.'

'I don't care what you tell her. I don't really care if she listens to you, or if you listen to me anymore. I've already done too much. The one thing I've learned is to keep out of other people's business. You stick your oar in and it gets snapped off.' William gestured at his face. 'All this is my fault. Now, I got to get some pills out and then I'm going somewhere I like to drink. *Alone.*'

He walked to the counter. He heard footsteps walking away behind him. The door to the surgery rung a shrill bell as it was pulled open. He was given some paperwork for his prescription from an unsmiling receptionist who didn't utter a word. When he limped back out into the sun, Rhiannon was stood at the end of the ramp. She was leaning on the railings, a bottle of cider in each hand.

'You don't listen very well do you?' he said.

'We have that in common.'

'What do you want from me?'

'Five minutes.' She held out one of the bottles. William made it to the bottom of the ramp, the handrail taking his weight. He snatched the bottle. He eyed the other.

'I didn't have you down as a cider drinker,' he said.

'It's for you. At the end of the five minutes. It's the same brand as all the empties at your place.'

William snorted and pushed off the handrail. 'Clever kid. Five minutes,' he grunted.

William knew a spot nearby. The Leas was a grassy expanse on a cliff top on the very edge of the town. For many it was a beauty spot where you could sit on one of the many benches, among manicured lawns and flowering beds and gaze out over the sea. William loved the sea view, too, but his choice of a place to sit was a footpath long since closed, the end of which had fallen away and the beginning of which was blocked by a gate with stern warning signs of cliff falls. William ignored them all. The padlock was thick and meant business. William used it to rest his foot on before he pushed his weight up and almost fell over the top. He couldn't help but groan in pain as he landed; his hand immediately moved to this thigh, then reached through to grab the cider he had put on the ground. Rhiannon didn't say anything, just scaled the gate and followed him along the path. Twenty metres along, it dropped down the cliff face and turned back on itself. William followed it round. He walked another few metres. The path became rougher, the part that had fallen away was clearly visible. He stopped a few metres short, where a break in the trees offered a clear view through to the shuffling sea. He fell to a sit, twisted the top off the cider and took a long swig. He said nothing, just gazed out at the sea. Today it was striped with different shades of blues and greens pierced by mini eruptions of white froth. Every day the colours were different. Rhiannon sat next to him.

'Nice spot,' she said.

'Yeah.'

'I can see why they closed it off, though.'

William looked over to where she was leant forward, looking down the slope on the other side of the steel railings. The path dug into the side of the cliff. Some of the rock and mud had slipped away from the side as well as collapsing at the end of the path. The slope on the other side was steeper and more sudden than it had been just a few months before.

'I'm glad they did. I like to drink in peace.'

'How did you find it?' Rhiannon said. She either hadn't picked up on the dig or chosen to ignore it completely.

'It was Janey's place. She brought me here. She's always loved the sea. We both have.'

'Something in common then.'

'We were both elsewhere. Both inland, living different lives. We both asked to be rehoused near the sea, thought it might help fight our addictions. Two different councils both fell for it. I always said the sea is what brought us together.'

'That sounds right to me. You would never have met otherwise.'

'No. And for all the shit, for it hurting now, I'm glad we did.'

'What happened with her?'

William was suddenly aware of himself. 'She died. Simple really.' He sniffed and shuffled to try and get more comfortable.

'Sorry. I shouldn't have asked.'

'Don't matter.'

'I lost my aunt. She died too. That's why I'm here. They put me in some emergency foster care.'

'And here we are.'

'What do you mean?'

'Me and Janey, we got brought together by the sea. Beautiful it is, nothing more beautiful on earth. Me and you, we got brought together by death, right? That's a sign we should stay away from each other, if ever I saw one.'

'Well, when you put it like that . . .'

William was aware of an awkward pause. He hadn't intended to sound quite so harsh. 'Do you like it?'

'What?'

'The foster placement? Where you're at?'

'I liked living with my aunty.'

'You should stay there. In your placement. You'll be safe there.'

'And what about you?'

'What about me?' William took another swig on his cider.

'Where are you safe if it's not at home?'

'Here? I'll be okay. I know enough about this world to know these people. They don't hang around long. And they won't do that again, as long as I don't stick my nose in.'

'But they're still at your home. And you can't stay here.'

'It stopped being my home when Janey left. I feel closer to her here. This feels more like my home. I'll spend some time here — go back when I need to sleep. This will pass. It always passes.'

'Do you think Sam's in danger?'

'I've told you enough. You're both in danger if you spend any more time with those people. You need to stay away.'

'That's what I told her.'

'Is she a good friend? Doesn't she listen to you?'

'I hardly know her, I guess. I mean, we met when I moved to the house a few days ago. But she was good to me, right from the start.'

'You need to look after yourself, though. You can't be worrying about her. Putting yourself at risk just for someone who was nice to you, that's madness.'

'We all need to look out for each other, right?'

William turned to take in Rhiannon. He lingered on her soft features, long enough that she gave a nervous chuckle and looked away, out over the sea. Her long hair drifted about her face in the light breeze, her legs were pulled up, her arms wrapped around her knees. She looked small, vulnerable. Beautiful.

'Who's looking out for you, though, Rhiannon? I've seen people like you before. A big heart, a pretty face. This world will chew you up and spit you out. That loveliness that you've got, you have to learn to switch that off. You need to be ruthless when it's called for. Trust me, you need to start looking out for yourself.'

'Thanks,' Rhiannon said.

'For what?'

'For talking to me today. For talking to your doctor, too. And for last night — when you forgot to be ruthless.' Rhiannon stood up. She placed the second bottle of cider next to him. He watched her as she disappeared from sight.

Chapter 15

Mo walked the pedestrianised area of Langthorne at midday. He had a hundred wraps in his underwear, a mix of heroin and cocaine. Every one of his senses felt heightened. This wasn't normally his role; he was never the mule. He had always looked after the money. Aaron had thrown his toys out of the pram that morning; he had suddenly decided that he wanted a switch of personnel. The issue he'd had with Danny was clearly still on his mind and they were all having to suffer for it.

Whatever. Mo just needed to make it another one hundred metres to where a road veered off from the High Street and into the grounds of the cemetery. Rosh should be there to meet him. Rosh was out doing the street deals today. Aaron had previously been using local users to deal the drugs — they worked for next to nothing and they took all the risks — but he was closing ranks. A hundred wraps was a lot to be carrying at any one time — around two thousand pounds in street value. The local dealers were given ten wraps at a time. They couldn't be trusted with any more.

Mo's heightened senses had picked out a tail. He couldn't be sure; maybe it was just that he was so aware that his mind was tricking him into believing anyone who looked at him must be someone to worry about. The man in question was stationary. He was leaning casually against a wall between two shop fronts. Too casual maybe, he had one leg up so the sole of his foot met the wall and he was idly flicking through his phone. It looked to Mo like he was trying to demonstrate just how little he was bothered about what was going on around him, yet all the while he was probably texting to update on Mo's movements. They would be surrounding him, ready to strike. Mo shook his head. *Stupid.* He was just another boy walking the busy High Street. There was no reason for undercover officers or rival gangs to take notice of him. Except for the hundred wraps of class A drugs in his underwear. He had refused to plug them; he drew the line at pushing them into his anal cavity. You wouldn't get that much even into an experienced mule and it rarely stopped the police finding it anyway, it just made it take longer.

Mo walked past the casual man. Ten metres more and he would need to take a right. The shop on the corner opposite was at an angle. It was glass-fronted, and the window provided Mo with an effective mirror. The man was now behind him. Mo saw him look up and push his phone back into his pocket. He pushed off the wall.

Mo took the turn. All his concerns were back in droves. He pulled his own phone from his pocket and wiped the messages as he walked, then the call history. There were only two contacts on the phone and he wiped them, too. The street towards the steps down into the cemetery was quieter. There was just a hairdressers and the shop front for the local Conservative MP. He picked up his pace. He wore a black baseball cap, a hoody and blue trackies. He turned the peak of the cap so it sat off-centre, a signal to Rosh that he had been compromised. He still wasn't certain, but better safe than sorry.

Mo made the steps. It gave him an elevated view of the grassy area of the church. As planned, he could see Rosh leaning on a stone wall on the opposite side, some way in the distance. Rosh stood up immediately and started walking away at pace. At the bottom of the steps, Mo turned quickly right, ducking behind the wall. He bent down, fiddled with his shoe as if he was tying his laces. He watched the end of the wall where the steps finished. He heard footsteps. The casual man appeared and his phone was now to his ear.

'It's a temporary loss — St Eanswythe Churchyard,' the man said. He turned to the right and his eyes met with Mo's. They flared wide.

Mo leapt to his feet and broke into a sprint. He pushed right past the man and back towards the High Street. He wanted to go in the opposite direction to Danny and he fancied his chances of getting lost in the crowd. He didn't look back. He made the High Street. There was another street directly opposite and he weaved through bodies to get to it. Just as he was about to break free, one of the bodies threw its arms out and gripped him tightly round his chest. Mo's momentum took him over and he sprawled onto the cobbles. The grip on him was released momentarily but then he felt it again, this time round his legs. It was tighter this time. He could hear shouted instructions. 'Stop resisting! Police!' Mo tried to kick out, to kick him off. He could barely move his legs, shackled as they were by bodyweight. The man who had chased back from the cemetery took hold of his arms.

'Police!' he bellowed. 'Keep your hands where I can see them!' Mo was bundled onto his front. He felt his arms wrenched round so his wrists met at the back. Then the cold metal of handcuffs; he heard them ratchet shut. He pushed his forehead into the concrete and scrunched his eyes closed. He didn't shout or complain. He knew he was done and he remembered what he had been told. He wouldn't be saying another thing.

* * *

'What happened?' Rosh took a step back as Aaron moved off the sofa.

'I was where we agreed at the time we said. I saw Mo. He was giving a signal that he had picked up some interest, so I walked away. I had a grand in my pocket, I didn't want to get picked up and lose it. I stashed the money up and by the time I made it back round to Mo there were three blokes on top of him. One of them was in a copper uniform, so I assume they were all cops.'

'FUCK!' Aaron roared. Rosh took another step back. Aaron's breathing was suddenly loud, like he was struggling to get it under control. His nostrils flared.

Rosh tried to calm him down. 'What did he have on him? A hundred wraps? We'll have to wear that and Mo's a juvenile with nothing for drugs. They should boot him back out with a court date. He'll probably get some community shit. He shouldn't even go to juvie—'

'You think I'm bothered about losing the *gear*? About *Mo*?'

'Well, yeah, I mean what else is there?'

'I fucking KNEW IT!' Aaron kicked out at the wall. His foot coursed through the outer layer and got stuck. Bits of plaster cracked and flecked onto the floor as he pulled it back out. 'I knew I had brought a load of amateurs down here with me. You can't do this with fucking amateurs!'

'Aaron, I know it's a shit day, but we—'

'A shit day! You don't get it, do you? I know it happens, you *can* lose a hundred wraps and get a soldier burnt and it ain't nothing. But this was Mo, and he was picked up just walking down the street. Why did they even look at him twice? I sent him out today for the *first* time and he gets burnt! Mo's the money man — I keep him away from the gear. I only put him out today because Danny's a fucking liability. They had to *know* about Mo, which means they have to *know* about the line, about *us*!'

Rosh shook his head. 'I dunno, we kinda stick out down here you know. We're not exactly local. Maybe they got a sniff that a black guy was out dealing in the town — they stopped the first black guy they saw and got lucky. It don't have to be that they knew about Mo.'

'And where did this sniff come from. Someone's been talking. Who do you think that might be? Who knows all about our little setup here?'

'No one who'd be grassing, surely?'

Aaron stepped suddenly towards Rosh. Rosh flinched, but Aaron walked right past him. He made for the door to William's bedroom and his boot came up again. The bedroom door folded in immediately. Nobody was in there. Rosh couldn't remember the last time he had seen or heard anyone in it. Aaron huffed again, his chest rising and falling with the exertion. He swung his fist this time and it thudded into the centre of the television hanging on the wall.

'I want the rummy. And I want the two girls.'

'You don't think—'

'I don't KNOW!' Aaron roared. He checked himself. 'I don't know. And that means I can't have no control and that don't sit well with me. I need to know who's talking and what they're talking about.'

'Maybe it's just one of the users. It happens. They speak to the cops, tell them there's a new setup in the area.'

Aaron was shaking his head. 'Users don't know Mo. They don't know much and they need us. I get that it can happen, the cops wave a twenty in their direction and they get loose lips, but they don't know Mo. The two girls, the rummy. I need to put a bit of pressure on them. One of them has been talking and I'm going to find out which one it is.'

'You want them here?'

'No. The cops might know about this place too. They might be on their way to search it. We should assume they know about it.'

'If they knew about it they'd be here already, right?'

'Assume they do. Assume they know everything. Take the car. Run it through a few ANPR cameras, past a few cop cars and give them the eyeball. See if you get pulled over and how you get treated. I need to know if they know about the car too. I'll call you when I'm somewhere else. I need to get this place cleared. Then I want you start rounding them up. I don't care who you can get to me first, just as long as I get an opportunity to start asking questions.'

'Then what?' Rosh said. He had seen Aaron like this before, but only a few times: his nostrils flaring, his eyes wide and unfocused. He had lost his control. His chest moved in and out, his fists were clenched by his side.

'Depends on the answers I get.'

Chapter 16

Rhiannon mounted the bottom step of her temporary home as her phone rang. She stopped on the steps and pulled it from her pocket. It was Danny. She pressed to cut the call and continued into the house. It had a stillness about it that told her she was home alone. She called out anyway. 'Rose! Hello?' No answer. She walked through to the kitchen and made a drink. Her phone rang again. She had put it down on the kitchen table. She could see it was Danny again. This time she let it ring out.

Ten minutes later and Rhiannon was in her bedroom. This time her phone rang and it was Sam.

'Sam,' Rhiannon said.

'Rhiannon, you okay?'

Rhiannon just wanted to be left alone. 'I'm fine yeah, you okay?'

'Yeah. Where are you?'

'I'm back at the house.'

'Okay. I wasn't going to go back there until later. Do you fancy meeting up? I think we should talk about all this shit. About what happened. We need to have a plan, yeah? You know, so we know what we're doing from here.'

‘A plan?’ All of Rhiannon’s exasperation was back. ‘What do you mean a plan? We stay the hell away from those boys and whatever it is they’re into and we stay safe. That’s my plan. It should be yours too.’

‘Yeah, I know, I reckon it is. I just think we should talk, you know. I want us to be cool. I feel bad. You know them boys because of me and the other night I couldn’t do nothing. I feel proper bad.’

‘I know that, Sam. It worked out okay in the end. Look, I can make my own decisions and I thought they seemed like nice lads. Well, Danny at least. It doesn’t matter now. Don’t worry about it.’

‘So, do you still want to meet? I’m in the town. There’s some street artist festival on down here or something. Most of them are shit but there’s some good stuff too. We could have a smoothie or something.’

Rhiannon sighed. She didn’t know if she wanted to see anyone, let alone spend time with them. But she didn’t have any plans for the rest of the afternoon and she knew Anais would be back soon. That meant staying in her room until tomorrow morning. She didn’t relish that idea.

‘I’ll come down. I can’t promise I’ll be out for long, though. I don’t really want to be cooped up in here all afternoon, I suppose.’

‘Nice one! Yeah, come down. Give me a call when you’re in the town. I’ve got some shops to do and then I’ll probably go sit in Costa. I’ll meet you there.’

Rhiannon sighed again, the call ended. She surveyed herself in the mirror. She was back in her jeans torn at the knees, pump trainers and a fitted T-shirt. She knew Sam wouldn’t approve, but right now she couldn’t care less. She put a brush through her hair and freshened up before leaving the house for the ten-minute bus ride into the town.

The coffee shop was busy. Everywhere was. Sam hadn’t described the activity too well; it was some big art festival with some roads closed. The High Street itself was closed off by a flickering police car. Rhiannon hadn't bothered calling Sam. She figured she would find a table with a drink on her own for a few minutes before she let her know she was there. Rhiannon liked to people watch. She would make up back-stories for all the people walking past the window or filling the other tables. The people and the families she saw in her mind's eye would always be happy and fulfilled, with perfect lives and bright futures. She ended up disliking them all.

Rhiannon found a table. She had a bright red smoothie with loads of ice. Sam's voice was immediately shrill in her ear.

'Rhiannon!' She turned towards the source. Sam was carrying several shopping bags — the brown card types you get from shopping for clothes.

'Hey, Sam. I was just going to call. Did you want a drink?'

Sam pushed her bags onto the table and vacant seat. 'Don't worry, I'll get something.' She strode towards the counter. Rhiannon watched her, sucking her drink through a straw. She thought Sam looked a little uncomfortable, unsure maybe. She was in a long grey dress, the type that looked like an extended jumper and clung tightly to her figure. Her blonde hair was straightened and she wore new-looking versions of Rhiannon's pumps to finish the outfit. It was clear her attention was very much back over with Rhiannon. She was turned to the side, but it was like she wanted to be able to see her all the time in her periphery. Every now and then she would turn to face Rhiannon and project a smile over. She also fidgeted with her phone.

Rhiannon turned away. She peered out the window at the people walking past. With their perfect, uncomplicated lives and families, they all looked so happy to her.

Sam made it back to the table. She put her cup down but stayed standing. She was leaning on the back of the chair when Rhiannon looked up.

'You okay? Are you not staying?' Rhiannon quipped. She was suddenly aware of a figure making straight for her. It was Danny. He held an awkward smile. Rhiannon immediately fixed back on Sam. Rhiannon picked up her drink and her phone that had been laid out on the table.

'He just wants to talk to you,' Sam said.

'I told you I don't want anything to do with him.' Danny was at the table. Rhiannon did her best to ignore him completely.

'Just a minute,' Danny spoke, 'one minute.'

'For what?' Rhiannon demanded, doing nothing to hide the emotion in her voice. She felt furious. That he was here, that Sam had set it up. That they both thought this should happen.

'I want to say I'm sorry.'

'For what?' Rhiannon snapped again.

'What do you mean, for what?'

'What are you sorry for? I want you to say it.' Rhiannon stood up. She shuffled to the end of the table and paused enough for a response. Danny was floundering.

'For getting you into all this shit. I shouldn't have got you involved. I'm sorry, yeah?'

Rhiannon took another moment. The frustration had built to the point where she was struggling to form words; she just wanted to lash out. Sam cut across them.

'I'll leave you two to it then.'

'Don't worry, Sam. I'm not staying. He can't even say what he did. This is pointless. He can't even be honest with himself, let alone with me.'

'I left you there,' Danny blurted. 'Okay, I know I did. I didn't want to, I hate myself. I haven't stopped thinking about it since—'

'At last! Some honesty! Too late though.' Rhiannon took a step towards the exit.

'Ask me anything!' Danny called out. Rhiannon stopped. She was aware that the occupants from other tables were looking over. Her exchange had been neither quiet nor subtle. 'Anything,' Danny persisted.

'And how would I know you were telling the truth? With anything you say.'

'You'll know when I say it. Because I know what you want to ask, what you want to talk about, what you think you know. I'll tell you everything.'

Sam made her excuses once again. This time she left. Rhiannon didn't even acknowledge her. All her attention was on Danny.

'Are you a drug dealer?' she asked. She was still aware she was being watched. It was clear from Danny's reaction that he was aware too. He met a few gazes from the strangers now paying them attention before his eyes settled back on her.

'Yes.' His voice was considerably lower than Rhiannon's had been.

'I don't need to know anything more then, do I?'

'Yes you do. Let's get out of here so I can explain.'

'I am getting out of here. But not with you.' Rhiannon made for the door. She bustled through a group of girls coming in, they made some angry comments towards her but she kept her head down and kept walking. She turned hard left and quickened her pace. She heard running from behind her. Danny caught her up.

'I just want you to be safe. You don't belong involved in all this shit. You're different.' He was breathy.

'So you keep saying. You tell me I'm different, you make me feel special and then you leave me with an alcoholic to be a prisoner in his stinking bedroom for the night, where he paid to rape me. And now you say you just want me to be safe?'

'He didn't though, did he? Touch you, I mean?'

'Rape me. That's what you mean. He didn't pay to touch me Danny, he paid to rape me, remember? You should remember. You were there when the deal was done.'

'I can explain.'

'No you can't. And no he didn't. But I got lucky, the man turned out to be looking out for me, which puts him way above you in my estimation. There is no explanation for what you did. I want you to leave me alone.'

'I will. If you want me to. I will leave you alone. But Aaron . . . he won't be so easy.'

'Why not? What have I ever done to him?'

'Nothing. It's not about what you've done to him, not for a bloke like that. It's all about losing face. It's about respect.'

'Well, that's his problem. And yours.'

'He will come for you, Rhiannon. Just hear me out. Once you have the full picture you can walk away, but at least you'll know.'

'You tell me everything. You tell me what you're up to and I will sit and listen. Once that's done I don't want to speak to you again, do you understand?'

'Sure, okay. I understand.'

Rhiannon finally slowed her pace. 'We're not far from Victoria Park. We can go there. I want to be somewhere public when you talk to me. If you give me any shit I will make a scene and I won't stop until someone calls the police. They'll be very interested to hear about you, I'm sure.'

Danny sort of chuckled. 'There won't be any need to make a scene. I just want you to listen to me, I want you to know about Aaron and what he's about and then I'm gone.'

'You shouldn't laugh. I'm not laughing Danny.'

'I'm sorry, okay. This is all stupid. I'm no threat to you.'

'Well, I am to you. Don't you forget that.'

Danny held his hands out as if he was surrendering. 'I ain't even arguing with you. I came here to talk.'

'So you keep saying. What more is there to talk about? You told me you're a drug dealer. That's all I need to know, right?'

'If that's all you want to know.'

'I wish I'd never met any of you to be honest.'

'You don't want to know about the operation? About the bigger picture? What we were doing the other night? None of that?'

'The other night was a drug deal.'

'That was part of it.'

'Okay, I do want to know why you suddenly feel so desperate to tell me all about it. Are you not just putting me in more danger?'

'No. I know you're not stupid enough to go and tell anyone else what you hear. I just want you to know what I got you involved in and how sorry I am. I reckon honesty might be the only way that you might trust me again. That you might see why I did what I did.'

'There's never going to be an excuse for why you left me with a man who had just paid to have sex with me against my will. You know that, right?'

'I do. I'm not excusing what I did. I just want you to understand.'

'So go on.'

Danny checked around him. They'd found a bench in the middle of the park. It was a pleasant day and there were other people about, walking their dogs, jogging or pushing prams. No one was close enough to hear them and no one was paying them any attention.

'We sell heroin and crack cocaine mainly. A lot of cannabis goes through us, too, but I don't get involved in that. The supply is run from London, where I come from. We have to go and pick it up. I've done it before but never on my own. Only Rosh goes on his own. I don't think Aaron trusts me enough.'

'But he trusts Rosh?'

'Seems to.'

'Are you brothers? You and Rosh?'

'Brothers?'

'Yeah, that Aaron, he called you brothers.'

'Oh. No, it's just what we call each other. I guess it's a gang thing. We're like soldiers, brothers in arms, that sort of thing.'

'Soldiers,' Rhiannon shook her head, she laughed, incredulous.

'Well, yeah. Look, I know how that sounds, but there is a fight for territory out there. We do okay up home but when you come outside of the city to towns like Langthorne you can proper take over. That's what we found. We know what we're doing. We know how to make ourselves known and pretty soon we were running the show.'

'How long have you been down here?'

'Just a couple of months. We moved around a bit, spent a lot of time in shit hotels — the sort that still take cash and don't ask too many questions.'

'How can you sell drugs in a hotel? Don't they notice all the people coming and going?'

'They would, definitely, if we did it from the hotel. We never did. You couldn't. Aaron targeted one of the locals who was already set up. He agreed to give us his list of users in the area. At least Aaron forced him to agree. It's just a list of phone numbers. Then all you need is a phone and a text message out telling them you're online. The calls and texts come in and you go out and meet your customers.'

'Isn't it dangerous? I mean, you don't know who these people are. They could be anyone.'

'They were anyone. You always get people that test you, who want to see what you're about. They know you're likely to have drugs and cash on you somewhere, so yeah you are vulnerable. But Aaron started it off. He was the face of the line to start with. Once people met him they realised that we were for real, that you weren't going to take from us easy. I know how he looks, I know how he comes across — I know that people are scared of him from the off. But I've seen him go too, I've seen him when he was backed into a corner and you have to know that he can back it up.'

'So you just go and pick up the drugs. That's your part?'

'No. I don't often touch the gear. We've spread out a little. We provide a few other towns with a reload. They break it down and get it out and pay us when we're done. I either pick up their money or sometimes I pick up the gear. We've started using a more local supplier — that was what I was doing the other night, but they wanted the money up front all of a sudden. They screwed me over.'

'I thought you said he didn't trust you to pick up the drugs on your own?'

'The local supply is just if we get caught out, if we run out of our main load. It's a much smaller amount. Same with the money. I pick up the small fry — it's bits and bobs — and I bring it back to Aaron who sticks it with the main stash.'

'And what happens to the money?'

'Aaron takes his cut. We get our cuts and the rest goes back up the line. I don't even know how much is going back up or how much we make. I know it's a lot. Aaron deals with that himself. He takes the money personally.'

'Does he keep it with him too?'

'Why do you want to know that?'

'Why wouldn't I? I thought I could know everything?'

'You're not going to rob him, are you?' Danny chuckled. It didn't sound natural.

'I don't think so, do you?'

'It's just stuffed in bags. He takes it back up to London personally, normally a couple of times a week but at least one trip. He doesn't normally keep the money far away. It's probably in the house somewhere, out of reach of the rummy.'

'The rummy? You mean William?'

'I think that's his name, yeah.'

'How come this Aaron is living there? I don't think William wants him to.'

'I think it suits both their needs to be honest. Aaron needed a place to stay in the middle of it all and your man William was suddenly on his own and maybe wanted some company.'

'He didn't — want the company, I mean.'

'Well, he doesn't mind taking the rum, I know that for sure. You two friends now?'

'I owe him. He kept me safe and when he made sure I got out in the morning your mate Aaron beat him unconscious.'

'He should have done what he was told.'

'Keep me there? So I could be sold for sex, you mean? You did what you were told. Seems this *rummy* is a far braver man than you are.'

'There are ways of dealing with Aaron. Butting up against him isn't one of them. That's a way to get yourself killed. I don't want to be here doing this. I got sucked into all this when I was young and stupid. I want to go home, Rhiannon, you have to believe me.'

'You're scared of him.'

'You should be, too. We all should be.'

'William isn't.'

'Then he will get himself hurt. Worse than he already has.'

'I still don't understand why you're telling me all of this. What am I supposed to do now?'

'You're supposed to be scared of him. You're supposed to see the bigger picture, so you know to stay away from it all. You're too good Rhiannon.'

'There you go again. But here I am.'

Danny swore. Rhiannon thought it was frustration at her at first but his hand jerked to his pocket like he had been stung. He took out his phone but hesitated as he looked down at it.

'That the boss?'

Danny snatched his eyes away to meet with hers. 'No, it's Rosh.'

'He's still above you right? Just how far down are you in the pecking order?'

'I don't care about the pecking order, Rhiannon. I don't care about any of it.'

Rhiannon saw the screen on his phone change and she guessed that he had rung off. 'Are you brave enough to ignore him?'

'I'm not ignoring him. I can't talk to him here.' Danny looked around. Rhiannon did the same and couldn't see anyone close enough to hear their conversation. He stood up. Rhiannon stayed seated, her way of making it clear that she wasn't going anywhere.

'Look, I've got to go and take this. I have to play the game. For now at least.'

'For now? I thought you said there was no way out, that this was your gang and there was no walking away.'

'I did, I mean, there isn't.'

'So this isn't for now then, is it Danny?' His eyes snatched back to his phone. Rhiannon could hear the vibration; it was ringing again.

'Look. I told you all this so you would stay away. You have to disappear. I think your rummy mate is about to blow the whistle. If he does, that Aaron's going to be on the warpath. I don't want you being in the way.'

'Blow the whistle? You mean to the cops? William?'

'Look, I have to go take this, yeah? But you need to go. Don't be where you're known. Just until this blows over.'

'What? Until what blows over?'

'Please, Rhiannon, be smart.' Danny still had his eyes fixed on Rhiannon but now he spoke into his phone. 'Yo, Rosh.' Rhiannon immediately saw fear in him. He stood still. Rhiannon shook her head as she strode away. She heard Danny behind her: 'Look, hold on Rosh . . . just a second,' he said, but then he was immediately backtracking. 'Yeah, I get this is important. Yeah I can speak now.' Rhiannon continued her walk until she was out of earshot. She didn't look back.

Chapter 17

'What are we doing here?' Sam said. Her voice was low, unsure, lacking any strength. She knew she wasn't going to get an answer. Rosh had picked her up. They had argued. She had told him how disgusted she was with what had happened the other night. He had checked she had got the money from Danny so she could go shopping and she had fallen silent. Then he said he was taking her somewhere to make up for it. Initially she had been pleased; she had believed him, like she always did with men. But now she wasn't sure this was a drive somewhere as part of an apology. Rosh had stayed sullen; he had barely spoken and wouldn't answer any questions on where they were going. She could tell his mood was black. She had learned to spot the danger signs in men the hard way, and the other night she had seen a side to Rosh that was colder than she had ever seen before.

Sam had been anxious during the car journey. This now turned to all out fear as they drove round the back of a grey industrial estate and pulled up outside a featureless, flat-fronted building. Rosh told her to get out. He was looking directly forward, still gripping the steering wheel.

He didn't look at her. They were on the edge of the historic town of Sandwich. She'd been to the town once, a few years before, having been invited to a party on a boat when there was some golf competition on nearby. Everywhere had been busy. She'd gotten off her head and taken some tablets. She couldn't remember much more than that.

Today she had never felt more sober. It was mid-afternoon and a little more overcast than Ashford had been. There didn't seem to be anyone around; the units all seemed to be locked up, unused even. At the far end she could see a fence and beyond that it looked like tall grass running down to a river. She could see part of it stretching away into the distance, catching the sun like a grey, sparkly ribbon. A large boat was up on stilts in a sort of dry dock outside the last of the units. The boat's bottom was a patchwork of repairs and it was a faded yellow. The boat had rolled on its stand and was pushing against the fence. She could see the name etched on the side from where she stood: *Angela's Dream*. It didn't look like it would ever sail again.

'I said, what are we doing here?' Sam persisted. She climbed out of the BMW but remained stood in the open door. Rosh stood out of the car too.

'We need to go in. We're just picking something up.'

'What?'

'Why are you asking so many questions all of a sudden? We're here to pick something up. You need to come in with me. That's all you need to know.'

'What if I don't want to?'

Rosh walked round to Sam's side. He pulled her roughly away from the car and pushed the door shut. He locked it remotely. Sam watched him walk towards one of the units. All of them were the same: a white, garage-style door covered two-thirds of the front and a smaller door, like the front door to a house, was on the right side of it. Rosh pushed the smaller door open. He stood on the threshold and looked back over at Sam. She took a last look around and walked to him.

'You don't have to push me,' she said.

'You're right. Do as you're told and I won't.'

'I'm not here to do as I'm told by you. What the fuck is all this about?' She hesitated by the door. Still Rosh didn't reply. She made a decision, tutted loudly and stepped into the unit. The door closed behind her.

'You might be right, you know!' a voice boomed out from a distance away, the other side of the space. Sam tried to peer over to the source. 'You're not here to do as you're told by him. You're here to answer my questions.' Sam recognised the voice: it was Aaron. The natural light was limited, coming through the top half of the small door they had just stepped through and a similar sized window at the rear. Sam could see through to it, it looked like it was in a kitchenette space. Aaron was blocking much of this light. He was stood in front of it and appeared as a silhouette.

'What do you want from me?' Sam's voice carried her fear now. She was aware of it but there was nothing she could do. She turned to Rosh. 'This why you brought me here? So your mate here can bully me, too? The way he did Rhiannon?'

'Rhiannon!' Aaron clicked his fingers. 'That's her name. Where is she, Sam? That's your first question.'

'I don't know. What do you want with her? I think you've had enough to do with her.'

Aaron stepped forward. Something metal scuttled along the floor, unsettled by his footfalls. Suddenly a strong light clicked on above them. Aaron still clung onto the power switch, a thick grey box that hung down from the ceiling. Sam had to narrow her eyes against the sudden light. The room was sparse and looked to her like it had once been a working garage. The floor was grey concrete with brown stains in places and an inspection pit with a bundle of blue material and a drum of brown fluid at the bottom.

'She your mate?'

'Who?'

'This Rhiannon. Don't start playing dumb with me, girl. Don't start acting like you don't know what I'm talking about. You know what I'm talking about. You know why we're here and you know why I need to talk to you.'

'I have literally no idea what you are talking about.' Sam's voice broke to a sob. Her legs suddenly felt weak. 'I ain't done nothing wrong. I ain't done nothing to you lot at all.'

'One of my soldiers got burnt today.'

Sam flicked from Aaron to Rosh and back to Aaron again. 'Soldiers? Who got burnt? What are you talking about?'

'The cops picked up one of our gang,' Rosh said, by way of explanation, his tone markedly softer than Aaron's.

Sam's eyes were watery. She sniffed so she could speak. 'I didn't know. I didn't even *know*. How would I know that? It's got nothing to do with me.'

'Someone ratted us out. Someone told them what we're doing down here.'

'I didn't! What, you think I did? Why would I tell the cops? I got no reason to go to the cops. You gotta believe me! Fuck!'

Aaron still hung from the light switch. He stepped away and it swung in shallow loops creating fidgeting shadows. 'Where are the others, Rosh?' Aaron said.

'The girl wasn't at the house and she isn't answering her phone. Danny is out looking for her. He reckons he can find out where she is at least and then I'll go pick them both up. Rummy hasn't been back to the house. He can't be far. The search party is out. He'll turn up in some gutter somewhere.'

'So, girl, which one ratted us out then if it weren't you? Tell me what you know and make sure I believe it.'

'I haven't been to no cops. Rhiannon wouldn't have either, I'm sure of it. I don't even know this rummy bloke. I've never said two words to him.'

'But it weren't you?'

'I told you. Of course it weren't me. I'm not stupid enough to go shouting my mouth off about other people's business. What you do is up to you. I thought me and Rosh were good, you know? I thought we were going strong.'

'You and Rosh.' Aaron's lips turned upwards in a smile. His teeth reflected the strong light. 'You and Rosh. Rosh and you. Like a proper couple, right? Lovers?'

Sam shrugged. 'I dunno, there's nothing wrong with spending a bit of time together. I thought we liked each other.'

Aaron turned to Rosh. He was still grinning. 'You and white trash here, are you together? Boyfriend and girlfriend?'

Rosh shrugged now. 'It's like she said . . . we're spending time together. Fucking about.'

'*Fucking* about! Is that what you're doing, white trash? Are you fucking my man Rosh, here?'

'What is this? I told you I ain't been speaking to no cops. I want to go home now.'

'Are you fucking my man?'

'What does that matter?'

'It's a simple question. You were brought here to answer my questions, white trash, and I will tell you now there's a reason I brought you to a place with a pit already dug. This place hasn't been used for months. There's no chance it will be used again any time soon. So then, are you fucking my man here?'

Sam eyed the inspection pit. She was stood a few metres from the edge. She took a step backwards. 'We mess about, sure. So what?'

'And you think that he loves you because you're fucking? Is that right? That he thinks you're special?'

'I don't know. Look, I answered your questions, yeah? Now Rosh can take me home. I'm done with all this.'

'I don't think you are. All of you need to realise who we are. You seem to think we're down here for a bit of a break, to *mess* about with, to fall in love and live happily ever after with. We're brothers, the lot of us. You ain't nothing to any of us.'

'I don't get in the way of your shit.'

'That's where you're wrong, see? You are in the way of my shit. And Rosh here, he couldn't care less about you. You're worthless white trash to me and you're worthless white trash to him. Do you understand?'

'Sure, whatever you say.' Sam could feel the anger building. She had listened to this enough. Why should she stand here and take his abuse? She hadn't spoken to the police and now he was just trying to humiliate her.

'Whatever I say? A demonstration perhaps?'

'What?'

'I say he doesn't give a shit about you and you don't believe me. So you need a demonstration.'

'I don't, I believe you. Look, fine. I see you have got your shit going on. You say I'm in the way. I get the message, okay? You won't see me again. Just drive me home and I'm gone.'

'Bring her over here!' Aaron snapped at Rosh.

'Boss?'

'That's right. *Boss.* Now bring her over here.'

Sam turned to Rosh. He was staring over at Aaron. She took in both men; they were locked in a stare. Rosh broke first.

'Go and see the boss, Sam.'

'No way, Rosh. What are you doing? You did this to Rhiannon. You don't have to do what he tells you. Stop being a pussy!'

'Go and see the boss. Please.'

'Please?' Aaron called out. 'What the fuck is please, Rosh. We don't ask when it comes to business. We make things happen. We're masters of our own destiny, remember? Bring her the fuck over here!'

Sam was facing Aaron. She heard movement behind her. She closed her eyes and grimaced. Sure enough she felt a sudden grip on her elbow. It pushed her forward.

'Please don't. Just take me home, Rosh. I promise you won't see me again.'

Sam stumbled a few steps forward. She was led round the outside of the pit. She cast a look in. She could see the blue material better now. It looked like a waterproof cover, like her uncle had used to cover his classic car. And she could see the drum of fluid was a plastic container with the top cut off leaving rough edges. The front read *SULPHURIC ACID — HANDLE WITH EXTREME CARE* in sharp black lettering. There was a bright warning sign above it.

'I'll just go, Rosh. You won't see me again, I promise. I didn't say nothing to no one. I don't even care what you do!'

She stopped when she was close to Aaron. She could smell his body odour, he smelled of stale sweat.

'What did you tell the cops?' Aaron said.

Sam kept her eyes shut. 'I didn't speak to no cops. I told you already. I got no reason to go speaking to cops.'

'And you think you're part of this gang? You think you're working with us?'

'Me and Rosh, we were just messing about.'

'You're nothing to us.'

'Okay.'

'Take off your clothes.'

'What?' Sam thrust her eyes open. Aaron had stepped closer. He suddenly reached out and snatched at her top. He pulled it up over her bra. In his other hand he held a knife, it sliced the material on her bra in an instant revealing her breasts. He leered at her body. He reached out and roughly grabbed her breast, and twisted so that she screamed out in pain.

'Aaron, this ain't necessary.' Rosh's voice came from behind her.

Aaron stepped towards her. He lifted the knife and thrust it over her shoulder. 'I don't need you telling me what is necessary. Down here, the people need to know who we are, *what* we are. This girl ain't nothing to you right? Right?'

'I said that already. But she didn't talk to no cops.'

'But she ain't nothing to you. That's a whole different thing.'

'She's got that.'

'No, she hasn't. We're not making our mark down here. People are thinking we're weak. They're not paying their dues. They think they can divide us, take away our loyalty.'

'Let me go,' Sam begged.

'You're worthless. You mean nothing to him and you mean nothing to me. Take off your jeans.'

'Please don't.'

Roughly Aaron reached out. Sam shut her eyes again. She could feel his hands in her waistband. She felt the button on her jeans pop and his hands pulling roughly at them. She felt Aaron step into her, his breath against her neck, his teeth on her nipples. And she heard the sound of receding footfalls behind her, the sound of someone walking away.

Chapter 18

Rhiannon had intended on staying in the town for a little longer, but after her conversation with Danny she suddenly felt a lot less comfortable among crowds. Instead, she had wandered until she had walked across the frontage of a cinema. It was the middle of the day, they were showing a film she had never heard of and the interior was just as she had hoped — dark and empty. She paid her money and took a seat. The feature was just background noise. She ate her way through a whole bag of chocolate peanuts and re-emerged two hours later with the sun noticeably lower in the sky. It was late afternoon, the bus stop was a short walk and again she was happy to see there were only a few other passengers on board. All were elderly and they gave her no attention at all.

She used the time to think. She had made up her mind to call Theresa Hart, her social worker. Theresa had told her that she would have to stay at the home for another couple of weeks — a month at the most. But Rhiannon reckoned she could lay it on thick, tell Theresa she was getting herself involved with the drug scene — blame the environment. She would play on being vulnerable at the moment. She reckoned she could speed up her exit. Maybe they would even be able to move her to another emergency placement. Rhiannon knew how it worked; she knew how much emphasis they put on *safeguarding* and she just needed to say the right buzz words to get a much faster response. If she could move towns again and keep her new location to herself, maybe she could just disappear. She felt like that was what she needed right now.

Rhiannon checked around her again. Still there was no one paying her any attention. She dialled Theresa's number. It rang out and she left a message asking to be called back. She considered giving a bit more information, or even sounding a bit more breathy and panicked while leaving her message but she didn't have the energy for dramatics. That would come later if she had to press her case.

She got off at her usual stop and walked to her home. She pushed open the door and could immediately hear movement in the kitchen. Rose was fussing at the oven. She pushed it shut.

'Rhiannon!' Rose always seemed so genuinely happy to see her.

'Hey, Rose.'

'Are you okay, love?'

'I'm okay.' Rhiannon was tired and made no effort to hide it.

'Are you sure? You seem a little preoccupied maybe?'

'I'm just tired. I think it's the stress, you know. I need to know what's going on. I called Theresa to see if there was any update.'

'Ah yes, you know I did the very same. I left her a message. I wanted to talk to her about schools. I wanted to see if we are going to get you in a local one — you know . . . if you're going to be staying in the area. I think it would be good for you to mix with kids your age, to get back into something like that, with structure. But only when you're ready, obviously!' She gave an encouraging smile.

'I hadn't even thought about school to be honest.'

Rose waved her away. 'And why would you? It's not a big concern for now. I'd like to try and get you back where you were. I know you said you liked it down there. But there's no point if you're going to be moving away, you know, to a different area . . . I'm sorry, I'm not helping am I?'

'It's not your fault. I called her to try and get the ball rolling. I like it here. I like being with you, Rose, but I need to get somewhere permanent. I need to start building a life again.'

'Of course you do. What did Theresa say?'

'No answer.'

'Ah. I could have guessed. Well, why don't you go and get freshened up. It's lasagne for dinner. Maybe you could check on Sam while you're up there, too. She came in and went straight to her bedroom. I couldn't get a word out of her.'

'Sam's in? No problem. I'll go and see if she's okay.'

Rhiannon could hear the shower running as she walked up the stairs. She put her phone and keys on the side in her bedroom. The television was on in the communal living room. She peered through and saw Anais side-on. She didn't bother trying to engage. Sam's bedroom door was slightly open and Rhiannon pushed her head around it to make sure she wasn't in there with the shower running. She wasn't. She walked to the bathroom door and stopped to listen. When Rhiannon was in the shower on her second day in the house Sam had let herself in and sat on the toilet for a full-blown conversation. Rhiannon couldn't see that she would mind if she did the same. She wanted to talk to her about what Danny had said. She wanted to see how much she knew.

'Sam?' Rhiannon just stuck her head round the door. The room was full of steam. She could tell from the sound of the water there was someone in the shower.

'Sam!' She tried again, this time a little louder. She peered through the mist. She couldn't see any clothes on the floor. There was no evidence of anyone being there at all. She stepped through the door and pushed the shower curtain aside enough to see in. It took a second for her to find the figure curled up on the shower floor. Sam was fully clothed. She had her legs crossed at the shins, her arms wrapped around her knees, her head bent in. The water ran all over her and her hair lay flat over her face.

'Sam . . . Jesus!' Rhiannon leant in, her hand moving towards Sam. Sam's head snapped back in reaction to it. She moved to look up and straight away Rhiannon could see the angry red mark across her face.

Rhiannon twisted the taps off. The water still dripped in a quick rhythm. 'What the hell happened? Sam?' Rhiannon crouched over her. Sam moved so she was facing back down, her soaking hair falling over her eyes. Her head suddenly twitched as she broke down in a sob. Rhiannon leant forward and swept her up as best she could in a strong hug. The whole of her front was instantly soaked.

'I'm so sorry. I'm so sorry I got you caught up in all this, Rhiannon. You were right, you were right all along.'

'What happened to you? What happened, Sam?'

'You need to go. You need to go away from here. They think someone talked to the cops. They want to talk to you about it.'

'Talked to the cops? What are you talking about? Who talked to the cops?'

'I don't know! The police got hold of someone from their gang. I don't know who. Danny wasn't there — maybe it was him?'

'I saw Danny today. Lunchtime.'

Sam lifted her head. 'What did you talk about? Did you arrange to meet him or anything? Is he taking you out? You can't believe these people, Rhiannon. Promise me you won't go out with him!'

'I won't. It was nothing like that. He just wanted to tell me all about it, all about what they are. It was weird actually. What did they do to you?'

'I can't even say it. I can't even say it, Rhiannon! I wouldn't get undressed so he pulled my clothes off. I couldn't do anything. He made me wipe it up with my own bra! Oh God . . .'

'When! When was this Sam?'

'Earlier. I just got back.'

'At the bungalow?'

'No. They're not there. They've been spooked. They still have their stuff there, I think.'

'Did they hurt you?'

Sam managed a hurried nod.

'In those clothes?'

She nodded again. 'Rosh has gone. Back home, I think. He fell out with the other one. But he didn't stop it — he didn't do anything. He just left!'

'Okay Sam, you need to get out of those clothes. Let's have a look at you, see where you're hurt.'

'Can you get rid of them?'

'Get rid of them?'

'My clothes. I can't do anything. I couldn't even touch them to take them off. Can you just get rid of them?'

'Yeah, of course, yes. What about a bath? I think a bath makes more sense.'

Another jerked nod. 'Can you burn them?' Sam's voice was now a whisper.

Rhiannon struggled to speak. Suddenly she was overcome with emotion herself. It was everything: guilt, sadness and rage. She swallowed hard. 'Yeah, I'll burn them. Don't you worry. I'll burn them all.'

Chapter 19

William woke confused, and with a sudden urge to pee. He felt cold, too, and his whole body was stiff as he tried to move.

'William?' The voice again, he had thought he was dreaming. The sun was low in the sky, almost dipping its toes in the sea. It shone directly in his face. He turned away, towards the voice. It was Rhiannon.

'Hey,' he said.

'You okay?'

William made it to a sit. His thigh throbbed with the movement, his back sore where he had passed out on the stone path. The same stone path where she had left him. His first instinct was to check the bottles of cider. They were both empty.

'Yeah, of course. Except I literally hurt all over. I reckon my head's the worst.'

'I'm not surprised. Did you drink all that cider?'

'Of course. Don't ever say I'm not committed to my cause.'

Rhiannon sat down next to him. She leant back against steel slats that had once been part of a fence and pulled her knees up to hug them. She narrowed her eyes to the sun.

'You okay? You look upset?' William said.

'I went home. Sam was there. Those bastards did something to her. Something horrible.'

'I can't say I'm surprised. I did warn you.'

'I know. I didn't come here for told-you-so's!' Rhiannon snapped.

'Why did you come here then?' William snapped right back, his hand rose to his throbbing head.

'Sorry. I don't know what I came here for. They had a go at Sam because they think someone talked to the police about them. She reckons they might think it was me or you. I wanted you to know they might come looking.'

William shook his head. 'Nah, they will have done their research. Damon would have told them that I've never spoken to a copper in my life. They chose me for a reason.'

'Which one is Damon?'

'You won't have met him. He's a local druggie, the one I owe thanks to for the introductions.'

'To Aaron?'

'To all of this.'

'And you said yes?'

'Of course I didn't. It was never going to matter what I said.'

'So maybe you did speak to the police? They haven't exactly treated you well. You might do it just to get back at them?'

'I didn't, Rhiannon, and it doesn't work like that. I understand the rules better than most. I don't speak to the police. I'm not the man I used to be, especially in a fight, so I'm not going to throw them out and they know my weakness for the drink. I've seen it happen to other people. It's always sad cases that get cuckooed. I guess I'm the sad case now.'

'Cuckooed?'

'Yeah. I think the police made it up. These boys come down from the city, or wherever and they take over the nest of someone weaker than them. I guess you could say they pop out from there to deal their drugs, too.'

'Every hour, on the hour.'

'It looked like they were a lot more regular than that. They had some money coming in.'

'Money. I suppose that's what this is all about? They're not making enough in the city so they come down here to make some more.'

'From what I know about the gangs it's not always just about the money. I mean, yeah, everything they do is motivated by cash, but you get a lot of politics. There's a hierarchy like in any organisation. I see some come down here after they've messed up in the city — it's like a punishment posting. Like any big business I suppose . . . you mess up, you risk losing your table at the head office.'

William had to get to his feet; his bladder was near to bursting. He'd been building himself up for it and sure enough his thigh gave a couple of sharp pains that almost knocked him right back down again. It immediately started to ache. He was aware that Rhiannon was watching him closely.

'You need to start looking after yourself better, William.'

'So you keep saying. Sounds like you could do with taking your own advice. I need to pee. I don't think I'll make it far.' William's gaze lingered on Rhiannon. She still sat against the fence, she was almost at his feet and her attention was down on the ground. She snatched up suddenly to look at him.

'Oh, here?'

'Well, not here, but the bush over there.' William walked a few paces to where the path fell away and merged with the steep cliff. A tall, slim gate blocked his path. Rhiannon hadn't moved. He tugged his flies down.

'Oh! Wait for me to get gone, I'll move away a minute.'

William was already urinating; he could hold it no longer. He heard her scuffle to move away. When he struggled back to his seating position Rhiannon was nowhere to be seen. The sun was now weakened by a little cloud cover, enough to watch comfortably. It was a warm orange, its edges distorted — his favourite type of sun.

'You're done then.' Rhiannon returned with two cups marked with the McDonald's brand. 'I got you a coffee.' She placed it beside William. She balanced two sugars on the plastic lid. 'And a wipe,' she added, blushing a little.

'I would have preferred something a little stronger.'

'I know that. You're welcome.'

'This will do, though. Thanks.' William ignored the wipe. He stirred both sugars into the froth. 'What do you do now then? Do you not think you're safe at your new home?'

'I don't think they'll come there. They'd be silly to.'

'I agree with you. You don't know the rules like I do. Whether they think you talked to the police or not, they would certainly be risking it if they turned up at your house. You should stay there. I know I said it before but I mean it.'

'Maybe I should talk to the police. I *can* stay away from these people. I could talk to them and maybe help get them out of your house.'

William fixed on Rhiannon. 'You can't do that! You'll get my house raided. That might get rid of Aaron and his mates but the ones you see are only ever the tip of the iceberg. If you rat out one gang member you can suddenly find a whole world of pain come looking for you. I made that mistake once. Never again.'

'I thought you said you never spoke to a copper in your life?'

'I haven't. Not squealing anyway. I got in a fight with a lad from a gang. It was a long time ago. Some scouse lad.

That was over a girl.' William couldn't help but chuckle. 'He was mugging her off, taking advantage of her and I wasn't having none of it. It was a good fight, we were evenly matched and I came out on top. I thought that would be the end of it. Before I knew it I had the population of Liverpool stomping round the town demanding my blood. I had to get out of the town.'

'They came down here?'

'It wasn't here, actually. A previous life. But it wasn't so far away.'

'So these people can just come down here and treat people any way they like because there's a lot of them?'

'Happens in all walks of life. You just have to learn to accept your place in it all. This Aaron and his mates are nothing. They're foot soldiers for something bigger. They give it all their attitude and they strut around like they're something special but they're the drug world's version of the minimum wage and they get sent away for weeks on end to live in some squat. You wouldn't swap your lifestyle with theirs, trust me on that. How many jobs are there out there where you start your working day by shoving a condom full of heroin up your arse? You couldn't pay me enough.'

'I guess, when you put it like that.'

'Did they hurt your mate bad?'

'Yeah. I don't think she'll be able to move on too soon, to "accept her place in life" like you said. I don't think I will be able to either.'

'You have to let it go, Rhiannon. You're not meant for this.'

'Maybe I am.'

'What do you mean?'

'You said you had it out in a fair fight and you still lost out in the long run. You can't fight these people — they're always going to have the advantage. You can't talk to the cops — so what's left?'

'The only option . . . you walk away. You thank your lucky stars it was your mate and not you. You do your best to make her feel better about the whole thing, and you walk away. Let nature take its course. This Aaron fella is somebody bigger's dinner. You just have to wait it out.'

'I want to see it. I want to be responsible for it. I want to bring the fucker down and for him to know that it was me.'

William chuckled a little.

'Don't laugh at me.'

'I didn't know you could swear, that's all.'

Rhiannon didn't reply. She sulked, her bottom lip jutting out further than her top, her brow furrowed. Suddenly William was reminded of who he was talking to. She was sixteen — a kid, and naïve with it. 'You don't get what you want. Not out here, Rhiannon. Not in this world. Go back to your foster home, wait for your new family to come and pick you out. They're going to be good people. That's how you get what you really want, which is a proper life. With a future.'

'And what about you, William? What do you have to look forward to? What's your future?'

William turned to focus on what was left of the sun. It was treading water now, just a third visible. 'I don't know now. Me and Janey, we had this thing about having a flat with a good view of the sea. It was all we wanted, all we hoped for. The council do have a few places. We were onto them and onto them but they said they would never promise a sea view. I mean, it's fair enough isn't it? We got in with a housing officer, though. She was a good lady. Deborah was her name. She was really trying for us, but she was getting on and we went in to see her and she wasn't there. One of her workmates told us she had suffered a massive heart attack. Just like that. I knew our chance died with her. Nobody else gave a damn.'

'Maybe you'll still get it.'

'The sea view? It was our thing. Me and Janey. After our girl was taken away, it was all we had left.' William had lowered his voice for the last part. Not enough, and immediately he wished he hadn't said it at all.

'Your girl?'

'It doesn't matter now, does it? None of it since Janey's gone.'

'You have a girl? A daughter?'

'We had one.'

'Oh, I'm sorry.'

'It's nothing like that. She's still out there somewhere. They took her off us.'

'Sorry.' Rhiannon said again. She sounded like she was struggling all of a sudden.

'Don't be. They were right to. We were both battling our own demons. I've always had the drink, Janey's always had the drugs. I was on both at the time. We were both a mess. It was no place for a kid.'

'And you couldn't sort yourself out? Did you not want to?' There was no mistaking the edge to Rhiannon's voice now.

'I never wanted to do anything more in my whole life. But no, I couldn't.'

'Why the hell not? You sound just like my mum. She was always telling me just how much she wanted to change. So we could be better, so I would be proud of her. I never wanted to be proud of her — I wanted the normal kid-parent relationship where I'm trying to make *her* proud of *me*. Where I wasn't carrying her to bed, or covering her over when she passed out drunk. Or covering for her at school or at Social meetings.'

'I won't make excuses. I don't need to make excuses to you.'

'No, you don't and you couldn't anyway. What if I was your daughter? If I was here and I was asking for your excuses, for your reasons, asking you why you couldn't just stop drinking and start being a parent like everyone else?'

William inhaled. He closed his eyes. 'I don't know. Every time I tried and failed I hit the bottle harder. I really got into the gear when they took her away. I would do anything to try and forget just what a fuck up I was. I just kept letting her down and every time I did, my addictions took a firmer hold. I haven't even said her name since she left. I'm not quite brave enough. It hurts so much.' William felt his voice break. He quickly sucked in the night air and swigged at his coffee. It was boiling hot, it burnt his lips and mouth but he forced it down.

'You're as bad as my mum. It's never her fault. It's always someone else or the way she's wired. She used to say that a lot . . . "I guess I'm just wired different."'

William wiped at his eyes and exhaled a sudden laugh.

'If a man does not keep pace with his companions, perhaps he hears a different drummer,' he said.

'What?'

'That was my comeback. Your mum would say to you she was wired different. Me, whenever it came up that the rest of my peers, my old work mates, my family were all leaving me behind with their normal jobs, looking after their kids, paying their mortgages, living their *normal* lives, I would quote that. I can't even remember where I heard it from — just that I liked it. It made sense to me to start with, I think it offered me a way out, an explanation as to why I'm such a fuck up.'

'Sounds about right.'

'Sounds like a load of crap to me now. Your mum is probably closer. We *are* all wired different. Some of us like coffee and some of us need a cider.' William struggled back to his feet. Rhiannon looked up at him. She still hugged her knees. 'Are you staying here?' he said.

'No. I'm going to go back. I'll speak to the Social in the morning about a move. I know all the right things to say about drugs and threats. It should be pretty immediate.'

'No names mentioned though, right?'

'No names mentioned. Doesn't mean I'm happy about it, though — about running away and leaving these people to do what they like.'

'They won't be around for long. And if you did manage to get rid of them, all four of them, there would be four more on the next train down.'

'And driving brand-new BMWs, I bet.'

'Hire cars. Everything's disposable. Belongs to someone else. These people don't have anything but cash on the hip and that don't last long. It's not a career you want.'

'What more do you need?'

'Well, it to be your own for a start. I saw a bag of money — it was stuffed in the loft. Who knows how much was in there. There were drugs up there too and a spare key to their hire car so if the police try and stop them they can ditch the key they have on them and just walk away. They don't actually have anything. They're a raid from the cops or a rival gang away from being right up shit creek.'

'Why throw away the key?'

'Eh?'

'The car key. You said they ditch it.'

'Ah, it's an old trick. The police try and pull them over and they get clear enough to park the car and lock it up and walk calmly away. They get stopped and searched and with no key on them there's no link to the car and they might just get to keep walking. And the car doesn't get searched. It's a way of keeping your gear.'

'What about forensics?'

'Cops don't do any forensic work until someone gets nicked. And for something serious. It's expensive all that.'

'Don't you get arrested for driving off from the police?'

'Maybe, assuming they can prove you were in it. The police stick the lights on and the gang might boot it round a corner or lose them in traffic, or run a red light. Nothing too serious. You park it up as soon as you can and swagger away. The police know the tactic but there's nothing they can do about it. But my point is that all the risk, all the sleeping with a knife tucked in your belt or a gun under your pillow — it's all for someone else. You might be skimming a bit off the top, but whatever it is, it isn't worth it. These people will soon be gone, living their miserable existence somewhere else.'

'So I just run away. And what? Wait for them to move on?'

'Exactly. And they will. You say they've had a bit of a scare, one of their lot got rumbled, right? They might already be out of there. I would be making myself scarce if I was them.'

'So you can go back then? To your home.'

'Soon. I'm okay here for now.'

'And maybe I don't need to be running away still.'

'What else do you have to stay here for? I would keep running if I were you. Not just because of them, there's nothing here for you.'

'What about that ruthless side of me? You told me I needed to be more ruthless.'

'That was about being nice. This is different. You have to pick your battles, Rhiannon. This is one you can't win.'

'Why does life have to be a *battle*? It isn't like that for everyone.'

'It isn't, you're right. I know it don't feel like it right now but you've got everything going for you. There's no reason you can't be that person with the good life. I reckon you'll have your own family, be all the better as a mum because you've seen how shit it can be.'

Rhiannon got to her feet. She rubbed some grit from her jeans. 'Be careful, William.'

'Don't you worry about me.'

'I am worried. Seems that your ruthlessness has really slipped.'

'I'm a survivor. That means I can be whatever I need to be, when I need to be. Don't look back, Rhiannon, not at me, not at this place. Not now, not ever.'

Chapter 20

Rhiannon pushed open the front door and she could immediately hear voices. They sounded agitated. One voice in particular was raised. It was Anais. She was talking to Rose in the kitchen. Rhiannon walked through to find out what was going on. Rose was sat on a chair, she had her head forward in her hands, her elbows resting on the table top. Anais was leaning on the table too, but from a standing position. She was talking to Rose, her tone was angry.

'You just need to get rid. You can't have someone bringing this sort of trouble to your home. It doesn't matter what she's been through.'

'Is everything okay?' Rhiannon said.

Anais spun round like she had been stung. Her cheeks were flushed, she immediately stepped in close to Rhiannon. 'You got some nerve coming back here! You're not welcome anymore. You're trouble and I knew it from the start.'

'Anais!' Rose scolded. She lifted her face. Rhiannon could immediately see reddening on her right cheek and around her eye. She had been crying, she had fresh tracks on her face.

'What happened?' Rhiannon demanded.

'Your mates! That's what happened!' Anais snapped.

'What are you talking about? What mates?'

'Two black boys, yeah? Your mates, who know your name? They came and hammered on our door. Rose answered and they told her they were coming in to see you. She told them you weren't here, but they wouldn't take it from her. They forced their way in and when she wouldn't tell them where you were they knocked her over. They made all sorts of threats. Rhiannon, what the hell have you brought to our door?'

'Jesus! Rose, I'm so sorry. This has all gotten out of hand. I don't know anything about it. I don't know why they would come here.'

'You know them though? You know who they are? They certainly know you.' Anais spat, she still fronted Rhiannon up. Rhiannon attempted to step round her, to ignore her so she could talk to Rose. She didn't care that Anais was upset.

'I know who they are, yes, but they're not here because of me. These are nasty people, I didn't mean to get involved with them—'

'I told you didn't I, Rhiannon?' Rose said, her voice quiet. She sounded meek. 'I told you to be careful who you spent your time with. I take it these boys are friends of our Sam, are they?'

Rhiannon shrugged. 'I think they are. But it's not Sam's fault either. These are just horrible people. I don't know why they came here to talk to me. Is Sam still here?'

'She's upstairs,' Anais cut in. 'She wouldn't even come down when they were here. That spineless bitch won't even talk to me.'

'Okay, Anais, that's enough.' Rose whispered.

'Yeah, Anais, that's enough.' Rhiannon flashed her a sneer. 'You've been looking for an excuse to get rid of me from the moment I walked through the door.'

'Yeah and I was right, weren't I?'

Rhiannon ignored Anais to talk to Rose. 'Did they hurt you?'

'Of course they did!' Anais yelled. 'You can see they did. Rose isn't used to this. She doesn't deserve this in her own home.'

Rhiannon stayed fixed on Rose, waiting for an answer.

Rose's whole body shook with a sniff. 'They forced their way in. They wouldn't listen when I told them to get out and they grabbed my phone when I said I was calling the police. They threw it. It's broken — it doesn't work anymore. One of them was bigger. He grabbed me by the throat . . .' Rose was back leaning into the table. The sniffs were now sobs. 'He pushed me to the floor. I banged my head.' Rose lifted watery eyes. 'They went up to your room. I . . . I tidied it back up . . .'

'Jesus, Rose. I'm so sorry. I'll sort this out, I can sort this out.'

'I don't think you can, Rhiannon.'

'I think you just need to go.' Anais stepped behind Rose and put her arm around her.

'Do you want me to go, Rose? Is that what you want?'

'I think . . . I don't know. I don't think you can stay here.'

Rhiannon stepped back. She used the kitchen side for support. This was so unfair. She hadn't asked for any of this. She hadn't done anything to make these people come looking for her.

'Okay. I understand, Rose. I'll call Theresa. Now. I was going to ask for a move anyway — to another town. I seem to have made a bit of a mess of this one. I reckon she'll be able to move me tomorrow.'

'She won't, that won't . . .' Rose shook her head. She looked awkward, embarrassed. 'You will need to phone her now, but you need to tell her that you're homeless. That's the only way you can get moved straight away.'

'Homeless? You're kicking me out?'

'I'm so sorry, Rhiannon. I know you've had a terrible time but I have to look after me. I'm too old to be roughed up, not here in my home. And I have to protect Anais, here — she's nothing to do with any of this. We don't deserve to be caught up.'

Rhiannon bit at her lip as she tried to quell the panic. 'No. I suppose you don't.'

Rhiannon walked up the stairs to her room in a daze, her face a fixed expression of shock. She considered Sam's room but changed her mind. She pushed her way into her own room. Immediately it looked different. All the surfaces were empty of her belongings, her backpack straining shut on the floor in front of her. Her bags already packed.

She felt the panic again. She wasn't going to be able to control it this time. She scooped up the bag and threw it on her back. She paced back down the stairs, conscious of keeping her footfalls quiet. She didn't want anyone to see her break down. She doubted Rose would be looking to meet her anyway, to talk her out of leaving, to say she had changed her mind.

She wasn't.

Rhiannon hurriedly tugged the front door open and left. Her eyes blurred with tears. It wasn't sadness or panic anymore. It was something else.

* * *

Aaron greeted Mo with a clenched fist held out. Mo bumped off it then Aaron wrapped him up in a hug.

'Good to see you, bro.'

'Cheers, man.' Mo stepped back. He eyed Danny who hesitated a little before stepping forward for the same embrace.

'You popped your cherry then,' Danny said, his smile seemed weak.

'I guess I did. It's no big deal.'

'Shit food, though?' Danny managed.

'Just boring.'

'Danny here wouldn't know about the prison cell experience,' Aaron said.

'You make that sound like it's a bad thing. You don't want us getting caught, right?'

Aaron smiled. 'There are some things you can't help, Danny. Like when someone rats you out.'

'Is that what happened?' Mo said, suddenly interested.

'Let's walk.'

As soon as Mo had been released from custody he had walked to the train station in the centre of Langthorne. It was a ten-minute walk. The cops had given him a rail warrant and a handwritten free pass so he could travel back up to London. Just as well, seeing as how they had also taken all of his money off him. Mo knew the plan if he got arrested. They all did. He had gone just one stop up the line before getting off the train to meet with Aaron and Danny. This was a village on the outskirts of Langthorne called Westenhanger. It had a rundown-looking pub on the way out. It seemed to double as sort of café too, the men sat at a table. Aaron got them all a bacon sandwich. Mo tore at it; he hadn't eaten well in the cells. He could see the sun falling over the shell of a derelict-looking racecourse through the window.

'You weren't followed?' Aaron said.

'Who knows, maybe onto the train. But nobody else got off.'

'Good,' Aaron smiled. That was the reason for going one stop. It was a possible tactic for the police to release a suspected gang member and then follow them to see who they met up with. They needed to build associations between members. Getting off at the first stop and a quiet location would make a follow impossible. Mo would still have to travel back to London — he was known now, he couldn't stay — but he would get the next one in an hour's time when he could be sure he was alone.

'So someone ratted me out?' Mo said.

'Must have. Danny here seems to think it was our rummy friend. We've got eyes out looking for him. I caught up with the blonde girl that Rosh has been messing about with. I'm pretty sure she didn't have anything to do with it.'

'What about the other girl? She wouldn't like me after I tried to stop her leaving.'

'She wouldn't say anything,' Danny cut in. 'She wouldn't know you would be carrying anyway. If she had spoken to the cops she would have told them about the house, not about you. They would have come through the door.'

Aaron stared at Danny. Mo could tell that their relationship was still fractious.

'Danny here has his theories,' Aaron said. 'We're looking for her, too. I want to be sure and I still need to send a message down here, seems it hasn't been getting through. It would make sense, though, if it was the rummy who spoke to the cops. He wouldn't want them to be coming through his own door. That would cause him problems with his housing and he would face getting lifted himself. It would make more sense for him to stitch you up for carrying.'

'So he gets us out of his house?'

'Yeah. If he tells them just enough that you get swept up away from his gaff, he figures the heat will be on us and we will have to move around, maybe even out of the town.'

'But we don't, right?'

'I don't see us moving out of the town for the sake of some fucking rummy. We'll be out of his house, but when we're done with him I don't reckon it will be any use to him anyway.'

'What are you doing with him?'

'Me? Nothing. Danny here is going to sort that one out.'

Mo saw Danny's stifle his reaction. He thought it might have been surprise. Or panic.

'You want me to sort it?' Danny said.

'Well, yeah. You offered your services. And you're still five grand in my debt, Danny, unless you've made a visit and got my money back? You need to start making some waves, showing me what you got, earning your wage. You think you can do that?'

'Yeah, of course,' Danny said. Mo wasn't convinced. He reckoned by the lingering look that Aaron wasn't either.

Aaron turned his attention back to Mo. 'What did they ask you about? Do you think they know much?'

'I don't think so. They asked me for my address and I said I didn't have one. They had my old lady's address up in London. They said they were going to knock down the door and search it. She's gonna be well pissed.'

'You been taken back there a few times by the cops, right? That's how they know it?'

'Yeah, a few years back I was always doing a bunk and the old lady would call them. Ain't nothing changed, she just don't call them no more.'

'Did they talk to you about where you're living down here?'

'They knew I had been staying somewhere but when they asked I just said "no comment" like you told me to.'

'What did they get?'

'I had the full load on me. I hadn't made the drop yet. I didn't give it up but they made me strip in one of the cells. One of them held my arms. I couldn't flush it or nothing. You should have seen their faces when it dropped. They were well smug.'

'What did you say about it?'

'I said I didn't know what it was. I said I was asked to carry it out of sight from one place to another. I played on being a kid. I had some suit, some legal bloke. He told me to make sure I said that at least. Everything else was "no comment."'

'They didn't keep you in, that's good, man,' Aaron said.

'Nah. The legal suit . . . he said they wouldn't want to because I'm only fifteen and they need to test the gear. I got a bail date. I got to go to court in a few weeks back down here. They gave me some shit I can't do or I'll get nicked again. I can't even come into this shitty county. I got to be living at my mum's address. I think that's it.'

'Nothing too heavy then.'

'Nothing I can't handle. Shame I got to go back, though. We were doing alright down here.'

'We still will. We'll get set back up, get your case done and then you can come back to work. First time offence, fifteen years old — you'll get a slap on your wrist and some fucking kudos on the street. This has been a good day for you — trust me on that. And don't worry about your cut.'

'Don't feel like a good day, Aaron. Where's Rosh?'

'He's gone home for a bit. He had some shit to do, personal shit.'

'Is he reloading too? You want me to hook up with him?'

'Nah, we're good for a couple of days and then I'll head up with the cash. We'll hook up when I'm back though, yeah? Me and Danny have got it covered down here. Danny here is going to impress me. This is perfect for him.'

'Get it done, Danny.' Mo locked eyes with Danny, who still looked more than a little uncomfortable.

'Get your train. Get your head down and I'll be in touch, yeah?' Aaron said.

The plates were empty. The meeting seemed to have come to a natural conclusion. They left the pub and Mo received the same hugs, Aaron still the more enthusiastic. Aaron's phone rang just before they parted. He caught Mo's eye and it made him curious, so he hung around. The conversation was a short one. Aaron smiled at Mo.

'What?' he said.

'That was Damon. He reckons he might have found the rummy. He reckons he might have slunk home.'

'Maybe he thinks we've gone already?' Danny said.

'He'll have a shock then, won't he?'

'Has this Damon actually seen him there?'

'No. He got told. He was on his way to check it out.'

'*Was* on his way?'

'Yeah. I told him not to bother. I said we would go. I said we needed to have a chat with him somewhere private and that would do just fine.' Aaron laughed. Mo joined in, Danny did too but it took him a moment.

Mo wished them good luck and walked back towards the train station.

Chapter 21

Rhiannon took in the frontage of the bungalow. The street was straight and wide. It was part of an estate that had been built when this was still the way to build houses, before the wave of new-build estates shaped by traffic calming and profitability. She had already walked the surrounding streets and couldn't see the BMW anywhere. She was opposite the bungalow, partly concealed by a hedge in the garden opposite. She still felt on show. She was beginning to think this was a bad idea, despite having watched for nearly twenty minutes without seeing any movement at the windows. She knew this didn't necessarily mean it was empty; she was going to have to get closer to find out. She had been putting this off for as long as she could.

She stepped out from the bushes and immediately felt exposed, vulnerable, a little panicked. She had a sudden urge to pick up her feet and run away. She fought it and kept moving forward. The neighbours all had their bins out, dragged to the edge of the pavement. She lifted a lid, it was two-thirds full with sacks but looked clean enough. She dropped in her rucksack. If she needed to run she didn't want the extra weight. The sun had slipped behind the town's houses. The streetlights hadn't yet flickered on and the day had a grey hue to it, that odd void where the night hasn't yet replaced the day. The gate was still jammed open as she had remembered it. The lounge window was to the front, beside the front door. If there was someone in the lounge they would likely see her coming up the path. She walked to the door. The damp mobility scooter resting against the wall hadn't moved. There was no movement at the window. She could see the net curtains, yellowed with holes eaten into them. Originally they would have formed a crescent shape with a semi-circle of clear glass at the bottom, but now they hung off-centre and lopsided. Her whole body was tense, ready to spring at the slightest movement. She knew she was fast. She had seen Aaron and Rosh up close and reckoned she could outrun them enough to get away. But she would need to be ready. She couldn't let them get hold of her.

She pushed herself up against the glass. She could see the sofa. It faced her; the table was still in front of it, the bedroom door off to the right looked like it was open. She could see right through to the back door; it was still sealed shut, the grime around it undisturbed. She looked back at the table. This had been the hub of the activity, busy with scales, ashtrays, money and packages spilling out. Now it was near empty. Just a limescale-stained pint glass with a finger of liquid left in the bottom. She couldn't see any of Aaron's belongings either. It looked to her like they had packed up and gone. Rhiannon knew she couldn't leave without checking to see if they had taken everything.

She pushed at the door. She remembered what William had told her: he never locked it, but the door was stiff and always seemed as if it was locked — it was where the frame had swelled. The door didn't budge. She pushed it harder and felt a bit of give — maybe. She backed away a couple of steps to fully apply her weight. The door folded inwards, she lost her balance and stumbled into the living room. The smell was the first thing that hit her, it was instantly familiar; she immediately associated it with being terrified, with wanting to be somewhere else — anywhere else. She had to get herself back under control. She spoke out loud to herself: 'There's no one here, Rhiannon. You're fine. Let's get this done and get out of here.'

She barged the front door shut. A single key jutted out. She spun it, hoping the door lock even worked. She cast her eyes upwards and tracked along the ceiling; the living room had no obvious hatches or voids. She put her hand to her mouth as she now saw the dried blood in spotted patterns across the ceiling. She had seen this before: one of her mum's mates. She knew it was a sure sign of a heroin user trying to find a place to inject. A needle in a thigh could easily cause the blood to reach the ceiling. She'd even seen it happen. She moved further into the house, into the kitchen. More dried blood spotted the yellowing ceiling. She had to put her hands to her face in reaction to the smell. There was a bin pushed against the back door; it was overflowing and there were two more bin bags either side of it. The bin itself was big and square topped with a white carrier bag that smacked of a takeaway delivery hanging out of the top. She took a closer look. 'Oh God!' The white plastic was writhing with maggots. She turned away to gag.

The kitchen was part enclosed; the inside wall was a partition that stopped a couple of feet short of the ceiling. She had to step through to see the whole of the ceiling. Sure enough she could see the outline of a hatch door. It had a brass catch and visible hinges. Rhiannon could reach it by climbing onto the work surface. Gingerly she pushed aside some dirty plates and cutlery and pushed herself up. She stood up but had to stoop a little where the ceiling closed in suddenly, but she could reach the clasp. It was stiff; it looked like it had been painted over carelessly when the ceiling had been done. The paint had been chipped away since. The loft hatch had definitely been used. It was impossible to tell how recently. Rhiannon gritted her teeth with the effort as she wiggled the catch. It clicked open and the door swung all at once. It was heavy and Rhiannon had to move quickly out of its way. She dropped back down to the floor. She couldn't reach the ceiling, or the opening from where she stood and it wasn't directly above the kitchen unit. She would need something to stand on. She peered around the kitchen — there was nothing that could assist. In the living room there was only the sofa and the table, and both were too large for her to move on her own. She wouldn't be able to get them through the opening to the kitchen. The only thing that might do was the bin.

She looked over to it again. She could still see the top of the bag moving where it was pulled tight in a double knot at the top. A filthy mop leant against the wall on her side of the back door. She picked it up and hit the bag. It rolled off the bin and hit the floor. A dozen or more of the maggots splayed out across the tiles. They bucked and twisted in their new environment. Rhiannon put her hand back to her mouth. She nudged the bin away from the wall using the mop. It took a few more pushes to move it under the open hatch; it was sticking to the layer of grime on the floor. The lid could now close. It was of a solid-looking, rectangular design and she pulled herself up on it, gingerly at first. She could feel the lid flexing under her feet. She started in a squat position then stood up, her arms reaching for the hole in the same movement. She heard the crack from the lid first, then felt it start to give. She managed to get high enough to get one of her arms into the loft space and gripped on something wooden. She allowed it to take her weight and it didn't budge. She grunted as she pulled herself up. She felt weak and it took every ounce of her strength, but she didn't have much bodyweight and she managed to drag herself into the darkness.

Rhiannon fiddled in her pocket for her phone. The light from the kitchen didn't travel far into the loft space. She could see puffy yellow material around the hatch that looked like the insides of a cheap duvet and irritated her skin. She got out her phone. It had a torch function and she flicked it on. The loft space was largely empty. Her expectations of what it might be like were based on the lived-in part of the bungalow, but all she could see were three boxes side-by-side along the eaves and a carrier bag on the other side of the hatch. The boxes had gathered the same amount of dust. The bag was orange and had a large white tick motif on it. It looked out of place — too clean. She stepped over the opening and snatched up the bag. At first she thought there was nothing in it, but a solid object swung in the bottom. It was a car key. It had a BMW badge in its centre. The spare!

She ran it over in her hands then made a decision and stuffed the key into her jean pocket. She swung the light from her phone around the loft once more to be satisfied she hadn't missed anything then hung her legs through the hatch and dropped back onto the bin. It held her weight for a matter of seconds, then, with a second, much louder crack, the lid gave in. She lost her balance and fell onto the kitchen floor. The bin went over too, items of rubbish and a pungent smell immediately filled the room.

Something hit the front door. Rhiannon froze, her eyes darted in that direction. She could just see through the gap to the window. There was movement! She ducked under the counter, immediately kicking out to push the bin towards the back door. It was still on its side. She picked up the mop, she held it by the head end and reached up with it towards where the hatch still swung gently from its hinges. She couldn't reach it from the floor — not even close. The door banged again. It wasn't a knock, it sounded to Rhiannon like someone expecting it to open with a big enough push, just as she had managed. Whoever it was, they had been here before. She heard voices now, frustrated, raised. She couldn't make out words. They were male voices. She leaned back round the counter as much as she dared. A figure filled the window and it was peering right in. *Fuck*! It was Aaron!

Rhiannon stood up. She was still hidden by the dividing wall in the kitchen. The door thudded again. This time it was a solid kick. It was obvious that the tactics had changed, that the persons trying to enter now had more determination. She couldn't be sure if Aaron had seen her. The door was kicked again. She heard a sound like wood splitting — it wasn't going to take much longer for them to get in. She pushed up with the mop. If someone was looking in now they would see the movement, but she didn't care: she had to close the hatch. The catch didn't take and the door sprung back open almost immediately. It caught Rhiannon by surprise, knocking the mop out of her hand. It clanged on the floor. The door was hit again. She tried to steady her hands and control her breathing. It was delicate trying to balance the heavy door on the end of the mop. It pushed back shut again and she gave it an extra shove. It seemed to stay shut. She moved the mop away gently. The front door gave in. Rhiannon could only do her best to run out of sight.

* * *

'What the FUCK!' Aaron shouted. Danny watched him strut into the bungalow, his arms swinging by this side, his chest puffed out. He turned back on the front door. It was hanging open, clear damage to the wooden frame where it had split as the lock had been kicked out. He pulled the key out and held it up for Danny to see. 'See! This is what I am talking about! These people don't respect us down here. They don't know who we are! These people need to fucking know who they're dealing with. They can't be locking us out.'

'Only one reason why he might be locking us out, Aaron.'

'The rummy?' Aaron raised his voice, he turned to project it towards the closed bedroom door. 'WHAT? YOU THINK HE MIGHT BE HIDING FROM US? THE FUCKING DIRTY RAT — THINKS HE CAN TALK TO THE COPS AND THEN HIDE FROM US?' Danny watched Aaron. He bit down on his lip and waited for a few seconds in silence. There was no reply. Not a sound.

'You think he's in there?' Danny said.

'It was locked from the inside, right? Of course he's in there. It's perfect, man. It means we get to have a nice little private chat — and on our terms. We're gonna find out just how much he said to the cops and then we're going to make him fucking regret that he ever opened his mouth. This is actually a good thing, Danny. This is a big opportunity for us — for you. We can send out a message here . . . We are not to be fucked with. You think you can do that?'

'Send a message?' Danny knew exactly what he meant. He tried to hide the uncertainty in his voice.

'A message. You need to impress me, Danny boy. Now take this, and you show me just how you deliver a message.' Aaron pulled a large hunting knife from his waistband and held the handle towards Danny. Danny reached out and took it. The knife immediately felt heavy in his hand. He knew the weapon: it was one of the first he had held when he was growing up. He had been nine years old on the streets of Lambeth, and Aaron was in his middle teens. He was talking about the gang, about the life you could have, about belonging to something. It had resonated with Danny: it was all he had ever wanted — to belong. It was an easy sell and at nine years old he was cut on the palm by that very knife. Brothers bonded in blood. He'd had no idea what it meant then.

Aaron took a step to the side and looked over at Danny expectantly. Danny knew that he meant for him to take the lead. He walked towards the bedroom door. It was pulled closed. He heard Aaron behind him.

'What the fuck's been going on in here?'

Danny looked over into the kitchen. He could see some bags of rubbish spilling out over the floor. The smell of the place was stronger than he remembered.

'Dirty BASTARD!' Aaron shouted — for the rummy's benefit.

Danny reached out for the door handle with his left hand. His right held the knife, tight in his knuckles and ready to go. It was heavy, a good quality weapon. He had seen Aaron use it in anger before too. It could do serious damage.

'We go in hard. Get him on the floor and don't start cutting him straight away.' Danny heard the words whispered into his ear, he felt Aaron's breath. Danny exhaled, then pushed down on the handle and pushed the door. He entered quickly; he could feel Aaron pushing him in the back.

Empty. Danny stepped to the left side of the mattress while Aaron stayed by the door.

'Shit!' Danny said, hoping he didn't lack conviction. Aaron was swearing too but there could be no doubting he was genuinely upset. He kicked out at the mattress.

'Give me that,' he said, gesturing at the knife. Danny passed it over. Aaron snatched it off him and immediately dropped to his knees. He slashed at the mattress, two long lines that crossed each other to form a giant X. He stood back up, his chest rising and falling from the exertion. Danny looked over and saw movement in the wardrobe behind. Just the tiniest amount, the blink of an eye perhaps, or a tremor. The wardrobe was three doors wide, but the middle one was missing. From this angle he could see just a slither of Rhiannon stood behind the right side door. She was inches from Aaron. He could see one of her hands held up, the palm flat against the wood, her right foot angled out like a clown's so she could fit. Aaron was straight on to where she was hiding; he wouldn't be able see her — but the tips of her trainers would be visible if Aaron was really looking. He was sideways on to her, the knife in his right hand and down by his side, his nostrils flared. Rhiannon stared right at Danny, her eyes wide. He stared right back. She mouthed a word, Danny was sure it was *please*!

'We need to find this fucker. Him and the fucking girl. Every hour we don't find them it looks worse on us.' Aaron rubbed at his forehead.

Danny moved his attention away from the wardrobe. 'Don't worry. I don't think the rummy will be hard to find.'

'We haven't found him though, have we? They're taking the piss out of us, Danny. It only takes one and all of a sudden you got a real problem. Everyone starts thinking they can take the piss. This will start affecting business, you can take my word on that.'

'We'll find him. He won't be far away.'

'Find him? Find *her*! Find them *when*?' Aaron lashed out with the knife in his right hand. He slammed it with all his might into the wardrobe door. The doors were thin and the point embedded itself in the wood. It pushed so far in, it was stuck. Aaron had to wiggle it up and down to get it free. Danny stepped instinctively towards the wardrobe, raised his hands and made a noise like a grunt. Aaron immediately turned to him. He held the freed knife up. Danny could see the tip was tainted red.

'What's the matter with you?'

'I, uh . . . Look, we'll find him, Aaron — the rummy. Give me the knife boss, yeah? When we do find him I want to be the one pointing it at him. You said I could.' Danny reached out and took the knife. Aaron offered no resistance and then turned for the bedroom door. Danny held, waiting for him to go, but he didn't make it out of the room before he turned back to Danny.

'Let's go then. You get the stuff out of the car. We can put it back in here for now. We've got a couple of lock barrels, too, right? We can swap that over. That should stop the rummy coming back here — or anyone else for that matter.'

'You want to leave the stuff here?'

'Yeah, no better place for it. We'll change the locks, stick the stuff back up in the loft and go have a little look for the rummy and your little bitch. Once we get hold of them we can bring them back here and make all the mess we want. Then we get some time to get out and we can take the stuff with us. I don't want it in the back of the car, we're running the risk of getting tugged by the cops.'

'Yeah, okay.' Danny followed Aaron out. He pulled the bedroom door shut. He picked up a cereal box from the floor and tore one of the flaps off. He folded it in half and jammed it in the bedroom door.

'What are you doing?' Aaron was watching him.

'Just in case we don't catch up with the rummy. This way we know if he's been back.'

'I wouldn't worry, Danny, we're finding him today. I don't see him coming back here without us knowing.'

'I reckon you're right. Just to be sure, though. Right?'

'Whatever. Get the kit from the car. I'll have a look at the front door.'

Danny walked out of the bungalow. His stomach was knotted with tension. Rhiannon was still in there, the cardboard ploy was more to keep Aaron from going back in there — not that he had any reason to anyway, but it wouldn't stop him if he wanted to. And what about Rhiannon? She was hurt, he could be certain of that, but how badly? That knife was about chest height he reckoned, it had to be somewhere around there. He hadn't been able to look at her — not even a glance. Maybe he should have stood up to Aaron right there and then. Maybe that was his moment to make a break, to get away from all this and to help Rhiannon. He shook his head. If he'd stood up to

Aaron in there he would have been killed, and so would Rhiannon. Danny lifted the knife to inspect the point. The light was bad, he could just tell it was darker. He wiped it in the long grass.

He bent into the boot of the BMW. There was a void on the left side with a symbol for a first aid kit. He pulled it open. A small tool bag was concealed in there. It had a pack of Eurolocks, the standard barrel locks used in most doors across the UK. Each of them had a key hanging out. He took the whole tool bag out. It also had a small drill with which he would drill out the existing barrel and a few other bits. Changing locks was becoming a fairly regular occurrence; Aaron had a habit of moving in somewhere and quickly making it his. By the time he got back to the door, Aaron had put the split wood surround back together. He pulled a screwdriver from the tool bag and started on securing the metal plate that the lock would push into. Danny struggled to focus on the task of changing the lock; his attention was very much in the other room. It took just a couple of minutes. Danny was ordered back to the car to pick up two bags, one a holdall style that contained their stash of drugs and the other a backpack with the money. He could reach the loft hatch from standing on tiptoes in the kitchen. The hatch swung open easier than he remembered, he had to shoot a hand out to stop it from striking him in the head. He threw the two bags up and then pushed the hatch back shut.

'That'll do. We need to go find this fucker. Once we find out what he said, we'll know where we can go from here.'

'Yeah, right,' Danny said.

'You ready for this Danny?'

'Yeah,' he said, 'I'm ready.' The door clicked shut behind them and Danny watched as Aaron lifted the handle and turned the key to deadlock the door. He pushed the key into his pocket and they walked away.

Chapter 22

In her rush to move, Rhiannon fell forward, the door pushed open and she sprawled out on the floor. The hand she put out to stop herself was slick with her own blood. She had been holding it as tight as she could against her left side to try and keep the pressure up, to restrict the bleeding.

She sat up and did her best to assess the wound. It was the left side of her chest. She wasn't sure how far the point of the knife had pushed in but she had felt it all the way. It had stung at first, but it was when it had started wiggling that the pain had very nearly brought her to her knees. She didn't know how bad it was but it bled profusely and she reckoned it would need a staple or stitches to make it stop. It still hurt like hell, perhaps more now than when the blade had first forced its way through the flimsy wooden panel, catching her completely by surprise. It had taken everything she had not to shout out. The wood panel had pushed in, too, and had caught her on the bridge of her nose. That was also spotted with blood and she heard the gristle creak as she surveyed it with her hand.

She moved carefully out into the kitchen and peered out from behind the dividing wall to make sure she was alone, then moved across into the bathroom where a few sheets of toilet paper clung apologetically to a cardboard roll. She snatched them up and dabbed at her wound. They were soaked instantly and it was clear that they were useless. For a few brief seconds, however, the blood was cleared enough for her to see a bright white gash of around a centimetre in length. She cursed and grimaced as she teased it apart. She could see it had gone deep enough to cut beyond the skin and into the fatty tissue below. It would definitely need some assistance to heal. Her Aunty Mel had been a nurse and had taught her the basics. She suddenly found herself wishing Mel was here with her more than ever. She searched the bathroom quickly for something that might help: more tissue, a clean towel — anything that she could use to assist with compression or cleaning. There was nothing. She moved back into the kitchen. The kitchen units were largely empty but the drawers were busy with unopened post, any number of keys, pillboxes, asthma pumps, lighters, empty bottles and other random items that painted a very clear picture of a man leading a chaotic life. There was no order, no sense to anything and nothing that could help. The last cupboard she checked was the largest of them all. It housed the boiler, a tool bag covered in thick spider webs, a dustpan with no brush and three paint pots stacked untidily. On top of the pots were a couple of brushes fused stiff with magnolia paint and a roll of Gorilla Tape. Finally, something that she could use.

She tugged at the tape, pulling out a decent length and she cut it with a kitchen knife that was so blunt she had to hack at it. The tape came free. She surveyed herself quickly. Her T-shirt was by no means clean. It was bloodstained around her wound and the rest was blackened from crawling around the loft space, but she reckoned it to be the cleanest material in the house. She used the knife to cut off one of her short sleeves. It came away in a good enough square. She pressed it over her wound and held it in place by wrapping the tape around her torso as tightly as she could manage. She took a moment to get her breath, the tape restricted her breathing a little but she could cope. At least this might stop the bleeding. She felt for her nose and her fingers came away with no fresh blood. She concentrated on breathing through her mouth.

Her attention turned to the loft hatch. Again she pulled herself up onto the kitchen bench. The pain in her left shoulder restricted her movements and she couldn't lift her left arm up, but she managed to drag herself up using her right. She popped the catch — it was getting easier every time — and the loft door swung open immediately. It swung hard and fast but Rhiannon was ready for it this time. Once more, she used the light on her phone to see into the gloom. There were two bags on the loft floor: a rucksack that teetered on the edge and a longer bag behind it. She was able to reach up with the mop and knock the first bag down to the floor with ease. The second took a little longer but she was able to hook one of the handles and, with a little manipulation and ignoring the shooting pains in her left shoulder, it finally toppled over. She opened the rucksack first. It was stuffed to bursting with money — all paper money, ten- and twenty-pound notes. Each bundle was tied off with an elastic band in what looked like equal amounts. She couldn't even guess how much was in there — thousands, surely. She zipped the bag back up and felt the weight of it. It was heavy. She pushed it to one side and pulled at the other bag. It was longer, rounded, but with a flat base and a zip along its full length. She pulled the zip all the way back to reveal brick-sized parcels wrapped in yellow-tinged plastic wrappers. Among these were zip bags of a solid white substance that looked to Rhiannon like lumps of chalk. This bag was heavy, too. She struggled to pull on the rucksack, having to grit her teeth to get her left arm through the strap. She could feel the tape pinching her skin. She dragged the other bag across the floor until she made it to the front door. It was time to leave. She leant on the door handle. It wouldn't budge.

'Shit!' Rhiannon spun back into the room. She had been able to suppress the panic up to this point but now it threatened to consume her. She dropped the rucksack and it dragged at the tape again, this time pulling at her wound and making her yelp. She tried to focus, to think how she could get out. She walked with purpose back into the kitchen and tugged the large cupboard open where the toolbox sat under the boiler. She scooped the spider webs gingerly from the top and folded it open. Inside she found a couple of chisels and a screwdriver, all browned with rust and age. She pulled the whole box out into the light and saw what she needed: a claw hammer, consumed in rust but it would do. She pushed open the bedroom door and threw the hammer onto the floor under the window. She stepped onto the filthy mattress and looked outside. The overgrown grass, weeds and thistles ran for about ten metres to where there was a grey stone wall. Rhiannon assumed this marked the end of the garden. Beyond that she could see trees and bushes, but the next house was some distance away, as if the gardens backed onto each other. She retrieved the two bags from the living room and took in what she could see of the next-door neighbour's garden. It was much better kept and smacked of an old person with a passion for a neat lawn, pots of colourful flowers and numerous cutesy ornaments. In the part of the garden that she could see, there was no movement.

Back in the bedroom she pulled the pillowcase off the only pillow and wrapped it around her right hand — ignoring its brown and yellow staining. She picked up the hammer and swung it hard, turning her head and closing her eyes when the hammer struck. It took three more blows to make a hole through both panes of glass. The hole wasn't big enough and shards of glass pointed up like teeth from the bottom of the window. She used the head of the hammer to knock these out as best she could, then put the dirty-looking pillow over the frame.

She threw the bags out first. They landed among other items that looked like they hadn't been there long: an old suitcase, a chest of drawers and some old novels that looked like they hadn't gotten wet from the rain yet. She struggled over the lip of the window. Despite her efforts, small shards of glass remained, enough to pick and pull at her clothes, and scratch her bare arms as she clambered through. She picked up the bags and battled her way to the bottom of the garden where a full-length gate had been concealed in the worst of the weeds and tall grass. She pushed them aside. The gate opened into an overgrown alleyway that seemed to run along the backs of all the houses. To her left it ran into a dead end. She took a right and then immediately dropped the long bag on the ground. She had no use for it; she had only taken it so that Aaron didn't have it anymore — or at least to make him think he didn't. She got to the end of the alleyway and took off the rucksack. She dropped this over a low fence with a hedge the other side. It wasn't a good hiding place but it would do — for now, at least. She peered around the corner, checking both ways. All was still and quiet. She moved quickly out onto the pavement.

Chapter 23

Damon Allcott's arm swung in long, smooth movements as he strutted down the steep slope towards the halfway point on the path where he could work discreetly. It was early evening. The moon was not long risen, but it was full and bright enough to cast its own shadows. He was on a footpath known locally as 'the zig-zag path,' which was very apt: it ran from the Leas, down the outside of the stone cliff, cutting back on itself regularly until it reached the coastal park at the bottom. At one point where the path turned, it dug into the rock to provide a natural shelter. This was where Damon was meeting Tony Jones. 'Tone,' as he was known, was a regular. He had been even before Damon had started out as a thirteen-year-old kid, acting as a lookout for his older brother. After his brother had died in prison Damon had lost his hold on the town they had once enjoyed exploiting. Now he was reduced to working as a small-time street dealer for whoever had a stranglehold on the town at that time. He had seen it change hands any number of times. Sometimes things had become bloody; sometimes a new setup was scared away by police action; sometimes they just upped and left for a bigger market.

Damon didn't care. There would always be someone for him to work for. There would always be the Tony Joneses of the world. And there would always be a little something left over at the end of the day to satisfy his own addiction.

'Hey, Tone.'

Tony Jones was already sitting on the makeshift bench. It was a simple design: wooden slats screwed into a shelf dug out of the rock face. Tone was little more than a silhouette with a red glow where a cigarette balanced between his lips. It jigged about as he spoke.

'Damo.'

'What's new?' Damon stood side-on, his attention sweeping all around him.

'Ain't nothing new round here, Damo. You know how it goes.'

'Yeah, I do. What do you need today?'

'Same, old man. Two brown, one white.'

'You don't wanna stock up?'

'I would, but I've got what I've got.'

Damon had an elevated view down to the coastal park. It was well lit by ornate lamps and deck lights sunk into wooden walkways. He had seen a jogger move across it from left to right when he had first walked down. He could see nothing moving down there now.

'This won't do you, will it, mate? I'll have to see you again tomorrow.'

'I know. Let me know where you are.'

Damon tutted. His hand moved down into his underpants and he pulled out a plastic egg that had once housed a child's Kinder toy. The egg came apart. He counted out three tiny parcels wrapped and twisted shut in bits of old carrier bag. Two of them were blue; the third was white. Tone already had his palm out, waiting. He folded them up in his fist. Damon knew his methods; they hadn't changed for as long as he had known him. Tone always held his gear in a clenched fist in his pocket. If he saw a potential threat — a copper or another druggie who might be looking to take them away, he would move them to his mouth. If he was challenged he would swallow. Tone didn't want to go to prison and he would still get what he wanted — he would just have to wait it out. It was how most users who had been on the gear for a while seemed to get their purchases home. Tried and tested.

Tone held out a twenty.

Damon eyed it but didn't take it straight away.

'It's still three for twenty, right?' Tone said.

'No, it ain't. It's back to thirty. Like it says in the text.'

Tone snatched his phone out of his pocket like he wanted to make a point. He squinted as the screen lit up, then he read slowly, like a primary school pupil: '*Back on for best of both. Two coffee one cream for twenty.*'

'Jesus fuck, Tone! Give me that!' Damon snatched the phone. 'That was two days ago. Look, you've had two messages since then and — oh, what a surprise! You've already opened them both! Today's message . . . *On now, best of both, good size ten bags.* Now you've got three, mate. So you okay with three times ten or is that a bit of a struggle?'

'Come on, Damo! You know me from old, right? I ain't got another ten. I thought it was twenty. I came here in good faith.'

'Don't go giving me shit, Tone! Not tonight. I got more important things to do. I got some fucking gang-banger wants me out looking for some pisshead. Reckons it's all my fault he can't be fucking trusted to keep his mouth shut. You and I both know how this plays out, Tone. We've both been doing it for years. Give me a tenner or you choose one of them wraps to come back to me. I promise you, you don't want to be wasting any more of my time.'

'What pisshead?'

'What does that matter? You ain't changing the subject on me. Now what is it to be?'

'Will? I heard you was in with Will. I saw him earlier. He looked all beat up. In a right bad way. Do you know what happened?'

'You saw Will?'

'Yeah, earlier.'

'You know where he is?'

'Might do.'

'Don't mess with me, Tone. Do you know where he is or not?'

'I know where he *was*.'

'Fine. So where *was* he?'

'How much are these three wraps, Damo? Only I'd rather not give this one back.'

Damon bared his teeth in an attempt at a smile. 'Okay then, Tone, let me make you a deal. You need to be seeing me tomorrow no matter what, right? You can have them three wraps for your twenty. You tell me where you saw our friend, Will, and I find him there still, we forget you owe me a tenner when we meet tomorrow. Needless to say, if I don't find him and you've been playing me along then you'll find the prices will be a little adjusted when we speak tomorrow. You in?'

'Yeah, I'm in. I saw him, I'm telling ya. We even had a chat. He seemed proper down.'

'Where?'

'Top of the Leas. Down the end near McDonald's. He was on one of the benches.'

'Which one?'

'The very last one down that end. But he weren't staying there. He was sort of leaning on it — I think his leg was giving him stick or something. Seemed to be in a lot of pain.'

'Fucking hell, Tone! That ain't gonna help me a lot, now, is it? So he moved off shortly after. Jesus—'

'No. I mean, yeah, he did. But when we spoke, I asked if he was alright, like, and he said he was but he was well pissed. He had a fresh one in his hand — cider, it was. He had just come out from where he was staying to get it. He was talking about his bird that died.'

'Janey, yeah.'

'Yeah, well they had a place they used to drink. It's just off the Leas, down one of the paths that ain't in use no more. You remember they shut a few off 'cause they were dangerous all of a sudden?'

'Yeah, I remember. Yeah. I used a couple of them in the past. No one can see you down there.'

'No, right. Well, I reckon that's where Will is. That's what he said earlier and it was only, like, a couple of hours ago. He looked like he had been staying out on the street. He looked rough, like, rougher than usual.'

'Alright. I'll go have a look.'

Damon turned to walk back up the slope. He heard Tone calling out from behind him.

'If you find him, you remember me tomorrow! Maybe that information is worth a little bit more, you know what I mean? I scratched your back there, Damo.'

'Yeah, you did. Like I'd forget about you!' Damon called back, then he lowered his voice to speak to himself, 'you wily old cunt.'

* * *

William pulled at his woollen hat, dragging it so it sat just over his eyes. The night had set in. The air temperature was still high but the ground was cooling swiftly, and he knew from experience that this could spread quickly through the bones. He had found a cardboard box that provided a layer between him and the ground and an old friend had given him a sleeping bag. It was a kid's one, he reckoned, not long enough to cover him completely, but it was clean and offered some protection. As long as it stayed dry he would be okay. He swigged at a bottle of cider and faced out towards the sea, which shimmered in the bright lights given off by the harbour arm. It had been redeveloped recently — a new lease of life for the locals. It had once been a train station — the end of the line — but it had been allowed to fall silent, and then derelict. Before the workmen had come, it had been his favourite place to sit and drink. It just had an incredible atmosphere, the sort you only got from areas that were once a melee of noise and movement and were now completely empty and forgotten. Like you could still sense it happening all around, but silent and hidden in the long shadows. Since then it had been redeveloped with train-carriage-themed wine bars and restaurants. Run down and industrial had become massively trendy all of a sudden and once again it was attracting the crowds. Will had seen one of the signs go up: *The Doddery Duck*. William remembered when a pub was a pub.

'Alright, Will!'

He turned to the voice and recognised it immediately as belonging to Damon Allcott. But the man himself remained a silhouette, complete with hands thrust in his pockets.

'Damon.'

'You living here now?'

'If I said I was, would you take this over too?'

'Now come on, Will. I never kicked you out of your house. I don't reckon them boys did either, I hear you upped and left.'

'You knew what they were doing, Damon. You knew who they were. That isn't for me, never has been. I can't have the housing people sniffing around. I'm already pushing my luck still being there.'

'You leaving doesn't help that though, does it? I mean you've just left them to get on with it.'

'I didn't want to die either.'

'Bit dramatic. Can't be that bad. You just got to keep your head down with this lot.'

'I shouldn't have to do anything in my own house. Why did you have to bring them to me?'

'As I remember, I asked you a question and it suited everyone involved.'

'You have a way of asking questions, Damon.'

'What do you mean by that?'

'A way about you. Your words form a question but there's no choice at the end of it. It takes some talent does that, I suppose. Probably comes from years of peddling out your filthy wraps to people that don't really want them.'

'Them people out there are begging me for them. I get calls all times of the day, I don't force nothing down no one's neck, Will, and you seem to have a very short memory. I never stuck nothing in your arm, or Janey's either.'

'You can leave Janey out of this, Damon.'

'I never gave her the hit. That was some new setup. They had a couple of near misses before Janey went. They've moved on. But I reckon if you wanted to find them I could—'

'I don't! Damon, I don't. What would I do if I found them? I'm an old man with a dodgy leg and a drink problem. The last time I reared up with a sense of injustice I lost my house and dislocated my jaw. I know my place and I know that Janey made her own choices in this world. She's the only person I could be angry at.'

'You miss her.'

'What brings you down here?' William asked. He swigged at his bottle, using it as an excuse to move it to where Damon couldn't reach it if he wanted to. Drinker's instincts.

'I ran into Tony Jones. He said he saw you. He said you were in a bad way. I came to make sure you were alright, like. I feel bad about all this. I thought this would work out well for us all.'

'These things never do, do they, Damon? These people, they don't mix well.'

'They really caught you, didn't they?' Damon had stepped closer. William was aware that he was inspecting his face. He sat down, a little too close for William. He was taking up the edge of his box.

'It was my own fault. I stuck my nose into their business. I should know better.'

'You live and learn, old man.'

'I thought I'd done all that.' William took another swig of his cider. 'Would you do me a favour?'

'I might do.' Damon's tone was guarded.

'Well, seeing as you feel bad for getting me into this shit and seeing me turfed out on the street I think you owe me this small thing.'

'A small thing I might be able to do.'

'These people, these drug lines, they don't last long. When they mess up and have to move on, for whatever reason, could you just let me know? Just let me know when I can go home. That's not too much to ask, is it?'

Damon chuckled again. He slapped William hard on his right knee and used it as a springboard to get back to his feet. William watched him walk away and saw he had a phone in his right hand that was all lit up.

'That sounds fair enough to me, Will. I'll keep my ear to the ground, yeah? When I hear these London boys have fucked off I'll come find you.'

'Nice one. You do that.'

'I take it you'll still be here, right?'

'I won't be going far, Damon. Reckon I'll be here for a while. With Janey.' Damon walked away. William held out his bottle of cider and lifted it to the stars. 'Here's to ya, Janey — I miss you.'

Chapter 24

Danny noticed the BMW slow for no reason. Aaron moved around in the driver's seat then he pulled his phone out from his pocket. He must have received a message — a long one; he kept flicking from his phone to the road to read it in its entirety.

'We found the rummy.' He grinned at Danny.

'The rummy? Where?'

'I dunno. Damon's sent some instructions — proper longwinded. I can't work it out from that, not while I'm driving. See if it makes sense to you.' Aaron threw his phone and it landed in Danny's lap. Danny lifted his arms instinctively, but stared at the phone like it was a lump of burning coal.

'Oh, great,' Danny managed. He took hold of the phone; the message was still on the screen. Damon wrote in pigeon English but he could translate enough of it to know that William was somewhere near the McDonald's in the centre of Langthorne.

'You ready for this, Danny?'

'Yeah, of course.'

'Can you see where we have to go?'

'Yeah, McDonald's in the town centre. You know it, right?'

'Yeah, of course.'

It didn't take them long. The night had set in and the shops were all shut. McDonald's wasn't yet, but there was just one occupied table and the only movement was from a couple of cleaners as they shimmied across the floor holding mops. Aaron had pulled over directly outside the restaurant. The BMW's hazard lights ticked.

'So where do you reckon this place is?' Aaron said. He leaned forward and squinted over the steering wheel.

Danny pointed towards the grassy area of the Leas. This was its start point. From here it ran along the top of the cliff towards Sandgate. 'He's just off the main path apparently. You see the big metal arch? If we walk under that there's a path off to the left. Damon says it's gated — signs and shit saying you can't go down the path. Our rummy is down there.'

Aaron seemed satisfied. He looked all around, suddenly agitated. 'Where do I stick this? It's all double yellows.'

'What does that matter? Just stick it anywhere. We're only gonna be a few minutes, right?'

'It does matter, Danny. Think about it. We get ourselves a ticket and it's a paper trail that the car was here. You gotta start thinking about these things.'

'Yeah, fair point.' Danny considered pointing out the CCTV cameras on a tall pole directly opposite them and on the other side of a small roundabout but thought better of it. 'There's some street parking after hours. You have to go left at the roundabout, behind the shops. It leads down to the graveyard where I was meeting Mo. It's tucked out of the way, too.'

'I wanted to be parked right here. I didn't want to be too far.'

'You worried about walking the rummy back? He ain't going to give us no trouble, Aaron.'

Aaron pulled away without replying. The BMW took the first left off the roundabout; an office block car park was immediately on the right with a barrier across it. On the left were some bays for the flats that ran along the top of the shops. One was free. Danny stood up out of the car. Aaron's head and shoulders appeared across the roof.

'You still got the blade?'

'Yeah.' Danny's hand fell to the lump in his waistband.

'You need to impress me, Danny. I expect to see just how strong you are. I need to see it for myself. A lot of people have been saying you haven't got what it takes, you know?'

'Let's go find the rummy.' Danny pushed his door shut and walked back the way they had come. Both men had instinctively pulled up their hoods. The streets were quiet. A solitary car moved up the hill and flashed them to walk over. Danny felt the knife's outline again, conscious of it, his mind playing tricks that everyone knew what he was carrying, and what he was thinking. They walked the Leas, the sea now visible on their left, but a hundred metres below them. They walked under a metal arch, where a plaque explained that it was a memorial to the fallen soldiers during both world wars, who had marched from this point down to their waiting boats. More recently it had been added to, in commemoration of police officers who had been killed in the town. Danny remembered it being on the news. There were wooden benches lined up. They must have had sensors that detected his movement because a tinny voice suddenly filled the air with the reading of an extract from a soldier's diary. It made Danny jump. He could feel Aaron looking over. He walked on.

The gate was obvious. It had a thick chain and bright signs with *DANGER!* written in bright red lettering. Aaron gestured for Danny to go first. He climbed it and dropped over. He heard Aaron drop behind him. The path sloped down gently. The light from the ornate street lighting reached what looked like a dead end. For a few seconds Danny felt a little upbeat. *Maybe the rummy wasn't here!* A few more steps and his heart sank again. It wasn't a dead end; the path turned back on itself. Danny turned with it. The artificial lighting was all but gone as the path slipped further down the cliff, the slope suddenly harsher. It took a few seconds for his eyes to adjust. Now the path was mainly black but lit with a silvery hue where the breaks in the trees allowed. A little way along, one of these silvery bands picked out the figure of someone sitting up, legs out straight. There were silhouettes of bottles where the feet ended. Danny knew it was their man.

'The fucker's here!' Aaron was excited. Danny could feel his breath as Aaron leaned into his back, clearly wanting to push straight on. 'It's fucking perfect, man. Do it here!'

Danny stayed still. His feet planted to the ground, he couldn't move forward. He felt another shove in the back.

'What are you waiting for, man? Let's get this done! Do it here! No one will even find him for days.'

'What if he's not alone?' Danny was still rooted. He was desperate.

'Go see!'

Danny moved this time — the insistent pushes were getting firmer. The seated figure moved, just the head turning towards him. Danny's eyes adjusted as he got closer. It was William. He was alone. There was no getting out of this now.

'Rummy!' Aaron called out over Danny. The path wasn't very wide but Danny pushed past. He stepped over to where William sat, to where Danny could now see that the path ended. Aaron looked through the gate and over the edge of the fence. He turned back to Danny and grinned. He had his thumb up.

'What brings you boys here?' William's words were a little slurred, no worse than normal.

'Danny here needs to talk to you, rummy.'

'Talk?' William's head rolled against the upright fence post as he moved from looking left at Aaron to take in Danny to his right. He lingered on Danny. 'He don't look like he's got the kahunas! Am I right?' He laughed, his head rolled back so he was facing towards Aaron.

Aaron didn't laugh with him. Instead he stared straight over at Danny. 'That's what *I* said. But it's always the quiet ones you gotta watch, right? They're the ones that can really surprise you when they need to step up.'

William's head rolled back to Danny. He sniffed. His eyes looked glazed. 'What are we talking about then, Danny? 'Cause I haven't got all night. I'm a busy man! Got a lot on!' William laughed. It sounded forced.

'What did you tell the cops?' Danny's voice was a growl. He tried his best to sound threatening though his mouth was dry, his heart was pounding in his chest and that knife was suddenly pushing much more firmly into his stomach.

'The cops, you say?'

'Yeah, the cops. Don't play dumb, rummy. We know you talked to them. We know you told them about Mo.'

'Mo? No, that ain't the name I gave.'

'What did you tell them? What name did you give?'

'I'll tell you what name . . . Jack Shit! The same name I always give them! I don't talk to the fucking cops. Never have, never will. That should be my nickname, you know — Never Will!'

'We know you did.' Danny's voice had lost some of its strength.

'You don't *know* fuck all!' William suddenly carried all the anger, all the strength. Danny couldn't let him seize the upper hand. Aaron was staring at him.

Danny strode forward. He swung his right foot as hard as he could into William's legs. He couldn't remember which one was already injured. William immediately shouted out in pain, he swung again. William's scream was louder now, but it was very suddenly cut short.

Aaron dropped to a squat and grabbed William by the throat. Suddenly William couldn't shout out and, judging by his bulging eyes, he couldn't breathe either.

'You think you can lie to us? You think we're just gonna listen to your shit and walk away? I don't need you to tell us what you did, I already know. You spoke to the filth — you told them about Mo and he got nicked. You didn't tell them about the house because you were worried about your miserable existence there. You were worried they would take that away. Well, guess what . . . we're here to take it all away.' Aaron loosened his grip enough for William to take a rushed breath. He looked like he was trying to speak. Aaron tightened back up.

'Fucking do it, Danny.' He twisted and stared at Danny, his eyes carried an intensity Danny had seen before; he was terrified of it. He reached down for the knife. It slid easily out of his waistband, the blade catching the moonlight. He levelled it, his grip firm. He stood over William, one foot either side of his outstretched legs. 'Do it, Danny!' Aaron screamed again.

William was staring up at him, his eyes wide, his lips parted but silent, Aaron still held him firmly round the neck. William had lifted his hands to pull at Aaron's wrists — his midriff was unguarded.

Danny thrust the knife. It struck hard, and the handle pushed back, bending Danny's thumb. He pulled the blade back out, it came easier than he expected and he stumbled backwards. Aaron let go of William, whose head fell immediately forwards, his hands fell, too, to where his shirt was now slick and reflecting the moon.

'Again!' Aaron screamed, his excitement peaking. Danny lunged forward again. He aimed for the abdomen, to where William's hands had moved. He pulled the knife back out then thrust it forward again, his whole body weight shifting so it was behind the blows. Danny paused. William lifted a hand in front of his shocked expression, his little finger hung by a flap of skin. Tears ran from his eyes and his hand dropped back to his lap. Danny saw Aaron stand and aim a kick. He heard it land but he had already turned away.

Danny walked the length of the path quickly. He almost made it back to the Leas. He was back in the artificial light and suddenly aware. The knife was still in his right hand, still protruding from his clenched fist. He threw it in a jerking motion and it landed in a bush. He climbed back over the gate, his hands slippery with blood. He heard Aaron right behind him. He was talking, his voice low. Danny didn't know what he was saying. He felt a gentle pull on his arm and let himself be led. A few minutes later and they were back at the BMW. Danny slid into the passenger seat.

'Keep your hands away from the car. We need to clean you up properly. You did well there, Danny. That was what I was looking for. Now we just need to find that bitch you were hanging out with. She's the last one, yeah? Don't worry, I'll deal with that. You did good.'

Danny didn't respond. His gaze was turned to the left, back out through the window. The scenery started moving, he let his vision blur, he was only aware of the passing of lights. The car picked up speed. Danny was frozen still, his hands rigid, palm up in his lap. They still dripped with William's blood.

Chapter 25

The phone rang out again. Theresa's irritating voice cut in, breathy and matter of fact, suggesting that Rhiannon leave her a message or call her during office hours. It gave an emergency number too, but Rhiannon couldn't face talking to a stranger. Where would she even start? She left a message this time.

'Hey, Theresa, it's Rhiannon. Rhiannon Davis. Look, I know you're doing what you can to get me somewhere, but . . . well, there's been a bit of a change in my circumstances. I'm homeless. That's the crux of it. It's not Rose's fault, I would have thrown me out too. Somehow I got mixed up with drug dealers. I didn't mean to — you have to know that. I haven't done anything wrong. Look, can you call me back when you get this message? I don't know what to do. I think they're looking for me. I think I might be in danger here. As soon as you get this, okay?' Rhiannon hung up. She didn't like sounding so pathetic but she had to lay it on a bit thick. She could just imagine Theresa's patronising face in the morning. She would have to bear it. She needed Theresa right now.

She pushed her phone back into her pocket. She was on a bench in the middle of a deserted Victoria Park in Ashford, all her possessions in a rucksack at her feet. The bus route wasn't far from here; she could get a bus down to Langthorne and sit with William. She knew she wasn't thinking straight. She knew there must be better options. She couldn't afford a hotel room right now, nor could she muster the energy to ask for one on the basis of goodwill. At least with William she would be safe.

She stood up and stretched. There was a breeze. She had been sitting under a big tree and its branches creaked as they moved. Its leaves shushed her. Suddenly her phone vibrated in her pocket. Maybe Theresa was picking up her messages out of hours? She pulled out the phone. Danny's name was across her screen. She hesitated long enough for it to ring off. The screen didn't have chance to go black before Danny was ringing back again.

'What?' she snapped. 'This isn't a good time, Danny. You've ruined my life so, you know—'

'Rhiannon, you're okay! I was so worried. You have to help me!' Danny's voice sounded panicked, his words so rushed he was falling over them.

'What's the matter?'

'I didn't want to do this. I didn't want to do any of it, Rhiannon. But Aaron was there. I knew if I didn't then it would be me. It wasn't real—'

'Danny, slow down. What's happened?'

'Aaron. He's on the warpath. He got hold of your friend and we found the rummy. Now he's looking for *you*, Rhiannon! I didn't want to do any of it!'

'What did you do, Danny? What's happened? Why did you come to my house? I got kicked out because of you.'

'I didn't want to. I didn't want to do any of it. The rummy, he made me hurt him!'

'You mean . . . William? What did you do?' Rhiannon fell back on the bench. She turned her head, trying to shelter from the wind. She could feel her pulse racing in her chest, Danny's panic rubbing off on her.

'I had a knife. Aaron made me carry it. I saw you in the house. I saw you and I didn't say anything. If I had — if I had said you were there he would have hurt you, Rhiannon. I don't know what he would have done. He's looking for you now.'

'What happened to William, Danny? What did you do?'

'That knife. I saw Aaron put it through the door. It had blood on it. Your blood, Rhiannon.'

'I'm fine, Danny. I'm fine. Calm down, please. What happened? What did you do to William?'

'Shit, Rhiannon! Shit! They're gonna know it was me. I think I killed him. I think he's dead. We left. I got his blood all over me. Aaron's gone into some flat. He's getting me some clothes to wear. We need to go get cleaned up.'

Rhiannon wanted to cut in. She wanted to shout, but she couldn't. She couldn't say a thing.

'Are you still there? Are you still there, Rhiannon? I think I hurt him bad. What if he's dead?'

'Where is he?' Rhiannon managed. She swallowed, tried to think, tried to focus on what she had been told.

'I left him there. He was down some path near McDonald's. He was drunk. I didn't want to. Aaron held him by the throat.'

'Do you think he's dead?'

'I don't know! I don't know. They're going to know it was me. I panicked. I threw the knife away. It's not far — they'll find it. I can't go back. Aaron doesn't know I threw it.'

Rhiannon stood back up. She picked out the path that would take her towards the town and started immediately down it, walking as fast as she could. Her mind was clearing. 'I can call the ambulance from here. I know where he is. I was with him there. I can tell them where to go—'

'You can't!' Danny cut in, his voice even more panicked. 'If you do that, Aaron will know! He'll know someone called the ambulance. He'll know I am the only other person who knows he is down there! No one can see him, Rhiannon. You can't do that! Promise me you won't do that! I think it was bad anyway. I don't think he's going to be okay.'

'Fine. Look, fine. I can go. I need to go. Maybe he's alive. Maybe he needs help.'

'But what if he tells the police it was me? What if he does? I can't go to prison, Rhiannon.'

'He won't. He always said he doesn't talk to the police. I need to go see him. I need to see if he's okay. Where exactly is the knife?'

'I walked back up the path. I got to the Leas and I was all lit up. I panicked. I threw it there. I don't know where exactly. Get it, Rhiannon. When you get it, put it somewhere they'll never find it. Please do that for me. I'm so sorry I got you into all this. I never meant to get you hurt. You don't belong here, Rhiannon — with all this. But today, when I saw you, I never said a word. I kept you safe. Please help me!'

Rhiannon reached the pavement. She knew there was a taxi rank another half a mile away. All of Danny's presence, all his arrogance was gone. All that was left was a desperate shell. 'Don't worry, Danny. I'll sort this out.'

'He's coming back . . . he's coming out, Rhiannon. I need to go!'

'Where? Where are you going now?'

'I need to clean up. The rummy's place, I think.'

Rhiannon pressed to end the call. She pushed the phone back into her pocket and broke into a run. The taxi rank office was closer than she remembered. She ran into the door so hard it thumped off the wall and there was movement behind the counter, the sound of someone in the back room springing to their feet.

'Sorry!' Rhiannon said. 'Have you got any cabs?'

She had given the middle-aged man with the swept-back hair a start. 'Yeah, where are you going?' He looked her up and down. She knew she was filthy, she had been crying and had a bloodied nose. She couldn't blame him for judging her immediately.

'Langthorne. The McDonald's in the town centre.'

'How soon?'

'Right away — I'm in a big rush.'

The man looked her up and down again. 'You got the cash?'

'Of course I have.'

'It's twenty from here. Pay it up front and I'll take you myself.'

Rhiannon reached into her pocket. She had some emergency funds that had been given to her when she was rehoused. She pulled out a crumpled twenty-pound note and laid it on the counter. 'But I need to go now.' The man still hesitated.

'Okay,' he said. He walked into a back room; he was gone a few seconds then reappeared. 'We're out the front.'

Rhiannon sat in the back of the taxi. The man didn't try and strike up any conversation, he just drove silently and quickly. Rhiannon was glad. She was aware that he was keeping his eye on her via his mirror and he was all the more interested when she reached up to the centre of the roof and turned on the interior light. She reached her hand up her top to her shoulder and it came back spotted with blood. The tape felt damp and the combination of sweat and blood had caused it to slip. She dug in her bag for the roll of tape she had taken from William's house. She lifted her top up, casting a disapproving look at the mirror. The driver snapped his eyes away. She pulled her T-shirt over her head. Her bra was stained with blood and there was a further trail of it down her chest and onto her stomach.

Some of it was congealed, but some was fresh. She had some more tissue and she bunched it together. She pulled the tape off her wound and gasped sharply as it tugged at her skin and pulled the wound apart. She pushed the tissue into the wound, which was back to bleeding freely. Rhiannon pulled some more tape from the roll, it crackled loudly and the driver's eyes were back on her.

'You okay, love?'

'I'm fine, thanks.'

'Is that blood?'

'Only a little.'

'What happened to you?'

'It's nothing. I walked into a nail or something I think. I'm clumsy like that.'

'I can take you to the hospital. We're kind of going away from it otherwise?'

'No need, thanks.'

'You sure, love? I mean . . . it's just up the road. I'll give you the money back, I don't—'

'No!' Rhiannon cut in. She calmed herself down immediately. 'No, it's fine. My aunt's a nurse. She can patch me up. It looks worse than it is.'

'Okay, love, whatever you say.'

Rhiannon managed a patch job. It was the best she could do in the back of a moving taxi with only the weak bulb of the interior light. She put an extra top on, a black hoody to give her a little more protection from the bag straps.

When they reached McDonald's in Langthorne town centre, the driver asked her one last time if she needed his help. She refused again, did her best to give a smile that was reassuring. He offered her her twenty back and she refused that too. She waved the taxi away, waiting for it to roll out of sight.

Rhiannon checked around. She was on her own. She sprinted for the Leas and the gate that led off it. It was still locked. She shimmied over and ran along the path until it turned back on itself. She turned the corner and froze. She could see a shape leaning against the railings, the outline of a man. He wasn't moving. There was no sound but the distant crashing of waves onto the beach and the clatter of rolling pebbles. The trees around shook and shushed. She moved along the path.

'William!' she called out, gently at first. 'WILLIAM!' Louder this time. She thought there was movement — from the head at least — but it might just have been moving shadows tricking her eyes. She got close enough to stand over him. He was still in the same dark, hooded top and woolly hat he had been wearing the last time she had seen him. His lower half was tucked into a sleeping bag, the cardboard under his buttocks was stained a dark red. If it was blood, it looked dry. 'William! Can you hear me?'

This time the movement of the head was definite. It lifted a little, the movement jerky. His hands appeared from where they had been tucked into the sleeping bag. The light was dim, just the silver of the moon, but she could see his hands were dark with blood, some of it fresh.

'Jesus, William, you're hurt! Danny told me what he did. I need to get you to a hospital.'

William seemed to smile. 'Ah, my little cuckoo!'

'You're hurt, William. I'll get an ambulance.'

She pulled her phone out of her pocket. It was so bright she had to squint. She didn't see William reach out. He pulled down on her phone in a clumsy movement. She dropped the phone. 'What are you doing?'

'You can't speak to the police. I thought I told you that!'

'I was calling an ambulance.'

'Same thing!' He chuckled a little, his voice just above a whisper. Rhiannon had bent down on one knee to be closer to him.

'You need an ambulance, William. You're bleeding. A lot.'

'It hurt a lot at first, Rhiannon. But it doesn't hurt anymore.'

'You've lost a lot of blood and its cold out here. You don't know what you're saying. I need to get an ambulance here. I don't have to go to the police as well.'

'You call in a stabbing and the police will come first. They have to. They have to be sure the ambulance staff aren't in danger.'

'Well, fine. I don't even need to be here. I can call and then walk away.'

'No, Rhiannon. They'll know it was you. They'll find you and they'll make you talk — about your mate, about what he told you.'

'He's not my mate.'

'Even more reason to keep you away from the police.'

'I'm not scared of him.'

'You should be.' William was struggling to talk now and his breathing was shallow.

Rhiannon picked her phone back up. She activated the torch. Immediately she could see that William was in a lot of trouble. His dark-coloured top was slick with blood, he had pulled it up a little from the bottom and his left hand was covering an open wound. Rhiannon pulled his arm out of the way. Immediately she could see puncture wounds. They were close together and some of his intestines were pushing through.

'I need to take you to hospital.'

William chuckled again. 'How are you going to do that? You got a car?'

'No. I can get a taxi.'

'You can't do that. The second we get in the taxi he'll be on the phone to call an ambulance. We can't call an ambulance here. There will be CCTV reviews and all sorts and they'll know you were here.'

'Fine. What about if we walk you a little further away? The cameras are only in the town centre bit — around

McDonald's. If we take you a bit further along the Leas, I can call someone to there?'

'They'll see us coming out on the cameras.'

'Jesus, William! Help me out a little here! What can we do?'

'It only hurt at first, Rhiannon.'

'Yeah, you said that. That doesn't help us if you bleed to death though, does it?'

'I am bleeding to death. But it's so peaceful, Rhiannon. This is my chance.' William's voice was even quieter now.

'Your chance? What chance? What are you talking about?'

'I get to go, quiet and peaceful. This is where I'm closest to Janey, right here and now I get to go to her. Leave me here, Rhiannon. Leave me in peace. I've got nothing left. This is my chance.'

'Don't be ridiculous! You can't just give up! I'm tired of it, of people just giving up because life is a little bit hard.' Rhiannon reached down, she took a firm hold of William's right arm, hooking hers underneath and trying to stand back up. William was a dead weight; he hardly moved.

'You can't carry me, love, and I can't walk. I'm too weak.'

Rhiannon changed her position, she grabbed hold of his hand to try and drag him, immediately she recoiled. 'William, your finger!' The little one on his left hand flapped like it had been almost completely severed. William looked at it, he was still smiling softly.

'Nothing hurts anymore, Rhiannon. Nothing. This is the best thing for me.'

'No, William. Please! For me, please try.' She reached back down. Again she hooked him under the arm and tried to stand. William shuffled, he grunted as he tried to get to his feet. Now he did wince in pain.

'You should just leave me here.'

'Just walk with me, please, William.' William struggled to move. He took tiny steps and pretty much all of his weight was on Rhiannon. It was hard going and it took every ounce of strength they both had to get back to the gate. Rhiannon tried to help him to the ground a few metres short but he ended up in an untidy mess. She saw him wince as he struggled to sit.

'You need to leave me here, Rhiannon. You can't be seen. Just leave me here and get on with your life.'

'I can't. Please don't ask me to.'

'This is it. I said you had to be more ruthless, love. I said you would know when it was the right time. This is the time. You need to let an old man like me slip away. I've got nothing left here now. But you? You've got a whole lifetime! Look after yourself.'

Rhiannon stared down at him. Her eyes flicked from him back to the gate. Even if she could get him to the gate there was no getting him over. She made her decision. She climbed back over the gate and dropped down the other side.

'Look after yourself, my little cuckoo!' William called out, his voice strained and mingling with the rustling of the trees.

'I'm so sorry!' Rhiannon's voice broke a little. She didn't wait for a reply. With tears stinging her eyes, she ran off into the darkness.

Chapter 26

Rhiannon ran the roads Danny had driven to get to William's bungalow on the other side of the town. She didn't think she'd taken the most direct route but then she had never walked the back streets of the town; she'd only taken buses or cars on the main roads. She couldn't afford to get lost. It wasn't a fast run; her bag was weighing her down and her arms were severely restricted. Her left arm was numb and she couldn't swing it. Instead, she was using her right to try and keep the bag's strap away from her wound. She was intensely relieved when she finally entered William's road.

Despite the street lamps, there were still pockets of darkness that could conceal a sixteen-year-old girl wearing a dark hooded top and a dark-coloured bag on her back while she caught her breath. She tugged at her hoody, trying to pull it away from her neck to get some airflow. She was hot from her run; she could feel the sweat slick on her back. It also ran off her front and had loosened the fresh tape on her wound. She could feel moisture running down her stomach. She couldn't be sure if it was sweat or blood.

A car turned into the road and moved slowly along. It seemed too slow. She ducked into the closest front garden — through a gate that squealed, and she immediately cursed her luck. It was a square slab of lawn, well lit by the light from the porch. The other gardens looked far darker and might have been better choices. This one did have a row of tall conifer trees on the outer perimeter at least, their tops trimmed neatly to form a solid square frontage. She pushed the gate shut. It squealed again and she moved behind the trees. They were thick and full and she couldn't be seen from the road. She was just a few doors up from William's place, but on the other side of the road.

She heard the car stop, then the distinctive sound of it reversing. She peered around the bush a little. She couldn't see the car but she could tell it was turned at an angle, its headlamps now skewed obliquely across the road. It was parking. Over the road it lit up a smart, white BMW parked directly outside William's. Rhiannon recognised it immediately. Beyond it she could see that lights were on in William's place. The curtains were half drawn; she could see a bulb hanging from the ceiling. She knew that was the living room. She had to move fast.

The parking car seemed to be taking an age to settle. Finally the engine was silenced and the lights were turned off. Rhiannon ducked back behind the conifers as she heard a car door open and close. Then, the sound of footsteps getting closer and a cough just the other side of the trees. Another car door opened and then she heard a voice.

'Here we are then, Mum. Safe and sound!'

'Thanks, love.'

'You left your lights on, look!'

'I do that, love, if I know I'll be home after dark.'

The two voices were female; the second sounded elderly. Rhiannon's attention was snatched suddenly back to the house in whose garden she was standing. It was a bungalow, in the same style as William's, only this one was far better kept and it had the addition of a solid-looking porch with a bright light that poured out through its glass sides, flooding the damp grass. *They were coming in here!*

Rhiannon looked for somewhere to hide. There was a flat lawn. She could see a bin on the path near to the gate and then two pot plants either side of where the path lifted gently to the front door. Nowhere to hide. She turned back to the conifers; they were thick — maybe thick enough. She could see one of the street lamps through the trees. This had to be where there was a gap between the trunks. She stepped into it, pushing with her head and her good shoulder as best she could. The tightly woven branches pushed back, resisting her entry, scratching and clawing at her face. She shifted her weight and they started to give. She managed to force her body a step and a half in and found a sort of void in the middle. She fell silent. She couldn't be sure her bag wasn't visible; it still clung to her back and she was pretty certain some of it was at least. The voices had stopped. She could only stay still and hope that no one was taking much notice.

She heard the gate squeak; someone had pushed it open. The voices started again but they were muffled — she couldn't make out the words. She'd had her eyes shut tight to protect them, but had felt a spiderweb push over her face. Now something ran onto her forehead. It moved down to her nose. Rhiannon held her breath, her eyes squeezed more tightly shut; she tried to shut off all her senses; she wanted to scream, to run back into the open and claw at her face.

She heard a noise behind her and thought it might be the front door closing. She held her breath for just a few more seconds. There were no more noises. She pushed herself back out into the open, bending forward and wiping at her face. She'd forgotten about her injury and now winced as she tried to lift her left arm. She watched a fat-bodied spider fall onto the damp grass and immediately scuttle back towards the conifers. Her whole body shivered.

Rhiannon checked all around her. She was happy that the road had returned to silence. The people had gone into the house; they couldn't have noticed her. She moved back out onto the pavement and used the parked cars as cover as she walked past William's house, still on the opposite side of the road. William's house had hedges, too, but they were unkempt and unruly. She got far enough so she couldn't be seen from his house and moved across the road. She continued along a road that went down the side of his house. The entrance to the alleyway she had come out of earlier that day was just a few metres up and concealed in shadow. She ducked into it. The two bags were still where she had left them and she ran the light from her smartphone over them in turn; they hadn't moved position at all. She knocked a couple of slugs off the bag with the drugs in it before picking it up and slogging around to the front of the house and to the rear of the BMW. She could see the lit window to her right and there was no movement inside. She felt exposed but, working on the logic that you can't see well out of a lit room, she ducked down at the rear of the BMW and pushed the bag with the drugs and her own personal bag under its rear. She moved back to the alley. The bag with the money in it was heavier. She had to lift it over the fence and onto her good shoulder, and she felt it tug at her wound. It made her draw a sharp intake of breath. She dragged the bag with the money back around to the BMW and dropped it on the pavement.

She pushed a hand into her pocket and felt for the BMW's spare key. She had to hold it up to the light to make out the right button. She pushed to unlock it. The car *clunked* and immediately lit up bright white in the interior and under all the door handles.

'Oh, shit!'

She snatched at the boot. It lifted quickly and she grabbed at the bags, bundling all three of them into the back. She jogged to the driver's door and pulled it open. She scrambled in and pulled the door shut. The interior light was still on — she was massively exposed. She dared to look right, up William's path to the front door. The light was still on there too — and still there was no movement. She prayed nobody had noticed she was even there.

Her attention shifted to the car's interior and she tried to remember what Danny had shown her. There was a button somewhere to start the car. She bent her head. The button was on the dash, behind the steering wheel. She rested her finger on it. In the silence of the car, she could hear her pulse in her ears; it was quick and strong. She was breathing heavily, too, and her mouth was dry with the tension. But she didn't press the button. She looked back out at the door to the bungalow. She couldn't help but wonder what was going on behind it. What had happened to Danny? They would surely know the bags were missing by now. Aaron would be looking for someone to blame. They might even have worked out it was her who had taken them. And what then for Danny?

She pushed open the door and stepped out. She was careful to lock the car so it fell back into darkness. The night was still, but with her heightened senses, every sound made her jump: a cat ran up and along a fence; glass was dumped into a bin a few streets over; a car passed at the far junction. She moved silently up the path to the bungalow. It was all as she remembered: the gate stuck open; the unruly bush that reached out over the entrance; the mobility scooter left to rust in the rain. She held her breath as she walked further up the path. Still she couldn't see any movement through the window. She stepped off the path into the long grass to get closer. Immediately her shins felt damp. She pressed up against the glass. She could see Aaron sitting down in his usual place on the sofa, practically facing her. His attention was focused downward. Danny appeared behind him wearing a pair of shorts and a clean-looking white jumper that clung to his body as if it was damp. His hair looked damp too. He had his hands on his head and his eyes were wide with what looked like fear. He said something. Aaron reacted immediately, his head jerking around. Then he sprang to his feet, his arms falling to his sides. He walked round the sofa and past Danny, veering off to the right where William's bedroom was. He was back out in just a few seconds. Danny had stayed rooted to the spot, his hands moved from his head to form a new gesture, it was aimed at Aaron; it looked like he was trying to calm him down. Aaron walked out into the kitchen and turned behind the dividing wall. Rhiannon couldn't see him anymore but she could see the loft hatch swing open. She saw movement around it, an arm maybe, a head moving into the space. Danny still hadn't moved.

Rhiannon watched as Aaron reappeared. He paced the floor directly towards Danny. He lifted his fist and lashed out at the last minute. The punch was well aimed, and Danny stumbled back and hit the floor. Aaron was over him, she could hear raised voices now and Aaron was shouting.

'You brought her here! Who else could have known?' There were other words too, but she could only pick out a few sentences through the window. Rhiannon ducked instinctively, she turned back towards the road, checking her exit.

'He could have told anyone! It don't have to be her!' Danny's voice, higher pitched than usual; she could tell he was terrified. She could pick out every one of his words, as he was closer to the window. She heard a thud, then another and someone shouted out in pain. She was certain it was Danny.

'Get her back, get her back, GET HER BACK!' Aaron's voice. More thuds and another shout of pain. Then all fell silent, not a single sound. Rhiannon wasn't sure how long the silence lasted but it gave her a bad feeling. As slow as she could manage and with her thighs burning she raised her head up to look back through the window. She couldn't see either man, the thuds had been close to the front door, which was to the left of the window. She tried to position herself so she could see the left side of the room. Her attention was drawn to movement directly in front. Aaron appeared from the kitchen carrying a hammer, the same hammer she had used before dropping it on William's mattress. Aaron's walk had menace, slow and deliberate, and he was looking at the hammer as if it was a thing of beauty. Suddenly she could hear a voice again, Danny's voice, the same high pitch.

'Aaron, listen, man! I can still sort this shit out. You gotta let me sort this out!' Danny carried on, but his voice dropped a little lower and Rhiannon couldn't make out the words.

Aaron smiled. Rhiannon wanted to duck away, to run off into the night, but she was transfixed. She watched him walk towards the front door. She still couldn't see Danny but she could guess his position. Aaron had stopped close to the window, right in front of her and looking down to her left. Danny had to be just the other side of the window, lying on the floor.

'I'M DONE! YOU'VE LET ME DOWN ONE TOO MANY TIMES!' Again there was more, but Rhiannon could only pick out the first sentence, which Aaron had shouted at the top of his voice.

Rhiannon heard a reply, then a scream, then a whimper. She couldn't make out words.

'BE A MAN, DANNY! AT LEAST BE A MAN NOW!'

Rhiannon heard more whimpering from the floor, then a few words. 'No, Aaron, don't! Don't, Aaron. DON'T!'

She ducked away and looked back at the street. She could see the BMW just a short sprint away. She reckoned she could be in it before anyone even got out of the house. She moved under the window then straightened up at the front door. Her hand rose in a fist, she held it at the door, hesitating. Then she pulled it away. Those words of advice from William — she couldn't shake them from her mind: *You can't be nice. Not round here. You're gonna have to be ruthless, Rhiannon. You'll know when.* She turned away and took a step towards the car. Suddenly she heard another thud, this one louder than those previous. It was sickening and accompanied by a horrific shout. Acting on instinct, she spun back to the door and rapped on it.

She froze. She couldn't believe she had done it. She stared at the door, focusing on the wood. There was nothing but silence. Then a single word projected from the other side.

'What?'

It fell silent again, the voice had been close — just the other side of the door. Rhiannon could still walk away. Aaron would think it was just some neighbour who couldn't hear their television over the noise. But then he'd go right back to Danny and she wouldn't have changed anything at all. She thought about shouting — but shouting *what*? She raised her fist and thumped again.

'Fuck OFF!' came Aaron's reply. Rhiannon's focus was back on the door. There was no spyhole and the three panes at the top were small and heavily frosted. She had to find her voice.

'It's Rhiannon! I thought you might want to know I have your stuff. You won't be seeing it again. Bye!'

Rhiannon twisted away from the step and she sprung towards the car. She was at the bottom of the path before she heard the door open and slam shut behind her. She could hear heavy footfalls, too. She already had the car keys in her hand and the lights were on where she had unlocked the car from the path. She grabbed at the driver's door and slammed it shut behind her, her eyes narrowing in the startlingly bright light. She tried to calm her hands, reaching out with her left for the button in the middle of the dash that locked the door. She pushed it firmly and heard a reassuring *clunk*. A split second later, she heard her door handle being rattled from the outside. The car rocked and she heard shouting. She tried to keep her focus forward, the movement in her driver's window caught up in her periphery. She remembered where the start button was. The engine fired immediately and the interior light faded to off. Her window thudded. A fist. Two hits in quick succession. Then all the noise stopped, she dared cast a look to the right, where she saw the image of Aaron running back up the path. Away from her. Her left hand moved to the gearshift. She spoke out loud: 'How did this work? How did this WORK!' She needed to steady her hands, silence her mind and focus. She pushed the handbrake down then grabbed the gearshift. She remembered it was a click down. She did that but something bonged at her to say she hadn't done it right. Her panicked eyes moved to the screen where it was pointing out her mistake.

The driver's window shattered into a million white fragments that instantly froze in place. It was like a dream, Rhiannon hadn't even known anyone was back. She ducked instinctively away from the noise, but she stared back at the vivid white pattern filling the window. Suddenly the window smashed in, a hammer carried through into the interior and coursed into the driver's seat, claw end first, clanging into the metal post of the headrest. Rhiannon could see Aaron's face, his eyes wide, his nostrils flaring as he tried to pull it back out for another blow. He couldn't. The claws of the hammer had lodged in the headrest. He let go of the handle and the hammer slipped down. Almost immediately she felt a blow to the right side of her face — Aaron's fist. It hit her so hard that her vision went fuzzy and she felt dazed. Instinctively she pushed out with her right hand, out through the shattered window and towards the noise. She felt her nails scrape skin and something soft and wet at the end of her fingertips. She heard Aaron scream in pain. He stepped away from the car, his hands lifted to his face. Rhiannon's attention moved back to the instrument panel. It showed the gearshift with an arrow pointed at the side. She grabbed the shift and could feel a raised button. She pushed it and pulled the stick back. She felt the car shudder under her and she lifted her foot off the brake. The car rolled immediately forward into the parked car in front causing her head to jerk forward. She took another blow to her right side but it was weaker than the first; her shoulder took some of the power. She could hear a hand scrabbling at her door — Aaron was trying to pull the inside door handle. If he got the door open she knew she was done.

Rhiannon pushed the button back in on the shifter, she pushed it forward and grabbed the wheel. The car slid backwards this time and she turned the wheel hard. She yelped as it struck another parked car behind her, this time at an angle. She snatched again at the shifter and the car lurched forward. She felt another blow to her right side, which knocked her sideways, her vision suddenly black. She could hear the door opening now, but all sounds were getting quieter. The sudden brightness of the interior light punctured her mind, snapping her back to awareness. She heard someone yell out in pain. She looked to her right and her door slammed back shut. She could hear a crunching sound; the car was still moving forward at an angle, but shuddering and rocking as it went. It moved out of the parking space, the driver's door scraping firmly against the car in front. She sat back up, trying to shake the last of the grogginess and looked over her shoulder. Aaron was moving, he was coming up to the passenger door. Her headlights lit up the road ahead. She stepped on the accelerator, she had to push her leg right out and lift her buttocks to reach it. The car lurched forward again — quicker this time. She saw Aaron jump back away from the car. She was now clear of the line of parked cars and she straightened up in the road, pointing down towards the junction. She took her foot back off the accelerator but the car still rolled onwards. The headlights picked out a figure limping out from between more parked cars further up the road. It was Danny. He stopped in the middle of the road. He was bleeding from a head wound and holding his shoulder as if it was damaged. He held his left arm up, his palm towards her.

'Rhiannon!' he shouted. His voice was still high pitched and scared. It was clear through the broken window. 'You need to stop. Just give him back the stuff and you can go, I swear. You can go, okay?'

Rhiannon saw movement by the passenger door, she heard the handle rattle again. Aaron was tugging at it. It was clear that he had no patience. And no intention of letting her go.

'Just stop the car!' Danny shouted. 'Stop the car and give him back the stuff. Then you can go, he just wants his stuff!' He forced a smile; it looked ridiculous covered in blood and as he held one eye closed. Aaron was moving again. He walked along the back of the car and was coming for her open window.

That loveliness that you've got . . . you have to learn to switch that off. You need to be ruthless when it's called for. William's words cut through the noise and confusion. Suddenly they were the only things that were clear. This was what he meant — exactly this.

Rhiannon stood on the accelerator. She still had to stretch for it — the seat was too far back. The car surged forward. From her position, she could just about see Danny's expression change from a reassuring smile to panic before she shut her eyes firmly. She felt and heard the thud at the same time. A split second later came a second thud; it was louder and it sounded closer. The car kept moving forward and she opened her eyes just as the junction rushed towards her. She moved to the brake, the wheels locked up with a sudden squeal and the car came to a stop. Rhiannon let out her breath. The windscreen had a circular dip and a spiderweb effect in the glass, it started from the top left and stretched to reach across in front of her. The circular part had hints of red and a clump of hair in its centre. In her mirror she could see a figure running towards the car up the middle of the road. She pulled the steering wheel right and pushed the accelerator again to move out of the junction and away. She picked up speed and the figure behind fell away.

Rhiannon burst into tears. Her body sagged where it had been stiff with fear. She suddenly felt something jabbing her in the back. She reached for it. It was the hammer Aaron had used; it had fallen behind her on the seat. She threw it into the footwell on the passenger side. She had to lean forward to see out through the shattered windscreen. She needed to pick out features, road signs — anything so she might know where she was, so she could tell how to get back to William. That was her only chance now. She needed to get back to him. He could make all of this right.

Chapter 27

The BMW bounced up the kerb. It struck harder than Rhiannon had expected and she yelped as the vibration jarred through her shoulder. She had found an area of the Leas where there was a big enough gap between the parked cars to cut through. She had been forced to drive past where she knew William was. She drove the car across the neat grass and turned hard left when the wheels met with the tarmac path. It was wide enough for the car, but she kept it slow; the headlights were dull compared with how she remembered them and she guessed she had damaged one getting away. She tried not to think too much about what might have struck the light, despite the clump of dark hair caught up in the cracked windscreen that shuffled in the wind.

She slowed even further as she got to roughly where she thought the gate was. Sure enough it came up on the right side. She turned hard left and moved out onto the grass. She then turned the car around so that she was facing directly towards the gate. She allowed the car to roll forward slowly until it was just a few feet away. She stepped on the brake and the car jolted to a halt.

Rhiannon let the car roll forward under its own steam. It bumped the gate at a slight angle — the gate flexed but held firm. She moved the shift to reverse and backed up until she was a bit further away. She shifted into drive and the car rolled forward; she squeezed the accelerator this time and the impact was harder than she expected. She had been leaning forward to get a clear view and the jolt pushed the steering wheel hard into her chest — her shoulder stung with pain. Once the car broke through the gate, the engine still drove the rear wheels and pushed the BMW forward towards the wooden fence on the other side. Rhiannon knew that a sharp drop awaited her there.

She moved her foot to the brake but was too late; the front of the car rode up the small bank and crashed into the fence. The boards splintered and pushed up over the bonnet as the car moved forward and lurched suddenly downwards. When the brakes finally caught, Rhiannon's head was once again thrown forwards. Her eyes slammed shut and she gritted her teeth. When she opened them she was looking down through a tree canopy. The trunk that sprouted it was a long way below and dug into the steep hill. The car groaned, it slipped forward a little, maybe just an inch, but it was enough to make Rhiannon jump. She yanked the handbrake as hard as she could and moved the shifter to reverse. She felt the car shudder under her as it engaged the gear and slipped another inch further forwards. She held her breath and let her foot off the brake. She held the handbrake in her left hand, her palms were soaked, partly from the tension and partly from the pain in her shoulder. She pushed in the button on the end of the handbrake then plunged the lever down.

The BMW jerked again. She could feel the rear wheels scrabbling and the car slipped sideways, slipping on the damp grass — then she felt a slide forwards as the wheels continued to spin. Suddenly the car shook and she felt a thud from the rear. The tyres gripped and the BMW rolled backwards. The view through the front window was suddenly out to sea, rather than a sharp drop. As she stopped the car across the path, Rhiannon suddenly erupted in tears. With some effort, she pushed open the driver's door. It had been creased in the earlier impact and it creaked as it opened. She sucked in the fresh air that was laden with the scent of the sea and took a second to calm herself.

Then she climbed out of the car and made for the path. The gate hung open; the chain had snapped. She could see where the wooden fence had broken, too — as well as the steep drop on the other side. She moved down the path quickly, pulling her phone from her pocket and activating the torch. William was still there, sitting upright where she had left him.

'William! I came back. I got a car.' There was no response. 'William?' Still nothing. She got to him. His head was turned away from her. She moved in closer, lit his face with the torch. She could see immediately that he was a different colour, his lips a dark blue, his face washed out, waxy, his eyes half open and unmoving. She touched the arm that lay across his stomach. It felt cold. She lifted it to try and feel his wrist for a pulse. His shirt came with it, stuck to him with dried blood. She dropped his hand and stumbled back. There was no need for her to check his pulse, no need for her to check anything. William was dead. She stood up and took one step back, her mind fuzzy again. She knew there was a way out of all of this, some way, somehow — she just couldn't focus on it now. She'd had it all worked out before; she thought she knew what she was doing. But William was dead. Danny, too, perhaps. She had run him down in a stolen car full of drugs and she didn't dare contemplate what might happen if Aaron caught up with her. Her mind cleared a little and she was back to thinking straight. Nothing much had changed. She could still pull this off. There was still a way out.

Rhiannon ran back to the car. The engine was still running. She pulled at the rear door and left it open as wide as it would go. She ran back to William and pulled him by the shoulders so he was leaning forward, his sad eyes turned down to the floor. She stepped in behind him, and reached down to take him in a firm grip under his arms. She had forgotten about her shoulder and it immediately shot through with pain. Rhiannon swore before looking around, desperate for anything that might help her. There was nothing. She took the same grip again and she heaved. The pain was excruciating but William's body shifted slightly. She heaved again. He'd turned so that he was facing down the path at least. Rhiannon took a deep breath. She tried to ignore the pain, braced herself and heaved again. William didn't move.

'Shit!' She had come all this way and now she was going to be beaten because she was too weak. She needed William in that car. Everything depended on it. She was back to looking around. Her eyes rested on where William had been sitting originally, down at the end of the path. She could see empty cider bottles, she could see his sleeping bag and she could see his cardboard box.

The cardboard box.

Rhiannon remembered shifting some furniture for her Aunty Mel. They hadn't been able to manage it and they had mocked one another's weakness before finally falling down laughing. Mel had had the idea of using cardboard. Rhiannon ran down the path and grabbed William's box. It was still dry — it had to be strong enough. She ran back to William. Her shoulder ached as she lifted his torso to put him in a sitting position. He wouldn't stay there and she had to lean him against her shoulder as she squatted down, positioning the box against him. She stood up and once again hooked him under the arms. She heaved, and he budged an inch backwards. She lifted him again, another inch onto the cardboard. Tears of pain rolled down her cheeks, but he had moved far enough. She reached back down and took a firm hold of the cardboard. She still had to support his head and she talked to him — her way of forgetting that she was moving a dead body.

'Come on, William. I would really appreciate you helping me out right now. There's a bottle of rum in it for you!' She tugged at the cardboard. It slid a few inches over the stone path and William came with it. He was still heavy and cumbersome, but he was moving.

'That's it. Good man. Is it because of what I said about the rum?' Rhiannon inched to the end of the path, where it met back up with the Leas. She was breathing heavily, near to exhaustion. She laid him down gently and moved back to the car. She positioned the back door as close to him as she could before grabbing William again under the arms. She knew this would be her last big effort. She braced herself, waited for the adrenalin to flood her veins, to mask the pain and to give her a last push. She screamed as she lifted, but she managed to get William sitting on the sill of the open door. She crawled back into the car. She took a deep breath and heaved again. William flopped awkwardly onto the back seat. Rhiannon folded in his limbs and leaned on the door to shut it. She stepped back and away, the realisation of having moved a dead body into a car hitting her all of a sudden. She had been able to put it out of her mind up to this point. She took a moment, her hand at her mouth, staring through the window. She could see him lying on his back, his opaque eyes towards the car's roof, his mouth open.

She needed to focus again. Her right hand plunged into her pocket. She pulled out her phone and activated the torch. She moved back to the broken gate, swinging the light around the base of the hedges and shrubs on the other side of the fence. It wasn't long before she saw an ugly blade reflecting the torchlight. It had to be the knife Danny had begged her to retrieve. It was some way in but she might be able to reach it. She put her phone back in her pocket and tore a strip off the cardboard box. She moved back to the fence; she could still see the outline of the knife. She gripped the cardboard and pushed her right hand through the gap in the iron posts. She had to turn her head a little to reach it. She used the cardboard like a grabber, folded over in her hand but it was slippery and the knife kept falling out. She managed to get it closer at least, close enough to reposition a little and to get a better grip on it. She pulled it back towards the fence and manoeuvred it through the posts. She lifted the boot of the BMW and, still gripping it through the cardboard, she threw it in. She slammed the boot back shut without even seeing where it landed. She moved round to the driver's seat and got in. She took a moment, a deep breath. She was nearly there; she just had to hold herself together for a few more minutes.

She knew Langthorne Police Station. Or at least she knew where it was. They had driven past it a couple of times when Rosh had taken them out as a foursome. It was on a main road through the town, in the more affluent west end. It was a long, wide road. She pulled into it and she could see the *Police* sign lit up in blue in the distance. She had seen a large set of gates just beyond that sign on the nearside. This must be where the police officers came out in their cars when they were responding to calls. The station was quiet now. The car's digital display was showing the time: just before 9 p.m. She didn't think it would be long before she saw some sort of movement. There were two gates: the one she had seen by the side of the road that led into a car park and then another, more solid-looking gate, that was further back and looked like the true perimeter of the police station. The second gate was part of a far higher fence and the cars parked on the other side had reflective police markings on them. She had parked across the first gate when she noticed sudden activity at the other. The gates slid back, an orange light spinning on the top, and the headlights of a vehicle flickered as the gates moved across it.

She knew she needed to act fast.

Rhiannon stepped out of the BMW. She pulled open the back door and grabbed William, again under the shoulders. She ignored the pain that was a constant now and yanked backwards. The leather seats gave him up easily and she was able to bundle William out of the car and onto the tarmac. He lay in the middle of the pavement near the entrance, his left leg hanging over the dropped curb. They couldn't miss him.

'Sorry, William,' she sniffed. 'This is me being ruthless.'

The light was suddenly brighter; the second gate was open. A police car moved through and came towards her. She ran to the driver's seat and moved away. The external gate lifted. She ducked her head — they were close enough that they might see her now. She checked her mirrors — the police car stayed still. Rhiannon didn't think they could get round William's body, even if they wanted to, but she had banked on them not moving, on them checking on the person lying in the road first.

Rhiannon followed the route Rosh had taken before, but in reverse. It took ten minutes to get to just a couple of streets over from William's house. She pulled into where a large church loomed on her right. She moved around the back. There was parking marked up for a Reverend Lucas and a few other names. It would do. She pulled the BMW across untidily and stepped out. She kept the door open and inspected the side of the driver's seat. There were three buttons and two of them were marked: one with the number 'one,' the other with the number 'two.' She remembered what Danny had said to her: *The boss is programmed in to the 'Number One' button. You just push that when you're done and he'll never know you were in his seat! It goes right back to how he sits.* She pressed the button. Immediately it slid back, the electric motor whirred and she stepped away. It slunk lower in the car, the backrest moved to a shallower angle too. Then it stopped.

Rhiannon slammed the driver's door shut and pulled open the boot. The bags were still there. There was a small green first aid kit that was also loose in the back. She picked it up and unzipped it. There were a few bandages, a pair of scissors — the usual stuff. There was also a folded-up rain jacket in a square pouch, an emergency measure for anyone lying in the road in the rain, she guessed. Whatever, it would suit her needs. She opened it up and tied off the sleeves. She laid it out flat on the floor, then stuffed the sleeves with wads of money from Aaron's bag — as many as would fit. She bundled it all up. She scooped up her own bag and threw it on her shoulder. Once again it tugged at the tape over her wound. She slammed the boot shut and walked to the front passenger side. She pulled one of her shoes off and threw it into the footwell. It came to a stop lying over the hammer.

Rhiannon scooped up the rain jacket stuffed with the money and limped out of the church grounds. She held the BMW key in her hand. She didn't have to walk far to come to a drain and she made sure she heard the key splash after she dropped it down there. As she stood up, she caught her reflection in the glass side of a parked minibus. Her face was scratched; she had dried blood on her chin, her cheeks and gathered in her nostrils. Her hair was a mess, her eyes puffy with emotion and exhaustion. She was holding her shoulder low, her hooded top was ripped and she could feel she was bleeding again from her chest wound. She was nearly there, though. She just had to find a place for the money and then get back to the phone box she had passed on the way and this could all be over.

Chapter 28

Aaron found a seat against the wall at the back. He was trying to keep his head down, trying to blend in. He'd intended on just dropping Danny off at the hospital and then leaving straight away, but he knew now that he couldn't do that; he knew he had to bide his time for the right opportunity. He'd managed to get Danny into a taxi. He didn't want to call an ambulance to the bungalow; he didn't want that address linked with them. The less information people had, the better. So he'd carried Danny to a nearby fish and chip shop on Dover Road and asked the staff for help. There had been a taxi driver getting his supper and he took one look at Danny draped over Aaron's shoulder and agreed immediately to drive them to hospital. The taxi driver, though, asked a lot of questions on the way over — too many questions. Aaron was already worried about him when they pulled up at A & E, but then when he insisted on coming in he knew the man was going to be a problem for him. He hung around while Aaron spoke to the receptionist giving Danny's details. Now the taxi driver was at the coffee machine in the waiting room, he scooped up two drinks. He had hardly taken his eyes off Aaron since they had arrived.

''Ere y'are, son. Get this down your neck.' The driver smiled reassuringly. He had said his name, but Aaron hadn't taken it in.

'Ah, yeah, thanks.'

'Your mate's gonna be alright. I can feel it.'

'Sure he is.' Aaron must have heard this ten times already. 'Look, man, you don't have to stick around. I know you got a job to do. I've got your number. I'll give you a bell later, like — tell you what the deal is. Thanks though, yeah?'

'Don't you worry about me! I know you said you ain't got no one down here. I'll stick around for the cup of tea at least. I'll tell you what, I'll go talk to reception again, see if there's any news.'

Aaron watched him go. He was due an update. When Aaron had carried Danny in, he'd been in a bad way. He'd taken a big hit to the head, he was in and out of consciousness and his breathing had become more and more shallow. Aaron didn't reckon he would make it. He didn't think that would bother him so much — but he'd still felt something when he had been shepherded into an area with waiting beds. Numerous medical personnel had seemed to come from nowhere. They'd buzzed around Danny, cutting his clothes off and barking questions about what had happened. Aaron had been vague, said simply that Danny had been hit by a car — but he, himself, hadn't seen it, he'd just heard the screech of tyres then his mate was lying on the road. He could tell from the looks they'd given him that they didn't believe him. Whatever. He didn't need them to. He'd only brought Danny to the hospital at all because that stupid bitch had made so much noise that people had come out of their houses. He had thought it best to pick him up and leave.

Aaron still watched the taxi driver. He was well over six foot and had to stoop to get close enough to the glass frontage of the reception desk to talk to the woman sitting behind it. She looked suddenly over to where Aaron was and her expression carried fear. She jerked her eyes away immediately and brought a phone to her ear.

It was time to go.

Aaron stood up. He turned swiftly away from the counter and towards the exit. He heard a shout — the taxi driver's voice. He didn't look back. He turned right into a corridor with the main entrance at the end. The doors were automatic. They parted for two incoming police officers in uniform. They made eye contact and the one on the right reached straight for his handcuffs. Aaron knew they were here for him.

He turned back on himself and broke into a run. The taxi driver was standing in his way. Aaron had enough momentum to push through him. He stumbled but he kept going. He turned right, away from the waiting area and into the main hospital. He could hear footfalls behind him. He turned hard left, a long, empty corridor stretched out in front of him where he could really build up some speed. A shadow stepped out of a door on the right — Aaron hardly had a chance to notice it, just that the head was down and a clipboard was out in front. They collided hard and Aaron was sent sprawling to the floor. He fell forward awkwardly, striking both elbows, and his chin bounced off the floor. Before he could shake his senses free he felt a knee on his back and a hand grabbing at his wrist. Then came the cold metal of handcuffs. His face was pushed into the floor. He lifted his head to spit and blood came with it.

'You're under arrest, mate,' growled a gruff voice from behind.

'No shit!' Aaron laughed. He spat again.

Chapter 29

Detective Sergeant Graham Wilson was fiddling with two sealed DVDs when Aaron strolled into the interview room of Langthorne House's custody block. He looked as if he was out for a walk on a lazy Sunday with not a care in the world. He was wearing an all-grey tracksuit that looked a size too small. He had rolled one of the legs higher up his shin than the other. The forensic people had taken their time stripping him, then swabbing his hands, face and arms. The tracksuit would have been what they had given him to wear after. His own clothes now formed part of the evidence and they would have their own analysis. They had asked to swab his genitals, too, but Wilson had been told how Aaron had told them to fuck off. He could refuse of course; it was his right. And, for Graham, this wasn't such a bad outcome — it could be used to cast doubt in the minds of a jury further down the line.

Aaron had been led to the largest of the interview rooms by a jailer who then left quickly. The room was dreary and oppressive, it had no natural light, and the walls and ceiling were all white, the same white tiles covering both. They were punctured all over with little grey holes that allowed the sound in. Behind some of these panels was the recording equipment that would pick up the audio from the room.

Graham had been standing when Aaron had entered. He moved quickly to one of the two fixed seats on the side of the table closest to the DVD machine, making it clear that Aaron should sit the other side. Aaron's solicitor was already on a chair opposite him anyway.

Aaron sat down next to her. He flashed her a big smile as his eyes moved over her body, enough for her to look a little uncomfortable and shift her position, crossing her legs. She was certainly an attractive woman. She wore a black pencil skirt with a matching jacket, a blouse unbuttoned a little from the top and killer heels. Her long brown hair was down with just a clip to keep it from falling over her dark, thick-rimmed glasses. She wore a touch of makeup, enough to retain a classy and business-like look overall. Graham had sat opposite her in interviews before and he knew she was sharp as a tack.

'Maddie.' Aaron winked at the solicitor. 'We still hooking up when this is all done?'

Maddie didn't return his smile. No doubt she had heard it all before. 'I don't mix work and pleasure, Mr Ayeko.'

'And I don't tend to worry about following the rules. We'll talk again later.'

'Perhaps we should get to the matter at hand first, before we talk about what you are doing afterwards.'

'Straight to business, Maddie. I appreciate that.' Aaron finally looked over the table to the detective sat opposite. 'Who the fuck are you then?'

Graham smiled cheerily. 'We'll do introductions as part of the interview.'

'Do what the fuck you like. I don't care. I ain't done nothing wrong.'

'The prisons are full of them.' This was a new voice. Detective Inspector Tim Brace entered the room, his face fixed and stern. He was a large man, both in bulk and stature, but he carried it well. Graham had been told he was ex-military. That certainly made sense. Tim stood still, his hands pulled together behind his back, his back and legs locked straight and his head slightly tilted. He wore an expensive-looking suit, a white shirt with blue pinstripes and a solid blue tie with a square knot. 'People that *ain't done nothing wrong,* I mean. Maybe we've been locking up the wrong people all this time? What do you think?'

Aaron relaxed back into his chair. He had crossed his arms and looked up at the inspector. 'You trying to be funny? You the funny man on the station?'

'No. They called me down from the other end of the county to speak to you, Aaron. I have a reputation for taking things like this very seriously. And for getting the right result. I am Detective Inspector Tim Brace. I'm one of the major crime inspectors in the county.'

Aaron shrugged then fell silent.

'I can call you, Aaron, right? That is your street name? I bet it's only your mother that calls you Abdullahi Ayeko, right? Maybe when you're in trouble. What do you reckon she would call you now if she was here?' This might have been an attempt at a joke. Graham honestly couldn't tell. Tim's facial expression didn't budge.

'You can call me what you like. I ain't gonna be here long.'

'Ah, I see. Well, that's fine then. I'll stick to Aaron for now. I take it that means you want to get on with this? I shall get started — if there are no objections?'

'Yeah, let's do this. You can get me a hot chocolate, though, before we start. Maddie, you want anything from the funny man here?'

The inspector sat next to Graham. He steepled his fingers and locked a stare on Aaron just long enough for things to get uncomfortable. Aaron stared right back, but he broke first, shaking his head and forcing a laugh. 'What is this? This all part of the act? You think you can intimidate me or summin'? This ain't my first time, man. You people don't bother me at all.'

'Of course it isn't. You're quite the seasoned *petty* criminal, aren't you, Aaron? But this is big time now. This is murder. This is rape. You might have come in here before full of your own piss and wind and you might have ordered yourself a chocolate and had some probationary officer tottering after your every whim, but this is all a bit different. I will get your drink. Then I will start the tapes. I have some very serious questions to ask. Do I make myself clear?'

'Just do whatever, man. I don't want to talk to you about the time of day. Ask me your questions and kick me the fuck out. That's all you've got to do. That's your job, right?'

'Locking up violent criminals. That is my job.'

'Good luck with that.'

Tim held his stare. Graham looked over at him, waiting to see what he'd do next. He was aware that Tim Brace had a reputation. It seemed people either loved working with him or hated it. Graham had a feeling he would have his own opinion by the end of this interview.

Tim stood up. He was gone less than a minute and returned with a hot chocolate. He also brought Maddie a water and a black tea for himself. The DVDs were noisy at the start, they got a little quieter as the machine warmed up. Tim covered all of the formal introductions. Aaron did his best to look apathetic, he even yawned at one point as Tim repeated the official police caution then checked his understanding of it. Everyone was ready to go. Tim was very much the focus of the room and everyone waited for him to ask the opening question. Even Graham peered across with his book open and his pen resting in his hand. Tim didn't have anything in front of him. He didn't look any more relaxed now he was sitting down; his back was still stiff and straight as he held his hands together on the table in front of him.

'You're under arrest for murder,' Tim said. 'I mean, this is very serious indeed. So tell me about that?'

Aaron turned to his solicitor. She had a piece of paper lying face down on the table in front of her. This was obviously her cue. She turned it over.

'My client has prepared a statement that I will read on his behalf. *I, Abdullahi Ayeko, came to Langthorne about two weeks ago. I came here with friends and to meet up with a girl I met on the internet. I found out some of my friends were members of a gang that operate in London. I am not a member of that gang, or of any gang and I do not deal drugs. I have not made any money from dealing drugs. I am on benefits and that is my only source of income. You will not find any money in my account. I am not a man of means. I have not harmed anyone since I have been down here. I have no idea why I have been arrested for murder or for a sexual assault. I will not answer any questions about these matters as I am confused and alarmed and I do not wish to incriminate myself.*'

Maddie reached out with the piece of paper towards Tim. He ignored her, staying fixed on Aaron. She put it on the table in front of him.

'So tell me about murder,' Tim said.

'Tell you what? What murder is? I know what murder is, but I don't know nothing about why I got nicked for it. I ain't murdered no one. This is shit.' Aaron stifled another yawn.

'Tell me that then.'

'What?'

'What murder is.'

'What murder is? Fuck you! This ain't no game. No comment!'

Tim leaned forward. He somehow seemed to increase his intensity, all of it fixed on Aaron. 'You seem to have the impression that you are in charge of this situation, Aaron. I understand that, because I think I know where that comes from. It's stupidity, it's naivety. You're too dumb to know where you are and why. Am I right?'

Aaron leaned forward himself a little. 'What the fuck? You can't sit there and call me dumb, man? I ain't done nothing wrong, plain and simple. If you can't understand that, you're the dumb one, man.'

'I know what you did and I know how you did it.'

'No comment!' Aaron smiled, seemingly enjoying himself all of a sudden.

'That's why I don't need to ask you a damned thing. But you *do* need to give me answers. You need to tell me how you're not guilty of murder, how you didn't kill your mate by running him down in your car, how you didn't stab a man to death in the street, how you didn't sexually assault a sixteen-year-old girl and how you're not here dealing heroin and crack cocaine. You need to tell me all that, Aaron, and I suggest you start from the top — from when you arrived in my county thinking you could come here and peddle your misery.'

Aaron flicked a look back to Maddie. He sat back and she sighed.

'I can only remind you, Mr Ayeko, of my advice in our consultation. That advice remains.'

Aaron turned back to the detective inspector. 'No comment.'

Tim took his time sipping at his tea. Then he reached down to where he had propped a folder against the wall. He pulled out some paperwork, A4 papers stapled together. It was a typed document with yellow highlighter running through it.

'When we have very serious allegations, particularly if they are from someone aged sixteen or less, we tend to interview someone on tape, rather than take a witness statement. No doubt Maddie here explained to you that we got our victim statement this way. Do you know Rhiannon Davis?'

Aaron's lips curled in a sneer. 'No comment.'

'She knows you. How does she know you?'

'No comment.'

'I interviewed her, late into the night. I've been doing this job a long time, Aaron. I've seen and heard some terrible things, but taking her account, that got to me. It really upset me. She's terrified of you, Aaron. Why is she so scared?'

Aaron shrugged. 'No comment.'

'Let me summarise the account she gave of you — so you know what she says happened. That's only fair, right? And I'll warn you now Aaron . . . I've wasted enough of my time in this stinking room with you already, so I'm just going to pause at the key bits and you can jump in and defend yourself if you want to. And if you don't, then I will just assume that it's right. Okay?'

'No comment.'

'With respect, Inspector, my client is exercising his right to make no reply to your rather oppressive questioning.' Maddie flushed red; she was clearly rattled. 'You cannot make assumptions that the allegation is correct because he chooses to continue with that right or because you've been upset by one side of a story.'

'You're right. Thank you.' Tim said, but his gaze was still fixed on Aaron, not wavering an inch. 'But a jury can. And they will, Aaron, they will ask themselves why an innocent man accused of murdering two people didn't shout his innocence from the rooftops the first chance he got.'

'I didn't murder no one,' Aaron said.

'Well, let's go through it, shall we? I'll keep it chronological, for everyone's ease, okay? So the drug dealing we know and accept. And you were doing that from William Dryden's house, right?'

'No comment.'

'Really? Okay, we'll come back to the drugs — they're the least of your worries, after all. Rhiannon Davis believes you were dealing drugs from William Dryden's house. She says she was brought to this house by someone called Danny. Who is Danny to you, Aaron?'

'No comment.'

'And you raped her.'

Aaron's eyes flashed wide. 'She's a lying bitch.'

'Mr Ayeko!' Maddie cut in. 'You will remember our conversation.'

Aaron's chest suddenly rose and fell as he took in deep gulps of air.

'So you did not rape her?' Tim said.

'She's a lying bitch, Maddie. I wanna talk. I wanna tell him it's bullshit. I never touched her!'

'You forced yourself on her in William Dryden's bungalow. You were so rough with her you didn't even get her fully undressed. She was still wearing her underwear. You just pushed it aside and you raped her.'

'She's *lying*!'

Tim lifted another sheet of A4. He turned it over to reveal the glossy photo of a pair of pink knickers with a white bow and a matching bra. They were packaged separately in clear bags with handwritten tags. 'This is Rhiannon Davis's underwear, or at least a picture of it. Have you seen these items before?'

Aaron shook his head. 'No comment.'

'You made her clean up your semen with it, Aaron.' Tim left the statement hanging. It took Aaron a few seconds to reply.

'I — I . . . no comment.'

'So your DNA will be all over it. And our analysts, they will be able to say it was semen too. *Your* semen. Can you explain that?'

'No comment.'

'Rhiannon was so traumatised that she ran home and got in the shower still fully clothed. She sat and wept for an hour, drenching herself under the shower. She didn't want to take her clothes off because she didn't want to see her own naked body. Finally she managed it. She bagged up her underwear to bring to us. It's still damp, but with the advances in DNA analysis, Aaron, we *will* have you on these. So I'll ask again, is there an innocent explanation for your semen being on the underwear of this sixteen-year-old girl?'

'She's lying.'

'You already said you didn't touch her. So if your semen is on there, it is fair for me to assume *you* are lying.'

'No comment, yeah? I got nothing more to say.'

Tim quickly moved back to scanning the statement. 'William Dryden was a witness to this incident. He wasn't there to start with, we are told, but he came in halfway through. You reacted by telling her to hide in the wardrobe. You had ripped her clothes — the sleeve of her T-shirt specifically — and she was upset and you were worried that he would know what you had done. Is this what happened?'

'No comment.'

'Rhiannon got in the wardrobe. She tried to hide but she was so upset she couldn't stay quiet. William heard her crying. You got angry, Aaron, you threw William out . . .' Tim paused.

Aaron shook his head. 'No comment.'

'When you went back into the bedroom, Rhiannon refused to come out. You got so angry you threatened her with a large knife. She told me she was so terrified at this point she couldn't have got out if she wanted to.'

'No comm—'

'You stabbed her through the wardrobe door causing a deep laceration to her chest.'

'I didn't! I don't . . . no comment.'

'You then drove her in your car back to her house. You have a white BMW that she describes as *looking new*. She ran into her house and that's when she got in the shower. Did you drive her home?'

'No comment.'

'Did you drive her home so you would know where she lived? Did you tell her that if she told anyone what had happened that you would break in and assault her foster carer?'

'No comm—'

'Rose Ansen. Her foster carer. She provides a statement saying someone matching your description and another man turned up at her house. They forced their way in under the premise of looking for Rhiannon and struck her to the floor—'

'That . . . no comment!'

Tim moved quickly back to his papers. 'Rhiannon got angry. After weeping for an hour in the shower, she cleared her head a little and went to find William Dryden. She wanted him to be a witness if she went to the police about what you did. She hung around outside William's bungalow. The BMW was gone and she could see Danny through the window. She dared to knock. Danny told her you had suddenly offered to take William to a McDonald's restaurant. He said you and William had both left together. Rhiannon went to the McDonald's in the town. There was no one around. Then she heard shouting, Aaron. That was you, wasn't it?'

'No comment.'

'She saw the BMW parked up. She looked inside, she could see the keys in the centre console near the handbrake and the door was unlocked. You must have parked in a hurry, Aaron?'

'No comment.'

'Or maybe you weren't planning on staying long?'

'No comment.'

'The shouting was down a path. She saw you walk back up it and she ducked out the way. She said you looked angry, Aaron — you were talking to yourself. You seemed agitated. She saw you throw something over the fence. You didn't get in your car — you carried on walking away. You had blood on you. She thinks maybe you didn't want to get blood in your car.'

'She's fucking lying!'

'So what's the truth, Aaron?'

'No comment. Shit! No *fucking* comment!'

'Rhiannon found William Dryden down the path you had just left. He was bleeding from three stab wounds that would later prove to be fatal. He said you had stabbed him. He said it was something about your mate getting arrested. You thought William had something to do with that . . .'

'No comment.'

'Was that Maurice Atlas? His street name is Mo, right?'

'No comment.'

'We can link him to you on the MET's intelligence system. Do you know him?'

'No comment.'

'How do you know him?'

'No comment.'

'Are you aware he was found in the town yesterday with one hundred wraps of heroin in his pants?'

'So what? No comment!'

'Those wraps will be DNA tested. Did you touch them, Aaron? I bet you did!'

'No comment.'

'Now's your chance to give me an explanation.'

'No comment.'

'Rhiannon wanted to take William to hospital but he refused. He said he had wanted to go back to his house to get something. A picture of his family that he said you had already damaged. It's the only thing of any value to him, but he knew he couldn't go back while you were there. And Rhiannon knows a bit of first aid, she thought she might be able to help a little back at William's place. She took him in the BMW expecting to get in and out before you could turn up. But when they arrived you were already there. She thinks maybe you got a taxi.'

Aaron was shaking his head. 'No comment.'

'You were furious. Rhiannon and William didn't even make it out of the car, you came from nowhere with a hammer. You smashed the car up . . .'

'No comment.'

'The hammer you used is still in the car. We'll have your DNA on that, fingerprints, too, I bet.'

'No comment.'

'You forced your way into the car. Danny came out. He'd gotten too close to Rhiannon — that pissed you off, right?'

'No comment.'

'Danny was injured already. But he saw you force your way in and he knew you were going to drive them off and you were going to harm them. He stood in your way, Aaron, didn't he?'

'No comment.'

'You ran him down, Aaron, didn't you? He's dead, Aaron. You killed him.'

'No comment.'

'Who is Danny?'

'No comment.'

'We haven't been able to identify him yet — that means we haven't been able to tell his mother that he isn't coming home. That he died a hundred miles from home. That his so-called mate ran him down. Who is he, Aaron?'

'No comment.'

'So after you fatally wounded Danny with your car, the white BMW, you forced Rhiannon and William into the back of the car, threatening them with a hammer. She didn't know where you were taking them. But when you passed the police station Rhiannon saw an opportunity and she tried to get out. You struggled with her in the car. She scratched your face trying to defend herself—'

'No.'

'No? That didn't happen?'

'No. No comment.'

'How did you get that nasty scratch on your face?'

'No comment.'

'We've taken skin from under her fingernails. She says it's yours. It will be yours, won't it, Aaron?'

'No comment.' Aaron had been sitting straighter and straighter under questioning. But Tim wasn't giving him a moment's rest between the questions. Now Aaron seemed to sag, his head suddenly rolled forward on his neck, his eyes stared down at the table.

Tim suddenly seemed energised, as if he was feeding off Aaron's body language. He leaned forward and rose a little off his seat. He was almost on his feet.

'You left the hammer in the car, Aaron. It was in the footwell and we have successfully pulled prints from it. The seat, you left that in your own saved position. Your DNA will be all over that car. You left the murder weapon you used on William — the knife — in the boot. It had blood on it. It was still wrapped in a piece of cardboard that *will* be a mechanical fit to the blood-soaked cardboard left down that path. Where you killed William Dryden! That cardboard is covered in his blood, Aaron! Rhiannon Davis is covered in your DNA! William Dryden was seen falling from your car by police officers. There is blood in your car — it will be William's and maybe Rhiannon's. There is blood smudged on the gate near where Rhiannon said you stabbed him, where you climbed out after you had done the deed! William had finger marks round his throat where he was grabbed and the pattern will match with your grip, Aaron! And, besides, you will have left your DNA . . .' Tim's face flushed, he sucked in a deep breath. Spittle had gathered on his lips and a vein stood out in his neck. He had planted his hands flat on the desk and Graham thought it was just as well; as if he had done it to be sure he had some control over them. He sat back down but he didn't seem to lose any of his intensity. 'And you still don't want to make any comment, Aaron? You still don't want to shout about how innocent you are?'

Aaron was collapsing in front of them as if in slow motion, his mouth gaped open; saliva had gathered and now fell to the surface of the table in a long string. His eyes were bloodshot and unblinking. 'No comment . . . no fucking comment,' he whispered, his head shaking from side to side.

Tim started up again — but quieter, a little more controlled. 'So you wrestle with Rhiannon Davis in the car — she's a brave girl, that one — I mean, you're a big man. But she's desperate, isn't she? She knows you're going to kill her next. Only she can't get out, Aaron, can she? But William Dryden? In the melee he falls out of the open door, right? He can't stop himself, Aaron, because he's now dead from the stab wound you inflicted. You suddenly realise you're right outside of this very police station and you panic. You drive away. You know you need to dump the car as soon as you can, so you take it round the back of a church, the first suitable place you see. Then you drag Rhiannon by the hair into the front. She fights you though, Aaron, doesn't she? She fights you all the fucking way. And she gets free. She loses her shoe, but she runs away, doesn't she? And so do you, Aaron, don't you?'

'No comment.'

'You were so desperate you left your bag of drugs in the boot and twenty thousand pounds in notes.'

'*Twenty* thousand?' Aaron exhaled a laugh. A tear dropped onto the table as he did so. 'Clever bitch.'

'Who is?'

'No comment.'

'Who is Aaron? Was there more? How much was in there?'

'No comment.'

'Your DNA, Aaron . . . it will be all over the bags, all over the contents of the bags, won't it? Can you tell me now why that might be?'

'No comment.'

'Is it because you're a drug dealer?'

'No comment.'

'Of course you are! It's the whole reason you're even in the town.'

'No comment.' Aaron's nose was almost touching the table. Tim finally let up; he relaxed a little and leant back in his chair. He took another sip of his tea. Maddie sighed, she pushed her glasses up her nose and scratched some notes on a leather-bound notebook.

'Let me tell you, Aaron, it's not often I get an allegation of something as serious as a murder or a sexual assault, and I can match every part of the victim's statement to physical evidence. You have to understand that the evidence is strong. This is early, too, Aaron. The investigation is only just beginning. We're in William Dryden's home right now. I took a call just before I came in here telling me there's a set of clothes soaking in bleach in the bath. I assume these are yours? There's a red staining to the water that I'm sure will turn out to be William's blood. There's a hole in the wardrobe door, just like Rhiannon said there would be and — guess what? There's blood on the other side. That will be Rhiannon's, right? We still have to review CCTV from the town, which we will do, and we will find your BMW in that area, the car that is hired in your name. We might not have coverage of where you killed Dryden, but we can show the car in the area at the material time. We have any number of witnesses that live on his road who are telling us about a white BMW smashing its way out of a car parking space. There's glass at the scene that will match. The BMW has damage, which includes Danny's hair and blood that was left in the windshield when you ran him down. It *will* be Danny's, won't it, Aaron? Rhiannon has half your face under her nails and we have no other explanation to go on other than Rhiannon Davis's. And everything she has said can be corroborated. Everything she has said makes sense.

So, you need to tell me now what's gone on, or I'm going to come to the only conclusion I can.'

Aaron did nothing. Neither detective spoke; they let the words sink in. Aaron lifted his head. He fixed Tim with a look like he wanted to say something. 'No comment,' he said.

'I really hoped you would say that.'

'She's got you all fooled, ain't she? I have to say, she's played a blinder here,' Aaron managed.

'Who?'

'Rhiannon fucking Davis.'

'You know her then?'

'I never said that.'

'She's a terrified sixteen-year-old girl, Aaron, and a slip of a thing. What are you saying? That she's made this all up? Planted evidence at every stage?'

'Maybe she has.'

'A sixteen-year-old girl? No criminal record? Not even a stop-check from uniform coppers and here she is, outwitting a hardened gang-banger?'

'This ain't any sixteen-year-old girl, Inspector. I see that now.'

Chapter 30

The man turned the key, pushed open the door and gestured for Rhiannon to follow. He wore a wide smile; he had been smiling from the second they had met, but it was one of those fake, fixed smiles, the sort that only estate agents could muster. He was young and good looking but a little too polished for Rhiannon. She got the impression that his three-piece suit and bright orange tie was a choice that had taken him a few attempts to get right. His hair was slicked over to one side, his parting as sharp as a ruler.

'This one's not been available for long but we've already had a lot of interest. I don't expect it to be an option for much longer. Someone will snap it up!'

Rhiannon stepped in behind him. The flat was on the seafront in Sandgate, the next town over from Langthorne. It was in a large apartment block. From what she could tell, most of the residents were elderly. The apartment opened up in front of her. It had kitchen units running down the left wall and an island with a polished tap marked the middle of the room. The whole of the right side of the room was open and bare. She could see by differing tones in the carpet where sofas and tables might have stood for the previous occupants. Nothing now remained except for a big brown plant plot housing a huge rubber plant that drooped a little, its leaves browning at the edges.

The only internal door that signified a separate room was immediately to the left. The estate agent pushed it open.

'This is the family bathroom. The two bedrooms are upstairs. The master bedroom has its own en suite.'

Rhiannon followed him in. The bathroom had a roll-top bath, a modern-looking square washbasin and a matching toilet. She left the bathroom and wandered further into the property. She could see a spiral staircase on her left that had been hidden by the bathroom. The frame was a grey metal, with dark wooden steps, which had up-lights embedded along the edges. She flicked her eyes around the interior, but her attention kept moving back to the bi-fold doors at the other end of the room. They covered half the entire width and she could see a balcony beyond. The lad must have seen her staring; he moved over to the door. He fiddled with the lock and the door swept back with ease, folding into itself. Straight away, she could hear hungry seagulls, excited children and the sea itself, its gentle rhythm against the beach. She moved across the floor and out onto the balcony.

'This sells it all by itself, right?'

'It does. I'll take it.' Rhiannon turned to the lad. He still held the smile. It still lacked conviction.

'It's eleven hundred a month. It's pricey.'

'That seems reasonable to me.'

'Well, good.' His smile fell away a little. 'And it comes as is. The owner would prefer someone willing to sign up with a twelve-month contract. It would also be necessary to pay two months' rent up front as a deposit. That holds the place, of course, and you would get that back when you moved out — assuming he had no issues with how it was left.'

'Okay.'

'And we would need proof of employment.'

Rhiannon scowled. 'What's that for?'

'Well, the owner would like to be sure they have someone in their place who can afford the rent. I work with a lot of landlords, they can be a bit twitchy for the first twelve months of any contract — you know, until they get to know their tenant.'

'I'll have to come back to you with proof of employment.' Rhiannon patted her pockets. 'I don't have it on me right now.' She knew how ridiculous she must have looked. She was stood in her old Converse pumps; they were falling apart but were the only shoes she had left after leaving one of her newer shoes in Aaron's car. She had changed her clothes, but nothing was clean really and everything was creased from being screwed up in the bag that still hung from her shoulder. She knew her face still had scratches and bruising. She had been with the police all night. They had wanted an account from her there and then; they had wanted swabs and samples, diagrams and photos. She'd done most of it but had refused the more intimate requests. She was so exhausted that she had nearly fallen asleep while standing up. She'd been jolted awake by flashes from the camera they were using. When they had finally finished they had offered a hotel — insisted at one point — but she'd refused. She was done with temporary fixes, with short stays *just for now*. She craved something that was hers, something that was permanent. This was it.

'I'm sorry, I know the landlords in places like this. They are quite insistent. He'll need a guarantee of sorts that he'll get his rent. I'm sure you understand.'

'What was it? Eleven hundred a month? Plus a deposit.'

'That's right, yes. Did you want to see the bedrooms? You know, before you make any firm decisions? Then maybe you can contact your employer and see what can be done?'

Rhiannon slipped the backpack from her shoulder. She had dumped a lot of her clothes — some of them were ruined anyway; she had needed to make room. She had worked out that the wads of cash from William's loft were in denominations of a thousand. She knelt on the floor and started pulling them out one by one.

'One, two, three . . .' She counted up to fifteen, leaving them in a pile on the floor. She pulled a few more notes out of a bundle and counted them out too. She stood back up as the lad looked on, open mouthed. 'Fifteen thousand, four hundred, right? By my maths, that covers me for a year.'

'I don't . . . I mean we don't . . . I've never had that before.' He flicked from the money to Rhiannon standing in front of him. She was too tired to care about whether or not she looked reassuring and trustworthy, or whether or not she had managed to get all of the dried blood off her face, neck and hands.

'I'm sure you can make it work, though, right?'

'I err . . . I just need to make a call.' He eyed the pile of money once more and stepped away. He walked back through the front door, leaving it ajar behind him.

Rhiannon pulled her bag open wider, pushing more wads of money aside as she searched. Her hands fell on what she was looking for: a solid wooden frame, smooth and cold to the touch. She lifted her eyes to the far wall. There was an electric fire, designed to look like a real coal fire. It had a bare wooden mantelpiece running along the top that finished almost level with the doors. She pulled the frame out of her bag and walked to the fireplace. She placed it in the middle of the mantelpiece, angled so that it was towards the door.

She walked out onto the balcony. The sea dominated everything in sight. It was as if a destructive child had ruined a sibling's drawing with a huge blue smudge. There was a small area of hardstanding immediately below her that ran up against where the pebbles started. The beach was perhaps fifty metres deep. She could hear the pebbles being turned over and dragged around where they met with the sea. The same pebbles sparkled in the bright sunshine. It was beautiful and it was calm.

Rhiannon heard the door behind her and turned to the estate agent. His smile seemed more genuine.

'Looks like we have a deal!' he announced.

'Great news.'

He made straight for the pile of money, but then his eyes started roving around the room. Rhiannon picked up on his need. She pushed back into her rucksack and pulled out the rainproof jacket with its arms tied off. She tipped out a few loose wads of cash that were still stuck in the sleeves and they fell back into her bag.

'Here, you can use this to carry it. It seems to do the trick.'

The lad looked unsure. Rhiannon laid the jacket down. She nudged the bundles of cash into the centre and wrapped it up before handing it over.

'Okay, thanks! I filled out a form while I was outside talking to the boss. This is basically your receipt. It'll cover the deposit and I've written on there by hand that you've paid twelve months upfront. You will get a more professional letter of confirmation. I will still need your proof of employment, as and when, and your ID. Usually I'd need references from previous landlords and a host of other stuff, but most of that won't be relevant now, I suppose. Look, I'll be back in touch if there's anything more we need, okay?'

'Fine.'

The lad looked at the bunched up jacket that was awkward under his arm. He looked awkward in general. 'So, I guess you'll need to arrange your furniture and such like? We have a bit of a tie-in with a removal firm. They're local and they do a discount for our clients. Do you want their number?'

'No, I can manage, thanks.'

'You're going to move your stuff in yourself?'

'I have already.' Rhiannon pursed her lips as the lad looked her up and down. He moved to look around the bare interior. He stopped at the frame on top of the fireplace.

'That your family?'

Rhiannon looked at it too. She remembered being sad when she had first seen it, as if it was out of place — William and his family looking so carefree. It didn't belong in that awful flat. It looked so much brighter here, happier. 'Yeah, I guess it is.'

'Is your dad going to help you? You know — to get started?'

'No, it's just me.'

'Really? No man? No knight in shining armour to turn up with a sofa and a takeaway?' The lad might have winked, his cheeks flushed a little.

'I'm not that kind of girl.'

Now his cheeks flushed even brighter. 'Sorry! I mean, I wasn't . . . you know . . . I was just making conversation.'

'It's okay. I know. I just meant I don't need a knight in shining armour. I always prefer the stories where the damsel rescues herself.'

He relaxed a little. 'Makes sense to me. Good luck then, Miss Davis. This is a lovely place. You should be very happy here.'

'I reckon you're right.'

He left, still looking a little awkward. It was a hurried exit. Rhiannon closed the door. She kicked off her shoes, enjoying the touch of the bare wood on her soles. She walked back out onto the balcony and turned so that the small of her back pushed against the railing. William looked out at her and the sea beyond. He was with his family — Janey and his daughter. He was happy.

'How do you like your view, William?' she said. 'I had to bring you here, just for a little while. I know you'd probably tell me not to be nice, not to think of you. You'd tell me to be more ruthless. You made it though. You all did.'

Chapter 31

The rain tried to conceal itself in the breeze but was fooling no one. Rhiannon had a long, black coat over black trousers and smart shoes. Only her face was exposed and her nose dripped with moisture. She had dug her hands deep into the pockets. She walked a stone path that was straight and wide and criss-crossed by much slimmer paths that carved up the expanse of flat, green lawns. The gravestones stood in a silent and orderly formation. Some ran with the rainwater, their slick, polished surfaces rebuffing the droplets so they ran straight off the gold lettering and surfaces flecked with glitter. Others absorbed it, sucking the moisture in tight, changing their whole tone to a duller, heavier looking grey.

She walked past a row of graves that bucked the trend and the atmosphere. They were bedecked with vivid colours and movement: tiny windmills spun in the breeze, each of the sails a different and bolder colour than the next. They had chimes, too, that clanged and clattered as they moved together among solar lamps and enclosed candles. They were children's graves. They broke Rhiannon's heart. She couldn't help but read a note taped to a candle on a grave that looked freshly dug. The ink on the note was starting to run: *Elliot — you were always scared of the dark. You don't need to be scared any more.*

Rhiannon shuddered. She wasn't sure if it was her environment or the water running down her back. Whatever the reason, she wanted to leave. She was just a hundred metres short of where the figure still stood. She had watched from a distance. She had seen the vicar come out. He held an umbrella in one hand and a big black book in the other. Rhiannon guessed it was the bible, it looked like he had read from it — something short — and then he had left the figure to it. It was a young girl, about Rhiannon's age, maybe a year or two older. And she had stayed there ever since.

Rhiannon made it over. The girl was standing with her back to her. She wore a long jacket that was similar to Rhiannon's but over a skirt, black tights and flat shoes. She was taller than Rhiannon but of a similar build and with darker hair. She stood in the middle of the two freshly prepared holes. Both had simple stones at their head. Rhiannon had decided to come at the last minute. The police had told her the time and the place and it had seemed like a good idea. Now she was here, she realised she hadn't considered for a second what she might say.

'Hey!' Rhiannon called out. She still wasn't ready and almost caught herself by surprise.

The girl turned towards her. She looked angry, as if she was ready for a fight.

'Sorry, I didn't mean to disturb you.' The girl's expression softened a little. Suddenly she had a spark of warmth in her eyes and her lips turned at the edges into a sort of smile. She looked instantly like her dad.

'You're alright,' she said, and turned to face away again.

'I'm sorry. About your loss, I mean.'

The girl turned back. This time she looked Rhiannon up and down. 'Why's that?'

'Why?'

'Why would you be sorry for me? We don't know each other, right?'

'Oh, no, we don't know each other. I knew your dad. I knew William.'

Her expression shifted back towards anger. 'So?'

'I mean, only for a few days. But I wanted to come down and speak to you. I wanted to . . .' Rhiannon suddenly realised she didn't know what she wanted. She hadn't quite sorted out the details in her mind.

'What? What did you want to do?'

'Talk to you, I guess.'

The girl turned away. Rhiannon stood still, a few paces behind her. She waited for the girl to speak again. 'I didn't really know him — not for a few years. He won't be a great loss to me. You can save your sympathy for someone who needs it. Whoever you are.'

'My name's Rhiannon. My mum, she's an alcoholic.' Rhiannon ran out of words again, she struggled with where to go next. 'I hate her, but just as much as I love her. She makes me so angry. Your dad made me angry too. It's like someone gave them a choice, the drink or us. And they choose the drink.'

The girl turned back to face her. The hard expression was gone. 'It used to bother me. It doesn't anymore. I've known for a long time that I would be looking down at my mum and dad's grave. I'm only surprised I got to eighteen before I did it. And it's just as I pictured it — a pauper's funeral in the rain. They had nothing. They died with nothing and they left nothing behind. A total waste of a life.'

'They left you.'

The girl's expression changed enough for Rhiannon to recognise surprise. It was only fleeting. 'They certainly did that.'

'I wanted to come and speak to you. I know how you must be feeling. I know how I would feel — totally let down. I didn't want that to be the last impression you had — not of William, at least.'

'You think you can change that? I can't see it, can you? My dad's never done a thing worth talking about in his life, let alone something for me to be proud of.'

Rhiannon smiled. She lifted her head slightly, pulled her hands out of her pockets and felt for the rain. 'These are private moments. You should take your time. But I'll hang around. I'd like to buy you a drink maybe, and then I'd like to tell you a story about a good man.' Rhiannon slid William's framed picture from her pocket. She pushed it into the girl's hand. 'I didn't break it, okay? Nor did William, it was all he cared about.'

The girl took it silently. She still didn't speak when Rhiannon turned to walk away.

THE END

Thank you for reading this book. If you enjoyed it please leave feedback on Amazon, and if there is anything we missed or you have a question about then please get in touch. The author and publishing team appreciate your feedback and time reading this book.

Our email is office@joffebooks.com

www.joffebooks.com

ALSO BY CHARLIE GALLAGHER

BODILY HARM
PANIC BUTTON
BLOOD MONEY
END GAME

MISSING

36382739R00153

Printed in Great Britain
by Amazon